I0761125

BY LISA PEERS

MOTOR CITY LOVE SONG

MOTOR CITY LOVE SONG

A NOVEL

LISA PEERS

THE DIAL PRESS • NEW YORK

The Dial Press
An imprint of Random House
A division of Penguin Random House LLC
1745 Broadway, New York, NY 10019
randomhousebooks.com
penguinrandomhouse.com

A Dial Press Trade Paperback Original

Library of Congress Cataloging-in-Publication Data
Names: Peers, Lisa author.
Title: Motor city love song: a novel / Lisa Peers.
Description: New York, NY: The Dial Press, 2026.
Identifiers: LCCN 2025031674 (print) | LCCN 2025031675 (ebook) |
ISBN 9780593736708 paperback: acid-free paper | ISBN 9780593736715 ebook
Subjects: LCGFT: Romance fiction | Novels | Fiction
Classification: LCC PS3616.E334 M66 2026 (print) | LCC PS3616.E334 (ebook)
LC record available at https://lccn.loc.gov/2025031674
LC ebook record available at https://lccn.loc.gov/2025031675

Printed in the United States of America

1st Printing

BOOK TEAM: Cindy Berman • Managing editor: Rebecca Berlant •
Production manager: Jennifer Backe • Copy editor: Rebecca Maines •
Proofreaders: Karen Ninnis, Karina Jha

Brick art: vlntn/Adobe Stock; CD art: dtuluu/Adobe Stock

The authorized representative in the EU for product safety and compliance is
Penguin Random House Ireland, Morrison Chambers, 32 Nassau Street,
Dublin D02 YH68, Ireland. https://eu-contact.penguin.ie.

FOR DANICA TOMICH:

Never forget you have the coolest parents in the world

JACE
DISC ONE
DISC ONE

1

WAY BACK WHEN

JUNE 7, 1997

Jace Randolph had to figure out what she was going to do before the crowd at the Artemis Club started lobbing beer bottles at one another. At 12:48 A.M. on a balmy Detroit summer night, it was like a boiler room inside the club, and the musicians, staff, and standing-room-only ticketholders had been waiting way too long for headliner Paloma Doralle to get her ass onstage and start her set. As music booker for the venue, it was Jace's responsibility to know where Paloma was, and, unfortunately, she had no fucking idea.

Jace collared Jerome, Paloma's bassist, in the wings. "When's the last time you heard from her?" she yelled over the throb of the music coming from the PA system.

"This afternoon," Jerome yelled back.

"This afternoon," Jace repeated as calmly as she could. "And at that time, she knew she was booked for midnight. Tonight."

Jerome nodded. "She said she'd meet us here. She wanted to go record shopping first."

Jace's stomach dropped. No record stores would be open at this hour. Had something happened to her—a car accident, or worse? "She had the map I gave you, right? She knew how to get here?"

The bassist shot her a sardonic smirk. "As far as I know." He pointed to Richie, the drummer, who was staring at a point on the floor backstage and twirling his sticks over and over through his fingers. "I mean, *we* got here, so . . ." As Jace turned to leave the stage, Jerome caught her arm. "Hey, if she doesn't show up, me and Richie can still do the gig. I'll take over lead vocals."

"And who'll play guitar?" Jace said. "Richie? While he's playing snare with his feet?"

Jerome had no answer for that.

Swearing under her breath, Jace skirted the crowd and entered the club's business office, which was shoehorned into the former coat check room at the front of the venue. Using the desk phone, she rang Paloma's listed home number, knowing full well she wouldn't be there to pick up. The call went to her answering machine, playing a greeting that Jace had suggested she make more professional: "*You have a mouth, so use it to leave me a message, cutie pie!*"

Jace hung up, frustrated. Was Paloma the type of musician who thought she could drop by whenever she felt like it instead of honoring her call time? Granted, Jace had almost no leverage over her. The Artemis Club paid a minimal appearance fee instead of a cut of ticket sales, and after a couple of failed experiments with an open bar, band members and their entourages could no longer drink for free. But Paloma Doralle had signed a binding contract, and if she didn't follow through, Jace could theoretically sue her in small claims court. Not that she would.

Folding her arms tightly, Jace perched on the corner of the desk and fumed. A faded, framed newspaper photo of the Artemis Club's founder, Stavros Galanis, stared at her from the opposite wall. Had he been alive to see what the club had devolved into seventy years after he'd opened it, he would have dropped dead from disgust. Mr. Galanis had been a civic-minded Greek immigrant driven by his conviction that the city needed a lecture hall dedicated to the appreciation of high culture, which he'd built here on Cass Avenue back in 1927. Now, Detroit was far from being the glittering Paris of the

Midwest it had been at the dawn of the auto industry. After decades of flight and blight, it was more like Rome in ruins, with the Artemis being a battered beacon for the survivors and artists who wouldn't or couldn't leave. These days, the concrete statue of Artemis, the Goddess of the Moon and the Hunt, that greeted patrons at the front entrance had been chipped, graffitied, pissed and shit on by dog and man, and occasionally outfitted with a red lace bra and matching panties on Valentine's Day. The performance space, which had boasted velvet flocked wallpaper and pastoral landscapes in its heyday, had been stripped down and plastered over with decades of posters from local rock bands and nationally known acts that passed through the Motor City on their way to LA or New York or London. The brass-and-glass chandeliers had been ripped out to make way for strips of stage lights; the porticos that had held replicas of Hellenic pottery were jammed with stacks of speakers. The stage was besmirched by duct tape residue and dents from mishaps with heavy equipment, and the floor where the general admission patrons stood had been stained over the years by puddles of beer and bodily fluids. The aroma of burnt popcorn, cigarette smoke, and BO was permanently singed into the air. The bathrooms ranged from tolerable to unspeakable.

This was Jace's place of business, and it was da bomb.

The Detroit punk and garage rock scene had blasted out of the exhaust pipes of the 1960s and fallen in and out of fashion ever since. These days, it was on the upswing once more, with another generation of Michiganders channeling their creative rage through secondhand guitars and dented drum kits, playing at venues that were scattered across the city like crumpled empty cigarette packs.

Jace had first entered the club as a Wayne State University freshman with her roommates, a blue Esprit jacket, and a fake ID to follow up on a rumor that Sammy Sinister would be doing a surprise appearance. Sabine Galanis, the Artemis Club's late-twenty-something owner—and great-niece of Stavros himself—was working the box office that night. Seeing Jace's disappointment when she learned that

Mr. Sinister had already left town, Sabine comped Jace and her friends to stay and hear a local band, Tiny Teacups, instead. As her roommates pressed toward the stage, Jace stayed near the back to take it all in: the décor, the crowd, the staff, and the band. The total chaos left her flushed with excitement. Tiny Teacups took the stage around one in the morning, and they were awful in the best way possible: bold in their ineptitude, ambitious in their mediocrity, and thrilling in their sheer nerve. They gave not one flying fuck what other people thought of them: the exact opposite of Jace's entire adolescence. She was mesmerized.

Her roommates had been ready to bail after one number, but Jace begged them to stay until closing time. Once the lights went on, while the other girls chatted up the lead guitarist, Jace was deep in conversation with Sabine about what she did for a living. Their flirting for naught, her roommates eventually pushed Jace toward the exit doors. She spotted Sabine in the lobby as she was waving the weary patrons on their way, and before she could be yanked out of the club, Jace asked her for a job.

Since graduating in 1992, Jace had grown out her dark brown hair into a Gina Gershon–inspired shag and become a bona fide indie music aficionado. She had heard a lot of bands since she started working for Sabine, and she had trained her ear to identify the ones she believed fit the Artemis Club vibe: formidable melodies, powerful lyrics, supreme showmanship, and, ideally, the ability to stay in tune. Jace scouted acts in college town clubs in Ann Arbor and Ypsilanti and sorted through piles of cassette tapes and CDs that eager musicians pressed into her hands. Sabine was relieved to have Jace handle the talent decisions as she aimed to raise the Artemis Club's profile as the premier place to play in the city. Before long, they'd gained a reputation for featuring musicians who were on their way to bigger things.

Musicians like Paloma Doralle, the twenty-seven-year-old singer-guitarist born and raised in Taylor, downriver from Detroit, who was making her debut at the club tonight. Paloma Doralle, whose physical presence aligned perfectly with the voice on the audition tape Jace had played on repeat for weeks: sultry, suggestive, and borderline dangerous.

Paloma Doralle, the flake who hadn't shown up for her set yet.

The door swung open, and Sabine entered the office, wearing a lace-trimmed black dress, ornate purple tights, and Doc Martens. With her overdyed black locks and large brown eyes, she looked like a petite background actor in a Tim Burton movie. After closing the door against the din of the concert hall, Sabine crossed her arms and looked at Jace with a bemused expression. "What do you propose we do?"

Jace ran her fingers through her wavy hair. "We have a few options. The guys from Cold-n-Flu are still here. We could bring them back on for another set."

"They don't have more than five songs, and none of them are more than two minutes long," Sabine said, perching on a corner of the Army surplus steel desk. "Once the ten minutes are up, then what?"

Jace was not willing to admit defeat. "I saw Manny Manto near the sound board. Maybe invite him to do a set?"

"He tripped over his girlfriend's cat and broke both wrists," Sabine said. "Between the plaster casts and the Percocet, he's in no shape to play."

"He could do a Q and A with the crowd about his cameo on *Buffy the Vampire Slayer.*"

Sabine was unmoved. "Never again."

Jace sighed heavily. "Fashion show? Musical chairs? Auction off one of the bathroom stalls?"

Sabine snorted. "It's up to you. You're the one who'll have to tell the audience."

Someone banged on the door before bursting in; it was a young butch gal in cargo shorts and a backward Tigers baseball cap. "Hey, are you Jace?"

As Jace nodded, Sabine said, "Jace, this is Mo. She's doing security tonight."

Mo nodded back. "Someone just pulled up out front. Said her name is Paloma."

Relieved and exasperated, Jace pushed past Mo to get to the sidewalk outside the front entrance and found a yellow cab parked at the curb. Its back door opened, and two long legs unfurled, one after the other. Despite her scarlet leather miniskirt and tight white sleeveless tee, Paloma looked like a waifish silent movie star who'd gotten caught in the rain, with her choppy bottle-blond bob, smudges of liner surrounding her olive-green eyes, and lips the color of a bruised plum. Stepping onto the sidewalk, she zeroed in on Jace and, with a toss of her head and a hitch in her smile, asked, "You ready for me?"

"Yes," Jace said with much less outrage than she'd intended.

"Which way to the stage?" Paloma asked.

Her mouth dry and her power of speech suddenly offline, Jace silently pointed toward the door on the right side of the building.

"Fantastic! Catch you after the show." With that, Paloma swanned past her toward the side entrance, leaving Jace in her wake to marvel.

"Hey," the driver called out, breaking Jace out of her trance. "She left her gear in the cab, and she said you'd pay her fare."

"Where did you pick her up?" Jace asked.

"Ann Arbor."

Jace's ire flared anew. Flipping the cabbie a few twenties and grabbing the guitar case out of the trunk, she hustled to the stage door, swearing all the way.

A few minutes later, Jace was at the sound board at the back of the room, the PA mic in her hand. As the last notes of the Motown classic "Detroit Dancing Days" by Melodee and the Makers faded from the speakers overhead, she called out in her most commanding Voice of God tone: "Ladies and gentlemen—and everyone else—please welcome PALOMA DORALLE!"

The stage lights brightened, and the house went dark. Paloma strode on, a black-and-white Stratocaster across her hips. The audience applauded as she plugged in and checked with Jerome and

Richie before stepping up to the mic stand, her eyes like green ice in the stage lights. She chuckled as she took in the crowd, then wrapped her fingers around the mic and brought it close to her lips.

"Okay, kids, let's play!"

With that, there was a rumble of guitar chords on top of a pulsing bass line echoing the beat of the drums leading into her opening number, "You Better Get Going." Paloma looked up from under her bangs and sang, her voice somewhere between a come-on and a snarl.

Why don't you love me?
Is it my hair?
Why don't you love me?
Can't stand my stare?
You have to love me 'cuz I told you to.
Love me now! Love me now! Love me now! LOVE ME NOW!

Half the audience chanted the lyrics along with Paloma, with the rest bouncing to the beat as she launched into the second verse:

You want to love me.
I know I'm hot.
You're scared to love me—
We might get caught.
I want your love, girl. I need it, too.
Love me now! Love me now! Love me now! LOVE ME NOW!

The band ripped into the instrumental verse. Her Strat bucked like a bronco as her guitar solo surged forward, and she bit her lower lip, her head tipping back as the music possessed her.

Even though Jace was standing well away from the stage, the aural blast from the columns of speakers—and the sizzling curve of Paloma's mouth as she sang the final verse—made her body buzz.

Just love me, girl,
Dissolve in my touch.
You are so, so sweet, girl,
And I don't bite . . . much.
You'll love what I can do. So why don't you
Love me now? Love me now! Love me now! LOVE ME NOW!

The song screamed to a close, and the audience whistled and whooped. Paloma acknowledged the applause with a gap-toothed smile that struck Jace like a lightning bolt. From the first number through her entire set list and as her second encore concluded, Jace was in her thrall. It wasn't simply that Paloma was arrestingly lovely from every angle, which was a documentable fact. It was the effortless certainty of her playing, the soul-incinerating power of her vocal delivery, the deceptively simple lyrics that burrowed into Jace's brain and gut: what lazy rock journalists would call "star power."

Jace found talent sexy. And Paloma was incredibly talented.

A couple of moments before two A.M., sweat-soaked and giddy, Paloma raised a hand and waved to the crowd. "Stay safe so you can see us again," she commanded. "Now get the fuck outta here!" The house lights went up, flooding the darkness and breaking the spell. As patrons filed out, Paloma cruised into the wings where Jace was waiting with bottles of water.

"Guys, great show," Jace said. "The best one I've seen you do so far."

"Thanks," Jerome said, passing a bottle of water to Richie then taking one for himself.

"Do you really think so?" Paloma asked without any of the bravado from her performance. "I totally fucked up the intro to 'Sell Myself.' It was embarrassing."

"No one noticed," Jace assured her with a hand on her forearm. "The show was amazing. You were amazing."

"Thanks," Paloma said, smiling and relaxing slightly. She handed her guitar to Jerome. "Could you put this away for me? I gotta go to the bathroom."

"So do I," Jace said.

"Make it fast," Jerome said, walking toward the instrument cases. "I gotta take a piss."

The two women walked farther backstage to the two-stall unisex restroom reserved for talent and crew, Jace following Paloma in. Paloma paused next to the sink, her green-eyed gaze meeting Jace's blue-eyed stare. Jace locked the door.

"Hey, babe," Paloma said, then kissed her hard and deep.

Paloma had a height advantage, along with impressive guitarist biceps, that made Jace feel damn near dainty in her arms. Paloma's fingers knotted in Jace's hair as she pressed into her, barely letting Jace come up for air long enough to moan before she went back for more. Breaking away, Paloma nipped Jace's earlobe. "Want to help me get out of these sweaty clothes?" she whispered, her breath hot against Jace's neck.

"Sure," Jace said, her eyes narrowing as she ran her hand up under Paloma's shirt. She smirked. "No bra?"

Paloma smirked back. "I left it at your place."

Jace spun them around and pressed Paloma up against the door jamb, pushing her soggy tee up and out of the way to taste the tang of her skin as she kissed a line down to her navel. "Christ, Jace," Paloma hissed as Jace's finger trailed up between her legs.

There was a sudden pounding on the other side of the door. "Hey, you two done yet? I told you, I gotta take a piss."

Startled, Jace jumped backward. "Coming!" she yelled.

"Almost, anyway," Paloma whispered, stifling a giggle. Jace clapped a hand over her own mouth to keep from laughing.

"Hurry up!" Jerome yelled back through the door.

Jace turned on the tap at the sink to give them a few extra seconds to tuck in their shirttails and grab a last smooch before opening the door.

"All yours," Paloma said innocently as they walked past the bassist on the way to the bar.

Jace and Paloma hung out with a smattering of friends and staff for another hour, even though Mo had already tossed out all their drinks and locked up the liquor cabinet to close the bar. They purposefully stayed away from each other; they'd only been dating since Jace saw Paloma play in Ann Arbor a few weeks earlier, and they weren't ready to go public quite yet.

A little after three A.M., Richie tapped on Paloma's shoulder to say, "We need to get to my cousin's. You ready?"

"Your cousin's?" Paloma asked.

Richie nodded. "Yeah, he said the three of us can crash in his basement tonight. Two sofas, one shag carpet. The carpet is a lot more comfortable than the sofas, so you can have that, Paloma."

Paloma shot Jace a "SAVE ME!" look.

"Sounds like a lot of testosterone," Jace said, casually placing her cup of water on the bar. "Paloma, you can stay with me if you want. My apartment has to smell better than Richie's cousin's carpet—no offense, Richie."

Thank you, Paloma mouthed.

Shortly thereafter, the ladies were tangled up in each other on Jace's futon at her studio apartment in Hamtramck. Finally alone, they were able to finish what they'd started in the Artemis backstage bathroom. Where they'd been frantic and feral before, now they could take their time. They were still in the discovery stage of their dating relationship, and Jace took careful notes whenever her fingers or tongue earned a languid growl from this spectacular woman, who was as tall and raw-boned as Jace was short and square-shouldered. And when Paloma kneeled at the foot of the futon and pulled Jace toward her to nuzzle her inner thighs, Jace thanked whatever god was listening for making this possible.

Later, lying in the red glow of her clock radio, Jace felt boneless and sated. Paloma rested her head on Jace's bare chest, humming as Jace idly stroked her hair.

"That's pretty," Jace said. "Is it a new song?"

"It could be," Paloma said, snuggling closer. "Maybe it'll be our song one day."

Jace breathed deep, catching notes of Paloma's lemony shampoo. *Our song,* she thought. *So this is what having a girlfriend is like.*

Jace had been the dateless wonder in high school, making clumsy passes at girls who inevitably were straight, closeted, or put off by the weird girl who'd bore them to tears after five minutes of yammering on and on about the LPs she'd discovered in the bargain bin at Harmony House. Once she got to college, she found people just as eager as she was to go to Goodwill and yard sales to dig through crates of records and talk until dawn about the legends of underground rock and roll: all guys, sadly. Sabine had done her best to set Jace up with some of her younger lady friends, but nothing clicked. Then Paloma had spotted her in the crowd at that tiny venue near the University of Michigan campus with a smile like a homing beacon, and, after listening to Jace sputter through her pitch for playing the Artemis, squeezed her forearm and asked if she could stay for a drink.

After that, everything clicked and seemed like it could keep on clicking, as long as Jace didn't blow it now with the proposition she was about to make.

"So, wanna tell me why you were so late tonight?" Jace began.

Paloma chuckled. "Didn't Jerome tell you? I was record shopping."

"More like shopping for a new crew," Jace said. "You were in Ann Arbor checking out other bands, weren't you?"

"Busted." Paloma sat up, pulling the sheet around her. "Look, I'm sorry I didn't tell you, and I'm really sorry I didn't have the cab fare. It's just that we're all sharing a car on this trip, and I didn't want the guys to know what I was doing. I feel awful."

Jace sat up next to her. "Jerome and Richie are okay musicians, but I agree that you need better. You deserve so much better." She looked into Paloma's eyes, shining in the light of a streetlamp streaking through the bedroom window. "Your career is about to break wide open. I've seen enough other bands to know this is the time. You've got the songs. Your sound is totally your own. And, babe, you've got a look that people remember."

Paloma pointed to the gap between her teeth. "Because I look like a hick."

Jace grabbed her hand. "Because you look like you take no bullshit and won't let anyone tell you who you're supposed to be. That's the essence of the Detroit sound right now. You're the one to introduce it to the rest of the world, and I want to help you do that."

"How?"

Jace took a deep breath. "I want to be your business manager."

Paloma snorted. "I have no business to manage. I don't even know where my next gig will be."

"That's why you need me," Jace said. "You focus on making the music. I'll focus on getting you gigs, doing publicity . . . and breaking the news to Jerome and Richie that they're being replaced."

"You'd do that?" Paloma asked. "Not just talk to the guys, but the other stuff, too?"

"Absolutely. I don't want anything, or anyone, to hold you back."

Paloma was quiet for a moment. "Do you really think I'm that good?"

It was as if Paloma had asked if water was wet. "Of course! Hasn't anyone else told you that?"

"I mean, yeah," she hedged, looking down at her lap. "Sometimes it's hard to know if people are lying to you to get something for themselves."

Jace laughed. "You saw that audience tonight. Do you think that crowd was jumping on top of one another and screaming their lungs out to trick you?" She guided Paloma's face upward, catching a glimpse of her self-doubt. "Trust me. You're that good. You're cover-of-*Rolling-Stone* good. Sold-out-world-tour good."

She was rewarded by an unbridled smile. "Get-on-*Late-Show-with-David-Letterman* good? That's where all the real talent goes."

"Yes!" Jace said with a sideways hug. "Don't doubt yourself."

"I'll try," Paloma said, her shoulders relaxing. "Look, this all sounds amazing, but I need to think about it, okay?"

"I get that." Jace looked at the clock. "Let's get some sleep, and we can talk about it in the morning." She lay down with her arm outstretched, pulling Paloma close to her again.

"So, if you become my manager, what happens to this?" Paloma asked, motioning between the two of them. "What happens to us?"

Us. Hearing Paloma say that tiny word was like an answered prayer.

"Well, we can have professional 'us' and personal 'us,'" Jace replied, concealing her delight. "We'll make it all work."

"Because I like personal 'us,'" Paloma said. "A lot."

"Me too," Jace said as their lips met. Then Paloma let out an enormous yawn and settled into Jace's arms, looking completely at peace. Jace was about to drift off as well when Paloma rolled on her side, half asleep, and said, "I would love to be on *Letterman* someday."

Jace spooned her. "I promise to make it happen for you. For us."

2

NOT LONG AGO

APRIL 22, 2023

When her iPod Classic went silent in the middle of "Cry Me the Detroit River" by Exclamation and the Points, Jace Randolph sucked in her breath. Suddenly, a *POP!* burst through her dashboard speakers, the song resumed, and she exhaled. The world was back in balance.

Going south on Woodward, Jace stopped for a red light at 9 Mile, braking her not-so-young Escalade gently so as not to jostle the ancient MP3 player back into silence. She knew it was living on borrowed time. Apple had stopped making this particular model ten years ago, but Jace loved its click wheel and 160 gigs of memory that put her entire music library of 20,000 songs in the palm of her hand. Last winter, her fix-it guy had retired, leaving her with the awkward prospect of explaining to folks at the Genius Bar why she didn't just stream music on her phone like everyone else. "Just old-fashioned, I guess," she'd say, so she wouldn't have to tell the truth about what that hunk of hardware represented: the time in her life when she considered herself the best indie rock-and-roll business manager in the country and had the live recordings, demo tracks, and limited releases, all stuffed onto one device, to prove it.

The iPod cut out again at Grand Boulevard, and after wiggling the cable didn't work, she huffed an aggravated sigh and turned on NPR. She had faith that the device would come to its senses before she drove home eighteen hours later, once the black-tie fundraiser she was producing was over. That was its usual MO.

Pulling around to the back of Little Caesars Arena, Jace waved a pass at the card reader and parked in a space on the ground floor. It was nearly six A.M. on what promised to be a beautiful April Saturday, not that she'd see any of the sunlight. Any minute, her crew would arrive in a fleet of black vans emblazoned with the Function Fest logo and start to unload their banks of video gear, sound boards, and laptops preloaded with looping PowerPoint tributes to the Adoption Academy, their client and host of that evening's "Holding Hands" benefit. The nonprofit was dedicated to matching children of all kinds to parents of all sorts, building families from a rainbow of races and genders, an array of physical and mental abilities, and more. Adoption Academy had helped her sister Joyce adopt Olivia and Kristi as a single mom more than two decades ago; through that connection, the agency became Jace's first major client when she launched Function Fest as an event management company shortly afterward. Since then, Jace's business had grown into a very profitable enterprise. The agency had kept her on retainer even when no one was having galas during the pandemic. She owed them a lot, and she was thrilled to be back yet again.

Actually, "thrilled" was way too strong a word. Obligated, maybe. Frustrated—definitely. More than a bit antsy. Kind of tired. She was thankful that Adoption Academy turned to Function Fest year after year, but lately Jace had been feeling less than inspired by a career that relied on her producing the same events the same way over and over. It was a far cry from supporting artists who were blazing their own trail.

"But tonight is for the kids," she told herself, bumping her fist against the steering wheel for emphasis. "Kids like Livvy and Kristi who need parents like Joyce. Pull it together for them, for fuck's sake."

Her affirmations complete, Jace checked the rearview mirror. She was grateful that her hair was graying tastefully—a little on the sides, a sprinkling through her wavy, chin-length shag. She was also glad her tortoiseshell horn-rims concealed a lot of the things she refused to plaster over with makeup or Botox: the under-eye puffiness, the frown lines that stuck around even when she was happy, the age spot above her left cheekbone that her dermatologist insisted on calling a "mark of character." She then pulled her computer bag and travel mug out of her SUV and headed toward the back entrance to the arena.

Playing this kind of venue hadn't even been on the wish list for most of the acts she'd managed in the '90s. None of them would have wanted to play this 20,000-seat behemoth, with its hydraulics and wraparound sound system and massive screens making it possible for folks in the cheap seats to experience the concert as if they were watching TV. To the old guard of the indie community, that was the epitome of selling out. Besides, what fun was doing a show if you couldn't sweat directly on your entire audience?

A question appeared, unbidden, in Jace's brain: Was that why Paloma dropped out of the public eye back in 2001? Did she think she was selling out? It hadn't seemed so at the time. More than twenty years later, Jace still didn't have a definitive answer.

After going through security, Jace made her way into the arena. There had been a Red Wings game the night before, and even though the ice was well below layers of flooring and carpet, she felt a slight chill in the stadium. She adjusted her black cashmere sweater over slim-fit jeans and straightened the chunky silver rings she wore on her right hand.

"Morning, boss!"

Jace looked up to see Louis Martin, Function Fest's senior producer, striding toward her, followed by a caravan of technicians in black polo shirts pushing carts of equipment into the arena. He had been Jace's first hire after she watched him jury-rig sound systems out of wooden crates and Radio Shack speakers at the dive bars where she'd booked Paloma at the start of their careers. He had an engineer's brain for solving technical glitches and kept his cool even when clients were screaming at him about why they looked like gorgons on the jumbo screens. He was a round-bellied, mustachioed sweetheart.

"So good to see you!" Jace said as she hugged him. Ever since the pandemic put meetings online, she rarely saw her staff in person anymore. As much as she liked working from home in sweats instead of getting into business drag and going to the office, she missed being around people. Especially her people.

Soon, she and Louis's team were huddled over their laptops, confirming every detail: when the stage build would be done, how long they had for each speaker to rehearse, the number of peonies in each centerpiece. As CEO, Jace's main role for the evening was to be chief schmoozer, liaising with the clients so her team could get their work done without tripping over any egos.

Hours later, as the doors opened and guests streamed in, the arena looked as if Adoption Academy was hosting a royal wedding. Rosy lighting focused attention away from the thousands of empty stadium seats and onto the main floor, which was abloom with floral arrangements the size of Roman columns and set with dozens of round tables and hundreds of folding chairs slipcovered in creamy brocade. The stage shimmered, its silver and blue backdrop framing the podium. Guests were nibbling crab cakes and mushroom wellingtons and sipping champagne as servers navigated the growing crowd.

Jace hung back at the tech table at the rear of the space. She'd changed into her black tuxedo, shirt, and tie, which was essentially a more expensive version of the all-black outfit she'd been wearing all day, headphones on so she could stay connected with the team.

About a half hour after the doors opened, Jace spotted Sabine and Mo at the bar. She gave them comps to Holding Hands every year so her friends could enjoy a glitzy night out on the town, and so they could all gossip about every detail of the event the next day.

Leaning into the "black" of the black-tie dress code, Sabine was wearing a vintage high-necked sheath with long sleeves and lace and sequin details that made her look like a tasteful raven, her pearl-gray hair speared with ebony sticks into a French twist. Mo wore a red brocade tux jacket, black velvet pants, and a starched white shirt with black piping around the points of the collar, a bit of pomade in her steely crew cut. Given that she was typically in scrubs before and after her shift at a physical therapy clinic, Jace almost didn't recognize her.

Pulling her headset down around her neck, Jace hugged them both. "Thanks for coming."

"Wouldn't miss it," Sabine said, raising her glass of champagne.

"You clean up well," Jace said to Mo.

"I'm surprised this getup still fits," Mo said, running her thumb under her waistband. "I swear, every day, part of my body's gone further south. Boobs, belly, ass. If I sneeze, stand back—this is all gonna blow."

"Who's covering for you at the Artemis tonight?" Jace asked Sabine.

"Rennie."

Mo snorted. "You sure that's a good idea?"

"They've worked for me for three years," Sabine said between sips. "They've handled everything from tending bar to breaking up fights. They'll be fine."

"Yeah, but did they bring their guitar?" Mo asked. "Please tell me they didn't bring their guitar."

"They brought their guitar," Sabine said.

Jace and Mo groaned simultaneously. "Rennie is a sweet kid but a terrible musician," Jace said.

"Give them a break. They're just starting out," Sabine retorted.

"They're the only guitarist I've ever heard who gets worse the more they practice," Mo said.

"Rennie has a bold, one-of-a-kind sound and an electrifying stage presence," Sabine corrected with a disapproving look. "They may not be to everyone's taste, but neither is any other musician. Cut them some slack."

"I'm not sure they're to anyone's taste," Mo said, setting her club soda and lime on the bar.

"It's a wonder that you two never dated," Jace said with a fond smile.

Mo laughed, then said, "Oh my God, listen! Can you believe what song they're playing?"

Jace tried to focus on the background music amid the chatter and clinking of glassware. "I can't hear it. What are they playing?"

"It's 'Heart Fire,'" Sabine said gently.

"Ouch," Mo said, grabbing some nuts from the bowl on the bar.

Jace closed her eyes and listened harder. Sure enough, that was "Heart Fire," Paloma's biggest hit. The song that got her national, then international, attention. The song she played on *Late Show with David Letterman* in 2001, which ended up being her last public appearance, professionally and personally. The song that Paloma had said was inspired by her love for Jace, which now seemed like a sick joke.

Jace opened her eyes and put on a brave smile. "I told the DJ to focus on recent hits. I'm surprised this got on the playlist."

Sabine squeezed Jace's arm sympathetically. "It's back on the charts, hon. It was featured on that Netflix show a few weeks ago, the one with all those Greek gods disguised as movie stars."

"*Olympia, California.* The season finale," Mo said. "Everyone on TikTok is using it for a soundtrack."

"How would you know that?" Jace asked, truly curious.

"TikTok is not just for the youths, my friend." Mo grinned. "You get any royalties on Paloma's songs?"

"No," Jace said. "I insisted she retain all her publishing rights, since she was the artist."

Mo snorted. "Too bad. You'd be making bank." Then she saw Jace's pained expression. "Sorry."

The song wrapped with three descending chords blasting pure energy to prime a live audience to scream and applaud. This evening, though, there was no audience reaction, and the next tune on the playlist kicked in immediately.

Mo put a hand on Jace's shoulder. "You know what I think? You're overdue for a new relationship. Have you ever thought about taking a night off from work once in a while to start dating again? After all, happiness is the best revenge."

Jace knew Mo meant to make her feel better. It didn't work.

"Can you get a drink with us later, Jace?" Sabine said, thankfully changing the subject.

Jace shook her head. "I have to stay until all the equipment is packed up. It's going to be a long night." She looked over to the control desk and saw Louis signaling she needed to get back on headset. "I have to go. We'll chat tomorrow at your place, Sab. Have fun tonight!"

"Break a leg," Mo said.

"*Merde*," Sabine seconded.

Jace put her headset back on and pressed the call button. "What's up, Louis?"

"Client's got a last-minute add to the visuals."

Returning to the control desk, Jace found Madeleine Grady-Poole, the head of fundraising for the Adoption Academy, expertly coiffed and delicately poured into an expensive evening gown. "Sorry to be your least favorite person at the last minute, Jace."

"Not a problem."

During the many years they'd worked together, Jace appreciated how much Madeleine loved Adoption Academy and its mission. Madeleine had also been an advocate for Function Fest and how their expertise was well worth their fees, referring lots of new business their way.

Jace looked at her watch; they had three minutes before the emcee was scheduled to get on stage. "What do you need?"

Madeleine handed her a thumb drive. "Our new board member wants to say a few words. Here's his title slide. He goes after the CEO, right before I introduce the auction."

"Anything for the teleprompter?" Jace asked as Louis uploaded the slide.

"He plans to speak off the cuff."

Jace had worked with Madeleine long enough to have developed an "If you see something, say something" rapport. "That's not a good idea."

Madeleine nodded. "It's a terrible idea—especially since he's a couple of Sazerac slings in—but he just bought his way onto the board with a massive contribution, so the CEO can't wait to give him a microphone and a captive audience."

"Swell," Jace said as she watched Louis flip through the graphics for the big screen. Madeleine gave her a thumbs-up then headed toward her seat. A minute later, Jace heard the stage manager count down the cue, and the emcee came to the podium to welcome the crowd.

Jace took a chair behind Louis to view the various monitors as they captured video, ran the slides, and cued up the walk-on music. Things clicked along as planned right up until the new board member unsteadily stepped up to the podium, looking as if he'd indulged in a couple more cocktails. "Here we go," she muttered.

"Because of Adoption Academy, hundreds of children have found families," the board member began. "Kids who were so desperate they'd take anybody who wanted be their parent. Parents who couldn't have . . . uh, natural children."

"We knew he needed a script," Louis said.

"And time to sober up," Jace added.

"Parents are the first line of defense in society," he went on. "Protecting their children from harmful ideas. Teaching them values, getting them the kind of education that puts them on the right path."

Jace crossed her arms. Nothing this man was saying was technically offensive or incorrect, but his word choice had her on high alert.

He pressed on. "And as a board member, it's my goal to connect these poor children with people who *deserve* to be parents. People with strong values, who won't confuse kids about who they are and what they should be."

Louis cocked an eyebrow.

"And when I say parents, I mean one of each."

"Shit," Jace said.

"Men and women parents—together," he rambled on. "None of that 'lifestyle' stuff. No wonder so many kids are confused about their identity. If you ask me—"

"Shit, shit, SHIT!" Jace turned off her headset and shook Louis's shoulder. "Cut the mic!" she hissed.

"Did Madeleine give you a sign or—"

"CUT THE MIC!"

The microphone went silent, and the room went still. Standing in the shadows, her stomach in knots, Jace watched as the board member tapped the microphone before slurring, "What the fuck is this? Censorship?"

In a sequined flash, Madeleine was on stage. She pulled the board member close enough to whisper something that calmed him down, then addressed the crowd with all the poise of a career diplomat. "My goodness, I apologize. We're having technical difficulties with our sound system," she announced with a professional smile. "While we take a moment or two to fix the problem, please join me in thanking Mr. Drew Kensington for his support and commitment to Adoption Academy. We'll be right back." During the applause, she descended the stairs and strode straight back to Jace.

"I need a word with you. Now," Madeleine said close to Jace's ear.

"Of course."

Jace followed her out into a corridor well away from the party guests. Checking to ensure no one was near, Madeleine half whispered, half yelled, "Did you turn off Drew's microphone on purpose?"

"I acted in the best interest of my client," Jace said calmly, her arms at her sides, her feet planted.

"How so? You embarrassed one of our CEO's good friends and one of Adoption Academy's major donors."

That broke Jace's composure. "He was insinuating there's something wrong with single parents, queer parents—queer kids even!"

"He's funding our operations for the next three years, Jace!"

Jace watched in silence as Madeleine Grady-Poole drew herself to her full height.

"Per our CEO, Function Fest's contract will terminate at the close of this evening's event. Look for an email from my office." With that, she stalked away.

The rest of the event, Jace sat in the dark at the tech table, close to the crew. She didn't leave to go to the bathroom or get a bottle of water, in case she'd bump into an executive from Adoption Academy. Even once the guests were long gone, she said nothing about what happened to anyone, not wanting to break their focus with so much work to do. She'd brief Louis and the team once Madeleine's email had arrived and the situation was official.

In the wee hours, Jace finally drove home, exhausted and heartsick. She sped north on Woodward in silence, rehashing every moment of the disastrous evening, her anger at Madeleine and the Adoption Academy board member flaring up at every stoplight. But it wasn't just losing Function Fest's most lucrative client for all the wrong reasons that had her in a fury spiral. As she turned off Woodward past the Royal Oak town line and headed toward her house in Clawson, she couldn't stop ruminating about one more thing:

How could "Heart Fire" become a hit again without me even realizing it?

Couldn't Paloma have contacted me to let me know?

Do I matter to her at all?

Did I ever?

Once home, she dumped her bags in the dining room and headed straight to the bathroom, iPod in hand. Not long after Paloma abandoned her, Jace had created a playlist designed to thrash pain and agony out of her system. She was going to take a hot shower and play the music as loud as she could without bothering the neighbors.

But when Jace settled the iPod into its docking station, she was greeted by a pixelated cartoon face with Xs for eyes and a frown.

Her iPod was completely, irrecoverably dead.

For the first time all night—for the first time really since Paloma had left her—Jace collapsed onto the floor and sobbed.

3

NOT LONG AGO

APRIL 23, 2023

A few hours later, Jace sat at Sabine's dining room table, staring into an empty coffee mug and nursing a tension headache. She'd agreed weeks ago to come over for brunch as her friends' thank you for treating them to tickets to the fundraiser. Given last evening's fiasco, she'd thought about canceling, but after a sleepless night, she needed some TLC. Sabine's little Victorian in Corktown was the epitome of cozy: squishy pillows on the purple velvet sofa, a window seat where her regal feline did her birdwatching, and kitchen cupboards stocked with everything from Sleepytime tea to top-shelf liquor. Plus, her friend was a talented cook, and Jace was all for drowning her misery in carbohydrates and caffeine.

Mo and Sabine listened patiently as Jace took them through the backstage drama, then dove in with advice as soon as she'd finished the recap, despite Jace's protests that she'd figure things out.

"Is there any chance Adoption Academy will reconsider?" Sabine asked, putting a pancake on Jace's plate.

"She already emailed me the termination notice," Jace said. "And just like that, more than half of my annual revenue went *poof!* and, with Madeleine knowing most of the CEOs in southeast Michigan, it won't be easy to find new clients beyond the handful I already have."

"Good riddance, though," Mo said.

"Easy for you to say," Jace said, her temples pounding. "You're not going to have to face down my staff tomorrow, trying to explain how standing up for The Community is worth putting them on furlough."

"Maybe you can branch out to other lines of work," Sabine said, taking a second helping of strawberries. "Ever thought about doing weddings?"

Jace stopped chewing mid-bite. "There is not enough money in the world for me to go into the Bridezilla business."

"You could probably get a lot of jobs in Oakland County," Mo offered. "Those suburban parents will throw down crates of cash to capture every minute of their kids' lives. I took my nephew to his friend's seventh birthday party last week, and I swear the mom hired a film crew."

"No," Jace said, going into the kitchen to nab some more coffee.

"If you don't like kids, they do the same thing for their dogs," Mo yelled after her.

"Again, no." Jace came back and sat down with a loud sigh. "Let's face it: I feel like I've been treading water for years. Maybe the universe is telling me to do something else. Something that makes me feel like I'm living my life on purpose."

Sabine looked at her, dark eyes hopeful. "Go back to managing bands!"

Jace's stomach tightened. She'd considered this on and off for two decades, yet every time she thought about it too long, she'd recall how her talent management career imploded the first time around. "I don't exactly have a stellar record. I had one good act, and she bailed on me. And the others I tried to make happen? Well, we don't exactly hear their tunes on TV shows, now do we?"

"C'mon, Booty Bar was a killer act," Mo said with exaggerated enthusiasm. "And Bitemother? Timeless."

"That proves my point," Jace said. "My management career was a very public disaster."

"That was Paloma's fault, not yours," Mo said.

"Paloma was an idiot!" Sabine fired off, balling up her napkin and tossing it onto the table. "She would have been living in her car and burning demo tapes for warmth if you hadn't entered her life. And I will never forgive her for breaking up with you by leaving New York without so much as a thank-you for getting her the gig of a lifetime. You deserved so much more, so much better."

As grateful as she was to have Sabine rise to her defense, Jace wished she would stop talking. She hadn't dragged herself from Clawson to Corktown on fifteen minutes' sleep to feel worse than she did when she arrived.

No such luck.

"All those frantic weeks you searched for her, worrying that she was on drugs or suicidal when she was just being selfish," Sabine continued, her volume rising. "All those months you spent on my couch, piecing your broken heart back together. And the fact that you haven't had another long-term relationship since then? I blame Paloma for that, too!"

Seeing Jace wince, Mo spoke up. "Okay, enough reopening old wounds. What we're telling you, Jace, is that you were a great talent manager back in the day and could be one again if you wanted to get back into it. Right, Sab?"

Sabine looked sheepish. "Right. That's exactly what I meant. You've still got it."

"Thanks," Jace said with a grateful nod to Mo. "Let's face facts, though. All my promo work was before social media, and most of my contacts retired or lost my number long ago."

"So make new contacts," Mo said, pushing the rest of her scrambled eggs onto her fork with her thumb.

"And you can hire someone for the publicity and social media stuff," Sabine added. "I did that for the Artemis."

"Who?" Jace asked.

"Rennie."

Mo hooted. "What is it about Rennie that you've got them doing every odd job at the club? Do they owe you money or something?"

"I appreciate a striver," Sabine said. "They love the club, they will do anything to help us succeed, and in the last few months, they've tripled our Instagram followers."

"So now you have nine?" Mo snorted.

Sabine ignored her. "Jace, getting back to what you want to do with the next chapter of your life—"

Before Sabine could finish her thought, Jace put up a hand to silence her; she thought she heard somebody walking down the stairs from the second floor. "Is someone else here?"

On cue, a tall and lanky twenty-something in flannel pajama bottoms and an oversized Grand Valley State University T-shirt trundled into the kitchen. Jace and Mo watched with interest as they rummaged through Sabine's fridge, extracted a bottle of oat milk, and fixed themself a mug of coffee. As they meandered back toward the staircase, oblivious to the fact that there were people staring at them from the dining room, Mo called out, "Rennie?"

They turned and pushed a shock of magenta bangs off their forehead to reveal lovely hazel eyes and a silver bridge piercing with delicate chains connected to the pointed studs. "Hey, friends," they said, lifting the mug in a salute and smiling broadly.

"I did not expect to see you here," Jace said, her mind full of tantalizing questions for Sabine.

"Me either," Mo said, tamping down a giggle. "You live here now?"

"Sabine is letting me crash until my lease starts next month," Rennie said after taking a sip. "Thanks again, Sabine. That was super cool of you. You're a lifesaver."

"You're welcome," Sabine said affectionately. "Would you like something to eat?" she asked, gesturing to the half-empty platters and bowls on the table.

"No thanks: band practice. I appreciate the offer, though." Rennie looked at Jace and Mo in turn. "Nice to see you all," they said and padded back up the stairs, mug in hand.

There was a beat of charged silence before Mo blurted out, "So you and Rennie are a thing now? I totally understand. That smile is something else."

"No," Sabine said curtly. "I have an extra bedroom, and they needed to get away from a toxic roommate. It's platonic."

"You sure Rennie thinks so?" Jace asked. "They work for you plus they want to get on stage at your club. And now they're sleeping two doors down from your bedroom. You gotta wonder why they're spending all their time at your elbow."

Sabine waved off her friend's concern with a *pfft!* "Rennie is trying to get busy with some barista, and I have no desire to relive my twenties, vicariously or otherwise. Besides, you know my spare room is always available for those who need it. Believe me: There's no funny business between me and Rennie. I'm just here to help."

"That's too bad." Mo shook her head. "I mean, look at us three single ladies. We were so randy when we were Rennie's age, but now? It's fucking depressing."

"I wasn't sure you wanted to start dating again," Sabine said.

Mo's bravado softened. "I will never love anyone like I did Gabby, but she's been gone for five years. Right before she died, she told me she'd come back and haunt me if I didn't find someone new. And she will, too."

"I've decided I don't want to start with someone new at this point," Sabine said firmly. "It would take a decade's worth of dates to go through all my backstory and baggage, and I have better things to do."

"I don't want to date because I don't want to settle," Jace said.

"You're worried that no woman wants to settle for *you,*" Mo said.

Even though she was teasing, Mo wasn't wrong.

"I don't even know anymore," Jace said. "When I was in college, all I wanted was sex. Then with Paloma, I still wanted sex, but I also wanted a life we could build together from every angle. Then that went completely to shit, and I decided to aim lower: find someone who'd like to have a few laughs. But when I went on a few dates in my thirties, it seemed like every woman I met wanted to raise kids or run a dog rescue."

"Not all of them," Sabine chided. "Some wanted to own cat cafés."

Jace continued her rant. "By the time I hit forty, all the women I was matching with online were as bad as I am. They're so focused on their careers and their hobbies and their friends and ex-lovers that they don't want to venture outside of that comfort zone to meet anyone new. Then I make it to fifty, and *bam!* The pandemic hits at the same time as menopause. I've pretty much lost interest in the whole dating game. I gotta accept that my time has passed."

"Or, you could just say, 'Fuck it!,' get a YOLO tattoo, and not give up yet," Mo said with a laugh.

"You first," Jace retorted.

Mo turned to Sabine. "Related topic: I'd like to book the club for my fifty-fifth birthday party the weekend before Thanksgiving, but I'm flexible on the date and . . . whoa, whoa, whoa! Why are you crying?"

Jace looked over to Sabine, who was unexpectedly teary-eyed and making small huffing noises. She put her hand on her friend's shoulder and drew close. "Hey, what's wrong?"

Mo looked stricken. "Did I say something wrong? Was it me talking about dating or being so much younger than you or—"

"No, no, that's not it," Sabine snurfled.

"Then what is it?" Jace asked.

Sabine looked at each of them and said in a quiet, broken voice, "I have to close the club."

Jace felt as if all the air had been sucked out of the room. "What?"

"No! Why?" Mo demanded.

"You remember the remodel I did in 2019? Upgrading the bar area and deep cleaning the floors?"

"Yeah," Mo said. "I was so glad you did that. I was tired of sticking to the linoleum."

"At first, it was going to be a minor update, just paint and plaster,"

Sabine explained. "But every time we started fixing one problem, another one came up. The bathrooms weren't up to code, the roof caused an ice dam, we needed a new HVAC system. It got way more expensive that I'd planned for, but I figured I could handle it. Bookings were strong. Some bands were scheduling a year in advance. But then the pandemic . . ." Sabine trailed off.

"Oh, Sab," Jace said, handing her a clean napkin.

Sabine mouthed a thank-you and continued. "I had already cut back on bookings to finish the renovations before everything shut down, then I didn't have any income for more than a year. No one was touring and the locals didn't want to play indoors, and there's no space around the building for an outdoor stage. And when they announced the PPP loans during Covid, I'd already borrowed so much, I didn't want to take on any more debt."

"The bands are back now, though," Jace said in an encouraging tone. "And you've added all those extra events, like Taco Twednesdays and Butch Bingo. The last time I dropped by, you were doing good business."

"Not enough to make up for all the revenue I lost," Sabine replied. "I've missed a bunch of loan payments, and now the bank is threatening to foreclose."

Jace's brain began to whir, considering her friend's options. "Have you talked to a lawyer?"

Sabine shook her head. "If I can't afford to pay the banks, how am I going to pay for a lawyer?"

"Do you have a CPA? Could they help?" Jace asked.

"I do my own books!" Sabine said, the tears returning. "I feel so stupid. I can't believe I let things get so bad."

Jace took Sabine's hand. "Hey, I don't think you're stupid. The last three years have sucked in every way possible, and you did what you thought was right at the time."

Mo put a reassuring arm around Sabine's shoulder. "It's going to be okay. We'll help you find a way through this. But take a few slow breaths first." Sabine nodded and complied.

"So, how much debt are we talking?" Jace asked.

Sabine didn't look her in the eye. "About two hundred thousand dollars."

"Holy shit!" Mo blurted. "Why didn't you tell us earlier?"

"I didn't want you to worry about something you couldn't fix, Mo," Sabine explained. "And, Jace, you have your hands full with Function Fest."

"At least I did," Jace muttered.

Looking over at Sabine, her head bowed, her face despondent, dread started to gnaw Jace's stomach lining. Sabine had never let anything defeat her before. If the bar sink stopped up, she'd be there with a plunger. If a fight broke out in the audience, she'd stop it dead with an air horn and a phalanx of lesbian security guards. No problem had ever been insurmountable for her, and no club owner had ever loved their venue as intimately and thoroughly as Sabine loved the Artemis. Without it, Jace was sure she'd lose her life's purpose . . . and as someone who was scrambling to find her *own* life's purpose, Jace didn't want that to happen to her oldest friend.

Then an idea dropped into her brain. A terrible idea, but perhaps the only one that could possibly work.

"What if we did a benefit concert to save the Artemis?" Jace said. "It might not be hard to put together. You've had so many acts at the club over the years, we could pull together an amazing lineup."

Sabine sat up, her face brightening. "Do you think they'd want to help?"

"Of course! They owe you," Mo said. "I saw how many times you broke your 'no free drinks' policy when I was tending bar. And you didn't just give them a few beers. You gave them a place to crash. You cooked for them, gave them gas money, convinced other clubs to book them. Face it: You're the den mother of the Detroit music scene."

"And going to a concert at the Artemis was a rite of passage for so many music fans," Jace added. "None of them want to see it close, and a lot of people would pay a premium to see a star-studded show while saving a piece of musical history." She got out her phone and opened the calculator app. "What's the venue capacity?"

"About five hundred," Sabine said.

Jace typed for a few seconds. "So if we're trying to cover two hundred thousand plus have a surplus for show expenses plus other unanticipated costs at the Artemis—"

Mo whistled. "That's more than four hundred dollars per ticket already."

"Not necessarily," Jace said. "We'll make a chunk of money off of food and beverage, and if we can get that donated we'll pull in even more. Plus we can charge more for VIP packages: special seating, meet-and-greets with the musicians, autographed merchandise . . ."

Mo grinned. "Just think, Sab, you can finally get rid of all those neon T-shirts in the basement. Excuse me, I meant to say 'vintage Artemis merch.'"

"Special seating?" Sabine said, a little deflated. "Our space is general admission, standing room only."

"Yeah, and a lot of folks won't go to a show if they can't sit down," Mo added.

Jace was undeterred. "We'll work something out: risers and folding chairs, barstools. Don't worry; I'll give you some options, and we can charge a couple hundred more for them."

"A lot of our clientele can't afford to pay that much for a ticket," Sabine said. "We need to offer some tickets for a lot less, like twenty-five bucks."

"You're joking, right?" Mo said. "This is a fundraiser, Sab. *You're* the charity, not the audience."

Jace saw the resolve in Sabine's gaze and knew she wasn't going to budge. "We might be able to offset some lower-cost tickets through higher-priced VIP packages, but we'd need a lineup of heavy hitters to make that viable. Maybe even a musician who doesn't usually do gigs like this. We want to give people plenty of reasons to pony up for the pricier tickets."

Mo raised her hand like a schoolgirl, and Jace snickered. "Yes, Ms. McIlheny?"

"I have an idea, but I don't think either of you want to hear it."

"There are no bad ideas during a brainstorm," Jace said, parroting what she'd told many a Function Fest client.

Mo leaned in. "What if we could get Paloma as the headliner?"

"No!" Jace and Sabine roared in unison.

Mo raised her index finger. "Hear me out. If we were able to announce that Paloma Doralle was returning to the stage for the first time in twenty-odd years, we could charge whatever we wanted and sell out in a matter of seconds. And since 'Heart Fire' is huge right now, all kinds of new people would want to come. Then they'd fall in love with the Artemis and come back for future shows, too, so you aren't in this mess ever again. What do you say?"

Jace felt like she was having an out-of-body experience. Her brain was agreeing with every point Mo was making, but her heart had slowed to a stop. Sure, they could put together a banger of a lineup without Paloma, but there was little chance they'd make the money Sabine needed to put her financial trouble behind her for good. After so many years out of the spotlight, Paloma had transformed from a pop music sensation into a mythical creature, and lots of people would pay insane amounts of money for a glimpse of that unicorn.

Even though Jace would probably end up gored in the process.

Jace was lying to her friends when she said she was done with dating. She was actually done with love altogether. All these years after Paloma traipsed off into the unknown, Jace still had so much emotional scar tissue, she could barely feel her pulse. She had exited the music industry, founded her own business, and even gone through the motions with other women several times since then, but none of that could repair the damage. And even though she believed she'd been through the worst of it already, who knew how bad it might get if she saw Paloma again?

Mo was staring at her, awaiting her reply, and while Sabine's frown was set in granite, her eyes were pleading for help. Jace realized this situation wasn't about her feelings. It was about saving Sabine's livelihood and reputation. It was about being a professional who could put her own emotions aside because she had a job to do. And if the universe intended for her to live on purpose, what better way to start than by helping a dear friend in need? She really had no choice.

Before she could talk herself out of it, Jace spoke up. "Mo is right. Paloma could make or break this event."

"Forget it," Sabine said, folding her arms. "I'd rather go bankrupt than ask her to perform here again."

"Then I'll ask her," Jace said, doubling down to silence the protestations in her head. "I'll hunt her down and convince her to headline the show."

Sabine briskly shook her head. "Jace, you can't do that."

"You ought to know by now you can't tell me what to do," Jace said with a smile.

Sabine exhaled sharply. Normally aglow with hope and kindness, she now looked wrung out and tired in ways her makeup couldn't hide. She took Jace's hand and leaned in. "I don't want you to get hurt all over again. This is my problem, not yours. Don't do this to yourself."

Jace gave Sabine's hand a smooch. "You've been my friend longer than anyone else on earth. I love you, and I love the Artemis. Whether you want me to or not, I'm going to save you and your club by producing a blowout benefit concert with special guest star Paloma Doralle."

"Shit, that's so dope! How can I help?"

Mo, Sabine, and Jace swiveled their heads toward Rennie, who was standing in the hallway dressed in motorcycle leathers, sporting a guitar case and a big grin.

Putting her momentary surprise aside, Jace said, "I'll let you know."

"Got it, got it. Fantastic! Well, anyway, gotta go."

"Which outfit are you playing with these days, Rennie?" Mo asked.

"We call ourselves Purple Betty."

"Why?" Jace asked, worried that they'd named themselves after some sort of party drug.

"It took Flintstones vitamins twenty years to finally include Betty Rubble," they elaborated. "Me and the band consider her a symbol of being true to yourself and breaking free of gender-based repression. And grape is my favorite flavor, so Purple Betty!"

"Ah," Jace said.

"See ya!" With that, Rennie put on their helmet and strolled out the front door.

Jace watched them go, wondering what she'd just gotten herself into.

WAY BACK WHEN

MARCH 7, 1998

The pungency hit Jace and Paloma right as they opened the stage door: Burnt popcorn. Cigarette smoke. Body odor.

Eau de Artemis Club.

"This reeks worse than that shitty Quality Inn in Toledo," Paloma said, wrinkling her nose.

"Don't worry, it'll smell even worse once the audience gets here," Jace said, squeezing Paloma's hand.

The sun had barely set when Paloma and her rhythm section—Mary the bassist, who Jace poached from the Ice Floes out of Pontiac, and Colin the drummer, the brother of the lead guitarist of East Lansing's Hootchie Mama—got on stage to do their sound check. Jace had insisted they be precisely on time so they could fiddle with the light levels, brief the kid who was running the merch table, and still have plenty of time for a leisurely dinner instead of eating cold pizza backstage per usual. It was the first time Paloma Doralle was playing to a Detroit audience after months of humping across the country, and Jace wanted her to be relaxed and ready to wow the home crowd.

They were running through "Why Don't You?" when Paloma

halted mid-verse. "Louis, is my mic too hot?" Paloma asked, looking toward the back of the room. "I don't want to drown out Mary and Colin."

Sabine had upgraded the sound and light boards while Jace and Paloma had been out of town. She'd also brought in Louis as her primary tech for the evening; Jace remembered him as something of a MacGyver, handy with high-end electronics but not above taping microphones to broom handles back when Sabine didn't have enough money to buy mic stands.

Louis turned a couple of knobs on the mixing board. "Try it now."

The trio picked up where they left off, and Paloma threw Louis a thumbs-up in between chords. Next, they worked through "Taken for Granted" and "Seedy," a couple of the new songs Paloma wrote in the van as Jace drove the band from college town to college town. Now that schools were closed for spring break, she was ready to perform them in front of a roomful of grown-ups.

Thanks to Jace's relentless phone calls and emails to flaky students and overworked campus staff, Paloma Doralle had played several months of gigs rippling outward from metro Detroit to Ann Arbor and East Lansing, dipping down into Ohio and out to Wisconsin and Illinois. Jace's strategy was to build Paloma's following with Midwestern audiences, who would tell their friends across the country to check her out. She set up interviews for Paloma for local newspapers and radio stations. If she saw an indie music zine in a bookstore or record shop, Jace would track down the publisher and invite them to the next show. When they weren't playing, Jace would take Paloma to hole-in-the-wall venues to check out the talent and chat up the bar owners, engineers, and fans to find out who else they needed to meet and where else they needed to perform while they were touring. And Jace gave every person she talked to a business card featuring an artsy black-and-white photo of Paloma on one side and the address of her brand-new website on the other.

It had been a slog. Nothing was ever set up as promised, and Jace spent most performance days calling around town for cables, guitar strings, and even generators and light trees. They'd slept when and where they could and eaten at a lot of gas stations and 7-Elevens. After all that, the Artemis felt like Madison Square Garden.

Standing in the back next to Louis, watching the red and blue lights dapple Paloma's face as she grinned during a guitar riff, clearly overjoyed to be on a stage that wasn't a converted cafeteria for the first time in forever, Jace felt immensely proud. Their show was sold out with additional standing room, and Brother Uncle, a group Paloma wouldn't have dreamed to be on the same bill with not long ago, was her opening act. The best singer/songwriter/guitarist in recent memory was returning to Detroit as a rising star, and Jace was sure she'd continue to soar from here.

The sound check wrapped, and Jace helped the musicians stow their equipment offstage so the opening acts could set up. Sabine met them as they came offstage and gave Jace a hug.

"It feels like you've been gone for nine years, not nine months," Sabine said with a squeeze.

Jace smiled, picking up notes of Sabine's signature freesia perfume and face powder. "I've missed you, too."

"Great to have you back at the Artemis!" Sabine said to Paloma as she hugged her next. "Your new material is really something special. You've taken a leap since you played here last summer."

"Thanks," Paloma said. "I've been trying to sharpen my lyrics, say something more than just 'Time's up, are we gonna fuck or what?' You know?"

Sabine chuckled. "That's actually a great lyric. You should write that down."

Mary tapped Jace on the shoulder. "When does Brother Uncle go on? I sat in with them when they got started a few years ago."

"Ten o'clock."

"Great. I'll be back by then," Mary said, zipping up her pink Naugahyde jacket and fluffing her jet-black bob before going out through the lobby.

"I'm out, too," Colin said, his hands stuffed into the pockets of his skinny red 501s. "My brother and I are going to catch his friend's band over at the Old Miami; they've got an early set."

"No fights this time," Jace called after him as he turned to go. "I don't have any more money for bail."

With the rhythm section out of the picture, Sabine turned to Paloma and Jace. "Well, ladies, the city is ours. Feel like Mexican?"

Before Jace and Paloma could weigh in, there was an enormous crash out in the hallway. Sabine ran toward the lobby, with the other two right behind her. When they opened the door, they heard a sound even louder than the crash: Mo yelling, "What the FUCK, Clem?"

Mo was towering over a pile of overturned cases of beer, with glass shards scattered across the lobby and pools of amber liquid creeping across the scuffed tile floor. A slightly built guy with a lopsided red undercut and a royal flush tattooed on his neck was on the other side of the pile, staring at his feet.

"I thought—" Clem said quietly.

"Oh, you *thought*?" Mo snapped. "Glad to know that's possible."

"Mo, be nice," Sabine interjected. "Clem, what happened?"

He continued to look at his shoes. "Since it's a long way from the delivery door to the bar, and those cases are heavy, I thought I could put the cases on a dolly cart and give them a push so they'd roll down the hall, and I'd catch them at the door. But they went a lot faster than I expected and smashed into the wall."

Mo's face tightened. "No kidding."

"I didn't know the floor sloped toward the doorway," Clem protested.

"You're blaming the floor now?" Mo asked.

Careful not to step on the wreckage, Sabine inserted herself between the two. "Okay, okay; what's done is done. How much did we lose?"

Mo scanned the boxes. "I'd say at least ten cases, and this is the fancy stuff. We charge more for this than the kegs of Crap on Tap."

Clem let out a sigh. "About the kegs . . ."

Mo froze. "What about them?"

"The delivery guy didn't have them. He said they got put on the wrong truck."

Sabine's mouth fell open. "You're kidding."

"And they didn't have the vodka or whiskey we ordered either. Something about an accident on the Ambassador Bridge, trucks not being able to come over from Canada. So that's not on me." Clem finally looked up at them, his apologetic water-blue eyes encased in black eyeliner.

Mo abruptly walked to the opposite end of the lobby, where she looked up at the ceiling and let out an unbridled "FUUUUUCK!" When she came back to the group, her face was much more relaxed. She pointed to Clem. "You are on cleanup duty. Get moving." He turned on the heel of his run-down Converse and raced to the supply closet.

She turned next to Sabine. "I'll do a quick inventory of what booze we've got on hand. We should have enough to keep people happy until I can get some more supplies. I need some cash, though. How much do you have?"

"I'll go check the safe," Sabine said, heading to her office.

Mo turned to Jace and Paloma. "You've got a van, right?" They nodded. "Jace, you remember how to get to the Liquor Coliseum?"

"In Dearborn?" Jace asked. "I think so."

Mo looked over at Paloma. "You comfortable chatting up strangers?"

"I've chatted up some strange people, if that counts," she answered with a side glance toward Jace.

Mo smiled and clapped her hands together. "Then let's go on a field trip, shall we?"

Forty-five minutes later and money in hand, they pulled into the barely lit parking lot next to the Liquor Coliseum in Jace's rust-ridden Aerostar. Under the terms of the Artemis Club's liquor license, they were not supposed to buy in bulk from local retailers, so they needed to make three large, seemingly unrelated purchases without raising suspicion. They entered the store with a clatter of sleigh bells as the front door opened, ready to follow the plan Mo had laid out for them on the drive over.

By the time Mo hoisted the kegs onto a flatbed and dragged them to the front register, Paloma was having a friendly conversation with the clerk, her purchases already paid for. Jace was quietly stocking her cart with cases of craft beer, keeping tabs on what was happening to make sure all was going smoothly.

"You're a guitarist, too?" Paloma said, leaning over the counter and ignoring Mo. "That's amazing! Where do you play?"

The clerk, who looked to be in his forties, puffed up. "I haven't performed in a while, but in the seventies our band would open for acts coming through the Grande Ballroom."

"That's iconic! I'm jealous!" Paloma gushed. The clerk scanned Mo's items without sparing her an extra glance, and she left the store without incident. "You've gotta have some stories," Paloma went on as Jace approached the register.

"How much time you got?" He peered over his glasses and chuckled along with Paloma. "Let's just say nothing gets the crazies to come out of the woodwork like a concert at the Grande."

"Oh my God!" Paloma said, ignoring Jace. "Ever think about going back on stage?"

He shook his head. "I'd had my fill of it by 1979. By then, my girlfriend was insisting on becoming my wife, and her dad wanted to sell his store, and then the kids came one, two, three, so: Welcome to the Liquor Coliseum."

"Nothing wrong with that," Paloma said. "Your kids are lucky to have such a cool dad."

"Not sure they'd agree with you," he said, handing Jace her receipt. "Here you go."

Jace dragged her cart to the door and looked over her shoulder to see Paloma hoisting her cardboard box full of handles of hard liquor and various mixers. "Thanks a bunch!" she told the clerk.

He started to walk around the counter. "Hey, I can help you with that."

"Oh, no, that's okay," Paloma said, walking backward through the door as Jace held it open for her without looking her in the eye. "If I can't lift it, I shouldn't drink it. Bye now!"

Within a few minutes, the booze was packed up in the van, and after a round of high fives, the women were back on I-94 speeding toward the club. Once they arrived, Mo located Clem, who was very eager to help them unload to make up for what had happened earlier, and Jace and Paloma went inside to find Sabine. While they probably didn't have time to eat anywhere beyond walking distance, Jace figured they could dine at a restaurant with placemats if they hurried.

They found Sabine in her office, holding the phone receiver to her ear. "No, we got her to leave on her own. You don't have to send anyone anymore; we're all set."

Once she hung up, Jace asked, "Who were you talking to? The cops?"

"Animal Control."

Jace's face tensed up. "What kind of animal were you controlling this time?"

"A bat."

Paloma's eyes went wide. "Those things live wild in Detroit?"

"The unlucky ones do. Thankfully, Mo was able to wrap the poor little thing in a towel and send her on her way." Sabine sighed heavily. "I'm sorry; I can't go out to dinner with you. Doors just opened, and being on critter patrol put me behind schedule."

"Want us to bring something back for you?" Jace asked.

"Thanks for asking, but no," Sabine said. "Mo and I will grab something later. You two go and have a good time."

Sabine shut the door behind her, and Paloma sidled up to Jace. "I'm so hungry, I'm about to eat my left arm. What's a decent place to eat around here?"

"Well, Lafayette Coney Island is not too far away, which is all we have time for if we're going to be back ahead of the opening act. Or I can grab a couple of pizzas and we can have a leisurely dinner backstage."

"Backstage pizza," Paloma said with small laugh. "My favorite."

"Wait: We'll eat here in the office instead, just in case they're hosing bat guano out of the dressing room."

Paloma giggled, and Jace kissed her lightly on the mouth. "I'll be right back."

Not long afterward, Jace walked from the stage door through the general admission audience, holding two large boxes aloft to avoid bumping into the gathering crowd. She stopped at the bar.

"Yo, Mo!"

Her friend looked up as she finished ringing up a couple of beers. "Yo, Jace!"

"Can I get that bubbly I bought tonight and a couple of cups?"

Mo reached into the bar fridge. "Here you go."

Balancing everything, Jace carefully tapped on the office door. When Paloma answered, Jace beamed and raised the bottle. "Happy homecoming, baby!"

As a group of Ferndale teenagers calling themselves the Propositions played their warm-up act, Jace and Paloma proceeded to gobble the pizza and polish off the Freixenet, with help from Mo and Sabine when they dropped in during a break. Paloma sat relaxed and laughing, and Jace took her in, wondering how someone so effortlessly sexy could exist in the same room as she did, much less the same bed at the end of the evening.

"So, are you nervous?" Mo asked Paloma, cadging a stray piece of pepperoni from the pizza box.

"Nervous about what?" Paloma responded.

"Bob Sarkisian coming tonight."

Paloma looked to Jace. "Bob who?"

"Sarkisian," Jace answered. "He's a producer."

"Not just any producer," Sabine added. "He's recorded half the bands who play around here, and he's got connections at most of the major labels on the West Coast."

"So why is he going to be here?" As Paloma said this, Jace noticed her eyes widening.

Jace kept her tone light. "You need someone to produce your EP, so I invited him to see the show, and he accepted."

"Which is an honor," Sabine added with a nod. "He doesn't do this for every band. He must believe you're worth seeing."

"Is this an audition?" Paloma asked.

"No," Jace said. "He just likes to check out the talent before he agrees to work with them in the studio."

"That sounds like an audition to me," Paloma said, the tension ticking up in her voice. "I've fucked up every audition I've ever done."

"Babe, just play like you always do," Jace assured her. "You have nothing to worry about."

"I'm not so sure, Jace," Paloma replied with a broken laugh. "Maybe the Propositions should do another set."

Jace knew she was joking—she *had* to be joking—but Sabine made a point of shooting her a look before saying, "Okay, break's over, Mo." As she walked past, she whispered to Jace, "Good luck fixing this, Talent Manager."

Jace took that to mean, *Don't let her cancel a sold-out show.*

She kneeled in front of Paloma, who was staring dejectedly at the floor. "Hey, what's wrong?"

"I know you worked hard to line this up, but if I see him in the audience, I'm going to fuck up. I know it." There was a desperation in Paloma's voice that told Jace that her beloved wasn't playing the diva or fishing for praise. She really was as freaked out as she sounded, and Jace's job was to help her get out of her own way.

She took Paloma's hands in hers. "You won't. You're a pro. Besides, there have been VIPs at your shows before, and they loved your music enough to stick around and tell you so. Tonight will be just the same."

"I didn't find out they were watching me until after the show was over," Paloma said with a crease in her brow. "That's a big difference; you know that."

"Well, I *didn't* know that," she said with an exasperated chuckle; there was a lot she didn't know about her a girlfriend a year into their relationship. She stood and pulled Paloma to her feet. "You're going to impress him. I wouldn't have invited him if you weren't ready to take this next step. Trust me, okay?"

Paloma's shoulders relaxed. "I trust you."

"I'll make sure he's seated out of your sight line."

"Thank you." Paloma pulled her close. "There is one person I do want to see from the stage, though. It's you. Somehow, I can spot you in the back of the house, no matter how dark or big the place is."

"Is that okay?"

She ran her fingers through Jace's wavy bob. "More than okay. That's how I know I'm not alone up there; you're here with me at all times. I love that."

Jace felt radiant. "I love you."

"Thank God."

They kissed until they heard a drum roll and crash of cymbals from the performance space. "Shit," Jace said, "it sounds like Brother Uncle is getting started."

"Time for this ragamuffin to turn into a princess," Paloma said, taking Jace's hand.

Paloma went backstage to change, and Jace stayed in the back to watch the opening act and greet Bob Sarkisian when he arrived. He looked older than Jace had expected, with gray splotches at the roots of his shoulder-length black curls and the hangdog face of someone who did most of his work at night.

"Thank you so much for coming," Jace said over the music pouring from the PA as she bought him a drink then pointed him toward the office. "There's gotta be a lot of bands asking you to check them out. I appreciate you making the time."

"The people whose taste I trust told me I couldn't miss this show,"

Bob said. "And that demo you sent me was pretty convincing, even though the sound quality was total shit. Where did she record it, the men's john at the Greyhound station?"

Jace chose not to explain to the top producer in Detroit, the one with the ear of execs at three major labels, that Paloma's demo was recorded on a four-track in an empty classroom in the Wayne State music department by a former classmate of Jace's who let them use his equipment for the cost of a case of beer. "This is a perfect night to see Paloma: packed house, brand-new audio system, lots of material from her time on the road plus crowd favorites she's been performing for a while that haven't officially been released yet. She's got more than enough cuts to choose from for a really strong EP."

Bob nodded. "Alrighty then. If I like what I see and hear out there and I think she's ready, I can start recording early next month."

Jace kept her cool, even though she wanted to jump up and down fist-bumping the air. "That should work. May I get you another Jack and Coke?"

Once Bob had his cocktail, Jace got him a chair to Louis's left at the sound board then took her usual place standing to his right. Once Mary and Colin got on stage, Louis took a microphone and with his best Voice of God said, "And now, Paloma Doralle."

The shrieks and whoops rushed toward the stage in a wave as Paloma walked to the microphone. She'd changed into her sequined Sun Records T-shirt over a black-and-white plaid skirt and bloodred tights, towering over her bass player in silver ankle boots. Butterfly barrettes kept her bangs off her face, and her makeup was leaning even further into 1920s Hollywood, with a cupid's bow of a mouth and outsized upper and lower lashes. Seeing her in the stage lights made Jace's breath catch.

The cheering had barely crested when Paloma brought the mic close to her lips and, with the grin of a little girl about to rip open her birthday presents, said:

"Okay, kids, let's play!"

5

NOT LONG AGO

MAY 6, 2023

Jace got to the tapas place fifteen minutes early for her third date with Lina, hoping to arrive first for once. She wanted to be in total control of the environment: stake out the table, touch base with her favorite waiter to ensure she got the check before Lina could offer to pay, confirm they were serving the flatiron steak and white sangria that night, the works.

Because this was their third date: the make-or-break date. The one where she either invited Lina to spend the night or broke things off to slink back home alone, frustrated, and even more convinced that she'd been stupid to try dating again in the first place.

Lina was a year older than Jace and ran a solo accounting practice from her house in Bloomfield Hills. During the pandemic, she had broken up with her girlfriend of four years when the quarantine had magnified the little things that bugged them into massive, multi-legged problems that no amount of couples' therapy could solve. Her friends had forced her to sign up for speed dating after she'd thrown her phone out the car window in a fit of pique over being ghosted one too many times on the dating apps.

Likewise, Jace had been strong-armed into giving speed dating a try by Sabine and Mo after the Adoption Academy contract went belly up. "You need to focus on something other than work, sweetie," Sabine had said, handing her the flyer when the three of them were doing dinner and a movie on a night when the Artemis was dark. "You have funneled way too much of your soul and psychic energy into your business, and you've put off dating way too long. You deserve to find someone who'll love you for who you are, not what you do for a living."

"I'm not interested in finding a life partner," Jace said.

"Well, shit, maybe you'll have to settle for sex," Mo added. "Poor you."

"This is coming from two women who haven't had a date since the Obama administration," Jace responded.

"Well, one of us has to blaze the trail, right?" Mo said. "If you can do this, there's hope for the two of us."

So Jace had speed dated, and Lina had caught her eye. At that first meeting, Jace discovered they both were small business owners, childless, terrible at any sport involving a ball, and haunted by their exes in ways they admitted were unhealthy. At their second meeting, Jace was pleased when Lina correctly identified the band (Chiaroscuro) and the title ("Love Bong") of the song playing overhead. And if that wasn't enough of a turn-on, it didn't hurt that Lina looked like Susan Sarandon as a sexy librarian, poised to take the clip out of her hair and loose her auburn tresses while removing her glasses to bat her long-lashed, wide brown eyes. Not that Jace sought out that kind of fantasy, but if the situation presented itself, she would be there for it, especially since Jace felt a jolt of electricity when Lina's fingers brushed against hers.

Yet there were some red flags. Most of Lina's anecdotes were about the horrors of tax season. She micromanaged tipping, sticking to a strict 15 percent on food and beverage (not the sales tax) and refusing to round up to the nearest dollar. And as for music, her tastes were squarely in the pop camp and set in amber prior to the 1995 edition of "Now That's What I Call Music."

Despite all that, Lina's hair clip seemed to promise something Jace hadn't experienced for more years than she'd care to admit. And she needed someone to desire her, remind her she wasn't dead—convince her that she was still capable of turning someone on at this point in her late-middle-aged life.

"You look beautiful," Jace said as Lina approached, wearing a fitted cotton dress printed with enormous yellow flowers and a pair of green, pointy-toed high heels.

"Thanks," Lina said. "I figured I'd step things up a notch." After a hug, she settled into the chair, looped her Chanel purse strap over its laddered back, and studied Jace for a moment. "Why does it seem like we dressed for two completely different dates?"

"Well, I told you this place is pretty casual," Jace said, folding her arms over her graphic tee with WELCOME TO SOUTH DETROIT printed over a Canadian flag. "And I dressed this way because I'm taking you somewhere special after dinner: I got us tickets to see the Loverladdies at the Magic Bag."

Lina's face fell. "A concert?"

"You said you liked MTV back in the day."

"I liked the music videos. I hated concerts. Hate concerts."

Jace was so shocked she couldn't stop herself from tittering. "Oh. Shit. Why?"

"I was forced to go with my brother to the Silver Dome when I was in high school," she said, her brows bunching up. "We were sitting miles away from the stage, and it was still way too loud. It took forever before the band he wanted to see went on stage because these other two shitty groups had to play first. Then the roof leaked, and we were stuck in the parking lot for an hour afterward because the guys with the light-up wands giving us directions didn't know their asses from a hole in the ground."

Even while dissing an experience Jace would have given her adolescent eye teeth to be a part of, Lina was overwhelmingly sexy, so she wanted to give her one last chance. "Not all concerts are like that. Not all venues are like that, either. The Magic Bag is a great space:

not too big, great sight lines. Lots of parking." When it didn't seem to sway her opinion, Jace added, "And the roof is watertight."

"If you say so." She leaned in, offering Jace a devilish smile and an unobstructed view of her cleavage. "But maybe we'll want to do something more exciting after dinner instead."

Lust flooded Jace's synapses as she contemplated the possibilities. "What do you have in mind?"

Lina unzipped her purse and pulled out her phone. "Let's find out." She opened an app and handed her phone to Jace, who half expected to see kinky photos of Lina, or maybe a still from *The Hunger,* with or without Catherine Deneuve. Instead, there were words. A lot of words.

"Is this a test?" Jace asked, confused.

"More like a 'getting to know you' quiz," Lina answered with a sly wink.

Jace scanned downward. There were pages and pages of questions about preferences relating to every element of a potential sexual situation: physical locations for both public and private encounters; body part nicknames; favorite brands of lotions and lubricants; body position in terms of degrees from horizontal; acceptable noise levels for various toys. She also noticed there was a button to view Lina's personalized report based on her own answers, but she refused to "Click Here."

Lust dissipating, confusion continuing, Jace asked, "Did you come up with this yourself?"

"I adapted it from an *Autostraddle* article I read a few years back," she replied. "They covered the basics, but I wanted extra layers of specificity."

The white sangria Jace had preordered arrived, and she didn't hesitate to pour herself a glass as she contemplated a dreadful question: Was everyone in the LGBTQ+ community expected to pass this sexual SAT test these days?

Jace poured some for Lina. "Kinda kills the spontaneity, doesn't it?"

"Spontaneity is overrated," she said. "At this point in my life, I don't want to fart around. I know what works for me, and if I have a heads-up on what the other person wants, I can lay in supplies and be ready to go. Everybody wins."

"I noticed there was nothing in there about relationships," Jace said after taking a large swig.

"Oh, that's a whole separate quiz," Lina said, sounding rather proud of herself. "It's pretty extensive, too. There are questions about polyamory, income inequality, and all that. Want me to show you?"

"No, I believe you," Jace responded, a little too quickly to be polite.

Lina had a point. Why waste each other's time if they were into different things? And Jace was on the prowl instead of looking for lasting love, and filling out some erotic paperwork—in the middle of a public place, which was more terrifying than titillating—might be worthwhile if it meant Lina was raring to go.

"So," Lina said in a foxy voice, "want to get started?"

Unbidden, a memory bloomed in Jace's brain from the night she met Paloma for the first time. After she'd finished her set at that sports bar in Ann Arbor, they'd found a corner away from the drunken frat boys so Jace could make her pitch about coming to the Artemis. Even as she tried to focus on business, she would lose her train of thought any time she looked at Paloma. It was like trying to hold a conversation with a beam of light, as Paloma seemed to glow brighter and more beautiful with every word Jace said. Jace had gotten to the point in her pitch where she'd try to hide the lousy performance fee behind a promise of "great exposure" when Paloma placed her hand on Jace's forearm, locked eyes with her, and said over the din, "Why don't we finish talking about this at my place?"

The next morning, Jace was putting on yesterday's clothes and scanning the room to make sure she had everything she'd come in with when she stopped in front of Paloma's Stratocaster case, lying open on the floor. The guitar was nestled in velvet, its pearl white face smudged and worn down, its jet-black body marred by nicks and scrapes. Jace stroked the strings, creating a muffled mash-up of notes. Paloma returned from the bathroom and kneeled next to her. "You ever play guitar?"

"No, I'm happier being a fan of those who can."

"Wanna try it anyway? Just for fun?"

Jace shook her head, staring at the Strat. "It looks fragile and expensive, and I don't want to break it."

"It's stronger than it looks," Paloma said, bumping Jace's shoulder with her own. "C'mon, I'll show you."

Paloma stood and picked up her guitar, then waved to Jace to join her on the other side of the room where her amp was. Once everything was plugged in, she looped the strap over Jace's head. Standing behind her, she positioned the fingers of Jace's left hand into an E5 chord and demonstrated how to hold the pick with her right.

"Ready?"

Without waiting for an answer, Paloma put her right hand over Jace's and strummed. The roar of that chord, the thrum of the guitar, the arc of Paloma's body echoing her own, the sheer joy of being with each other: Jace had never felt so in harmony with another human being before.

As Lina waited for her reply, Jace realized that sex really wasn't all she was after, after all. She wanted to see something, feel something, that promised more. She wanted that *click!* like when Paloma first put her hand on Jace's arm, completing a circuit between them that was amazing while it lasted and what she longed for even now.

Shit. She *did* want to find love.

Jace looked across the table. "Look, I'm sorry, but . . ."

Lina's confidence evaporated. "Oh," she muttered as she quickly slid her phone back into her purse.

Sensing her embarrassment, Jace wanted to keep things light. "It's good information to find out at some point, but it's a little too much, too soon for me. Hey, I don't even know if you're a vegetarian yet."

"It's clear this isn't going to work out," Lina said, ignoring Jace's attempt at a joke. "I should go. I'm sorry."

Jace saw her forlorn expression and couldn't help feeling bad for her. "Hey, no offense taken. Why don't you finish your drink before you go?"

"Why would you want me to?"

"Because you're a nice person, Lina," Jace said before pointing to the sangria. "And I can't drink this whole pitcher myself."

Lina scooted back in. "That's really kind of you."

Jace filled Lina's wineglass as she settled back into her seat. Lina took a sip then closed her eyes in shame. "Jesus, why did I think this stupid quiz was going to be the answer this time?"

"What do you mean?"

"As she was moving out, the last thing my ex said to me was, 'After all this time, you still don't know me at all.' And thinking about it later, she was right. When we got together, I was so overjoyed she wanted to be with me, I didn't dare say anything that might cause a rift. I'd keep my opinions to myself and do my best to accommodate her—sometimes at my own expense—but that wore me out and didn't make her happy anyway."

Jace froze, as if Lina had witnessed her final months with Paloma. "I understand how that can happen."

"I decided this time out, I'd leave no question unanswered. It was going to be honesty or nothing. I'd be upfront about myself and expect nothing less from whoever I was getting to know." She looked at her hands. "Anything not to be hurt again, you know?"

Jace knew. She had no intention of being hurt that badly again, either. But she also didn't want to settle.

Lina put down her drink. "Let me get this. It's the least I could do."

"It's already paid for," Jace assured her. "And don't feel awful on my account. You need to do what's best for you, and I hope you find someone who checks all your boxes."

"You, too."

Once Lina left the restaurant, Jace placed an order to go and texted Mo and Sabine.

Hey there! Date was a bust, so first one to reply gets to be my plus one to see the Loverladdies as long as you don't give me shit.

6

NOT LONG AGO

MAY 7, 2023

Jace was sitting in her sweats in her home office, a half-eaten bowl of pad prik king on her desk. She was FaceTiming with her niece Livvy over Sunday dinner, filling her in on all that had gone down over the past couple of weeks. After several minutes of monologuing interrupted by an occasional "Oh my God!" or "That sucks" from Livvy between her bites of a burrito bowl, Jace slumped back in her Aeron chair and stared into her laptop camera. "So . . . thoughts?"

Livvy adjusted her red-rimmed glasses. "You know that any sane person would have waited more than twenty-four hours after getting fired from one project to jump into another, even bigger project—for free—right?"

"What has sanity ever done for me before?"

Livvy giggled, and Jace smiled. Jace had instituted their weekly video calls ten years ago when Livvy was a freshman at Northwestern so she could stay in touch with her favorite niece; no disrespect to her older sister, but Kristi wasn't much of a music fan, and Livvy appreciated that her aunt's encyclopedic knowledge of deep-cut punk and indie music came in handy for DJing dances and dorm parties. Much to Jace's delight, they'd kept up the tradition post-college, even though Livvy was a full-on adult living in Chicago and working for a PR agency, with friends and hobbies and any number of other things that had to be more interesting than chatting with her aunt.

"I see it as a way to settle a karmic debt," Jace continued, tapping a spring roll into a tiny container of peanut sauce. "Sabine has always been there for me, and it's the least I can do for her now that she might lose her livelihood."

"But tracking down a long-lost lover who fucking broke you? That's beyond karma, Auntie. That's martyrdom."

Jace didn't want to admit that this had crossed her mind as well.

"Can I ask you a question without you calling me an ageist millennial or some shit?" Livvy asked.

"Sure," Jace replied, marveling at the fact that this was how her niece talked to her now. With her straight black hair in loose braids, Livvy still looked like the twelve-year-old who had to get her mom's permission to stay out after ten P.M. to go to a concert with Aunt Jace. "What do you want to know?"

"How old is Sabine?"

This was a topic Jace rarely contemplated. Ever since they'd first met when they were at either end of their twenties, Sabine had invested a lot of energy into creating a visual persona that transcended age. The magic of goth was that anyone could find their place regardless of gender, years, or body type as long as they had the patience to hunt down the appropriate garb and cosmetics. Jace did the math. "She's ten years older than I am, so sixty-three in June. Why?"

"Just surprised she doesn't want to retire," Livvy said.

"That is pretty ageist, Liv."

"People retire at any age. It's a fair question."

"God, no! She loves the Artemis and wants to work there forever. She's told me many times that running a venue is like hosting a non-stop family reunion, and she adores her family."

Livvy spooned up some more sofritas and guac. "Okay. I just

wanted to make sure this is worthwhile before you commit to doing all this work and reopening a painful part of your life."

Jace wiped peanut sauce off her fingers with her napkin. "So this means you'll help me find Paloma?"

"If you're serious about finding her, you should hire a private investigator."

"That's a last resort," Jace said. "I don't want this to get weird."

"It's already weird!" Livvy said with a theatrical eye roll. "Besides, I do have a job, you know."

"One that you told me was terminally boring and way beneath you."

"That's the definition of 'job,' Aunt Jace. That doesn't mean I have time for this."

Jace smiled craftily. "Does this mean you're dating?"

Livvy stared at her. "Are *you*?"

"I asked you first."

Seeing Livvy's dejected expression, though, Jace felt bad for teasing her. "Shit, I'm sorry. I thought that guy in Legal was a sure thing."

"Well, that guy had a girlfriend he didn't want to admit to, so . . ." Livvy trailed off, then looked back at Jace. "Why should I help you find your ex again?"

"You're bored. You love mystery podcasts about as much as you love indie rock music. And you're a fan of Paloma Doralle's."

"Who says?"

Jace stared hard into the screen. "You've liked her music ever since you were five and I snuck you into a sound check."

Livvy sighed. "You're right. I didn't want to be disloyal, but now that 'Heart Fire' is on every goddamn TikTok, I can't avoid hearing her anymore. As much as it pains me to say it, she's fucking amazing."

"You could stay off TikTok."

Livvy shuddered, horrified by the suggestion. "Side note: Why is it that so many punk and indie bands' biggest hit is a ballad? The rest of Paloma's catalogue is all muscular and up-tempo, and it wasn't until she slowed shit down that she got a Top 40 hit."

"Chicks love to slow dance?"

"Guess so."

"Anyway, can you do this favor for your favorite aunt?"

"*Only* aunt," Livvy interjected.

"And earn your place in the rock and roll history books as the woman who located the biggest enigma in twenty-first-century popular music?"

Livvy reached for a pen and an orange-covered journal, turned to a fresh page, and adjusted her glasses. "Challenge accepted."

"Thank you," Jace said, the tension in her shoulders easing.

"To confirm, you need me to research the whereabouts of Paloma Doralle, age fifty-three, last seen publicly at the Ed Sullivan Theater the evening of April 5, 2001."

"Correct."

"Is that her real name?"

"Yes. Her mother was a huge Picasso fan, and I think her dad's family was French Canadian or something."

"She lucked into a great stage name then," Livvy huffed. "Where was she living when she disappeared?"

"In Detroit. With me, at the house we were renting in Woodbridge." Jace had loved that place enough to have looked into buying it before Paloma split; she hadn't had the heart to drive by it in twenty years.

"You don't happen to have an old phone number for her, do you?"

"She deactivated it soon after she left."

"Did Paloma come by the house to drop off the keys or get her stuff?"

"Nope," Jace said. "Her brother Dustin came by a week later, but he had no idea what was hers, and I'd been too stressed out to have packed anything up, so it took forever. Then I moved to Clawson as soon as the lease was up, and that was that."

Livvy stopped taking notes and looked straight at Jace. "That's horrible. I can't imagine how hard that was."

Jace nodded, stopping short of telling Livvy that when she was moving out, she'd found a lavender bath bomb of Paloma's in the linen closet and didn't stop bawling for the rest of the afternoon.

Livvy set down her pen. "Are you sure you want to see this human being again?" she asked softly.

Jace sighed. "She has the ability to solve a huge problem for me—I mean, for Sabine. Next question."

"Did Dustin ever tell you where she went?"

"He was her proxy when we dissolved our business ties but never revealed her whereabouts. They weren't all that close; he may not have even known where she was."

Once Jace agreed to reach out to Dustin, Livvy continued to grill her about Paloma's hometown, old roommates, and past jobs. When that produced little of any use, she asked if any of their mutual friends might know more; Jace assured her she'd asked every last one of them more than once, and they didn't. After a half hour of this, Livvy put down her pen. "I hate to ask, but do you know for sure she's alive?"

Her heart froze for a moment before her brain took the wheel once more. "She has to be. It would have had to be in the news, or someone would have told me if . . . right?"

"Yeah, you're right," Livvy said with a reassuring smile. "Okay, I'll get going on this and let you know what I find out. Let me know if you hear anything from Dustin. Love you!"

"Love you, too." The screen went dark.

Jace hated Sunday nights. By the time dinner was over, it was too late to do anything meaningful but too early to go to bed. After taking her dishes to the kitchen, she grabbed a beer and plopped on the couch, a black leather three-seater she'd bought with her first major payout from Function Fest. She scanned Netflix for a lighthearted flick to help her downshift and maybe even prevent the insomnia she was sure was coming that evening, given the difficult week of work ahead of her. As she searched for something frothy and British, hopefully with lots of bustles and plummy Victorian accents, the poster for *Olympia, California* popped up. Frowning, she clicked on the image of Greek gods in sunglasses, which brought up the show synopsis and lists of episodes. Clicking through the menus, she located the finale of the most recent season. Her thumb hovered above the play button on the remote as she dared herself to find out how "Heart Fire" closed out the episode and thrust Paloma back into the public consciousness.

Instead, she set the remote down and went back into her office. After finding Dustin's email address in her old AOL account, she opened Gmail and typed a quick message with the subject line: *Please don't delete this.*

> *Hey, Dustin—I hope you are doing well.*
>
> *I'd appreciate it if you could let Paloma know that Sabine Galanis is in dire financial straits post-pandemic. I will be producing a benefit concert later this year to ensure the Artemis Club stays open. Given what Sabine has meant to all the musicians who have worked with her over the years, I hope your sister will come out of retirement and perform a few songs for this great cause. You can both reach me at the number below.*
>
> *I wish you and Paloma all the best.*
>
> *Jace*

Before she could torture herself by editing the message or worry about what she'd actually say if Paloma contacted her, Jace hit send. Then went back to the couch, queued up an Enola Holmes flick, and watched until she fell asleep.

7

WAY BACK WHEN

JUNE 30, 1998

Jace and Paloma stood on the front porch of a stately two-story brick house, doing their best to look creditworthy as they waited for the landlady to arrive with the keys. Today was the day they were moving to Detroit proper because, when they had returned to Jace's studio apartment in Hamtramck after the tour wrapped a few weeks before, three things were very clear.

One: Jace and Paloma wanted to live closer to the Detroit venues. The keyboardist from the Queenlords had been living in Woodbridge for a while and called when a FOR RENT sign went up in the window of a house two doors down from her. The hundred-year-old American Four Square offered loads of space for cheap, which was even more appealing now that they had to store all manner of equipment and merch. Jace was looking forward to setting up a home office with room for an answering machine and a copier/fax to manage Paloma's upcoming tour and the publicity that went with it. It would be good to have a spare room if Mary or Colin or anyone else needed to crash for the night. And Jace wanted a bedroom with enough space for a queen-size bed with a pillowtop mattress after years of making do on her sister's castoff futon, because . . .

Two: Jace wanted Paloma to live with her. There were a lot of practical reasons, like the money they could save and the fact that Paloma had been bouncing from place to place ever since they met. Lately, she'd been subletting a back bedroom in an Allen Park apartment from the lead singer of Bushwhipped, who littered his dirty boy laundry all over the living room and hairs of all types stuck in the shower drain, and she wanted out. Besides, the two of them were losing valuable sexy time with the commute to Jace's place after gigs.

But most important was three: Jace didn't want to be away from Paloma any minute she didn't have to be. After a year of sharing toothpaste and hamburgers and secrets and shower stalls on tour, Paloma had become half of Jace's whole. She knew how Jace liked her coffee (no sugar but enough half-and-half to turn it the color of a golden lab). She could find the upside in any situation, cutting Jace's cynicism down to size. She was relentlessly friendly, attracting strangers like moths to a porchlight and striking up an easy banter that Jace would never be able to master. And when Jace was overwhelmed by frustration and fatigue, Paloma would pull her close and whisper words of encouragement and carnal promises that broke the spell.

Jace had never experienced besottedness before: the Post-Its covered in hearts left for her on the bathroom mirror, Paloma's hand covering hers on the gear shift of their rattletrap van, the adoring glances from across the table at an all-night diner. She vowed to do anything to keep Paloma happy, especially since Jace felt she was punching above her weight. And moving into this place, with its sagging front steps and the black-painted eaves that made the house look like it was wearing a wig, was making Paloma enormously happy.

Paloma peeked through the front door window. "I can't believe this place has a foyer!" She looked at Jace and grinned. "I never thought I'd be able to afford a foyer."

Jace shared her glee. "You should be proud of yourself."

She was proud of herself, too. She'd negotiated larger fees from the clubs for Paloma as well as a cut of the cover charge. They were moving a lot of merch at Paloma's shows, too, including her first EP, *Grit-o-Matic,* and several record shops had placed reorders. With Jace as her manager, Paloma was finally making enough money performing to quit waitressing—and because she earned 20 percent of whatever Paloma pulled in, Jace could afford her half of the rent of a place with a foyer.

Paloma sat down in a once-pink rusty chair on the porch. "I'm twenty-eight years old, and I've never lived anywhere that wasn't sharing a wall with someone else. And there's even a front yard!"

Jace looked at the scrubby plot of weeds overwhelming the crumbling front walk and invading the cracks in the cement driveway. "I wouldn't call this a yard."

"Of course you wouldn't," Paloma snorted. "You grew up in a ritzy suburb."

"Sorry," Jace said. Even though she'd grown up in a middle-class neighborhood she'd never consider "ritzy," she didn't push back. She knew Paloma's parents had gotten married right out of high school with no idea how to run a home, raise kids, or make a living. Paloma didn't talk about her upbringing all that much, but when she did, her parents' screaming fights were the red thread that bound up her childhood memories. Jace would remember the handful of arguments she'd had with her parents, about nonsense like not putting gas in the car or wanting to dye her hair blue, and felt remarkably fortunate.

Paloma gave her a "don't worry about it" look and waved her over to sit in the rusty blue chair next to her. Jace pointed across the street at a banged-up Chevy Nova with its driver's side window busted in and the hubcaps missing. "Remind me to test the lock on the garage," she told Paloma.

"The price of living in the Big City," Paloma said, shaking her head.

"I wonder if our neighbors are okay with the fact that this house has been ceded to the Lesbian Nation. I don't want any of them to do this to *our* car."

"*Queer* Nation, hon. I'm bi, remember."

Jace winced. "I hadn't forgotten, but that word . . . echh."

"What, 'bi'?"

" 'Queer.' It's what Terri Roland used to yell at me every damn day in middle school."

Paloma squared her shoulders. "Can we hunt Terri down so I can beat her up for picking on my girlfriend?"

Jace was touched by the notion of Paloma being her bodyguard; usually Jace was the one on standby to keep the creeps at bay. "That's so sweet," she deadpanned.

Paloma rolled her eyes. "I don't care what the neighbors think of us. That's their problem, not ours."

After the landlady had dropped off the keys, they'd run back and forth from Hamtramck three times. By the time they'd unpacked what they needed to get through the next few days, they were too exhausted to put their new bedframe together. Instead, they set the mattress on the floor and tossed a couple of blankets on it before lying down, fully clothed, to take a break. They looked up at the ceiling fan, breathing in sync, enjoying the quiet.

The fan whirred above them. Paloma released a happy sigh. "Whatcha thinking about?" Jace asked.

"How I'd love to get a dog."

A faint alarm bell went off in Jace's mind. "A dog?"

"Yeah, now that we have a house and grass and places to walk around here."

"You can't be serious. We're out of town half the month, and when we're in town, we come home really late. And then there's the vet bills and— "

Paloma's face lost its dreamy cast. "I didn't mean we *should* get one. I just *wish* we could. Don't you?"

"Not really."

"Oh."

"I have enough to do taking care of the band. I'm sorry."

"No, I get it," Paloma said. "It was dumb of me to even suggest it."

"Hey, nothing wrong with wanting a dog," Jace said gently. "But you have to admit, that would be a huge step for the two of us. It's practically like having a baby."

Paloma's expression softened. "Would you want to have a baby together someday?"

The alarm bell went off again, louder this time. "Why, would you?"

"I asked you first."

Jace's mouth went dry. "I didn't think that was really in the cards because . . ."

"A lot of gay couples are becoming parents," Paloma said as she sat up on the mattress, re-energized. "My friend just had a baby with her partner in Ann Arbor. There's this sperm bank near the university that—"

"Whoa!" Jace scrambled to sit next to her, trying to sound even-keeled even as her heart raced. "I didn't mean because we're a gay couple. I meant because we're in the music business."

"Well, maybe we won't be in the music business forever," Paloma said, her forehead touching Jace's, her voice playful.

Jace did not want to have this conversation, especially right at this moment. She was exhausted and dehydrated, which was fueling her internal freakout about the possibility that the two of them weren't on the same page as a musical partnership, or as a couple. The way Jace saw it, Paloma was finally being mentioned in the same breath as some of the Detroit musicians she admired. Plus, her own career as a talent manager was beginning to prosper alongside Paloma. There was no room for a baby or anything else that would slow them down.

They did need to talk. Just not tonight.

She laced her fingers with Paloma's and kissed her on the shoulder. "Babe, we just moved in together. We need to unpack, do some repairs and painting, and get the West Coast leg of your tour set up. Can we hold off on talking about the long term until we get the short term taken care of? Please?"

Paloma gave a little laugh. "You're right. What the shit? We're here half a day, and suddenly I'm talking about babies and dogs. I'm probably scaring you to death."

Actually, Paloma *was* scaring her, so before she could say anything else, Jace kissed her, smoothing her hair with her hand. "I love you."

Paloma's shoulders eased. "Thank God."

Over the next few days, they threw themselves into settling in, with multiple trips to Target and Goodwill to fill in the blanks of their household items. This was the first time either of them had cohabitated with a girlfriend, so every choice they made as a couple was a milestone to celebrate, from the color of the lampshades to whether they got a bottle of Hunt's or Heinz. They stacked their white dinner plates in the kitchen's glass-doored cabinets with robin's-egg-blue trim and found a secondhand oak kitchen table and ladderback chairs so they could host up to eight people if everyone sat a little sideways. The wood-paneled parlor quickly filled up with shelves featuring their stereo system and extensive merged record and CD collections. They brightened up the square, sea-foam green living room with fairy lights and framed posters from some of their favorite gigs, and a print of Picasso's "Dove of Peace"—the artwork that had inspired Paloma's name—dominated the bedroom wall. Jace was thrilled to see the place come together, knowing that soon she'd come home from work to find Paloma sitting on *their* couch in *their* living room, and after a show, they could tumble into *their* bed. And bonus: They were about to show off their newfound domesticity to their friends at their first-ever Fourth of July barbecue.

Jace sent out the email invite since she had better spelling, and Paloma called the invitees a couple of days out to get a head count and confirm who could bring a charcoal grill, a couple of large coolers, and folding tables and chairs that they could wedge into their postage stamp of a backyard. Paloma had started to teach herself some simple recipes and could make a decent batch of chocolate chip cookies from scratch, and their guests brought plenty to share, too. Sabine provided cases of beer and pop, and Mo settled herself behind the grill with a KISS THE COOK chef's apron and handled the burgers and brats. Even the vegetarians ate well.

Over the course of the afternoon and evening, they had about thirty guests, a mix of members of Dunkman and the Queenlords and the Rousers and more. Paloma was in her element, leading impromptu house tours wearing a cardboard stars and stripes top hat then holding court in the backyard as she caught up on the latest band gossip. Jace socialized with folks as they waited for their hot dogs then reverted to staying on the periphery, tidying up, and making sure everyone was having a good time, which was how *she* had a good time at a party.

As Jace started on the dishes, she looked around the kitchen, imagining the renovations she'd like to do: put in a stainless double sink to replace the chipped porcelain; remove the wooden cabinets sticky from grease and too many coats of paint in favor of something sleek and modern. She was so engrossed in her imaginary kitchen redo that she jumped when Sabine tapped her on the shoulder.

Sabine giggled. "Ope! Sorry to startle you."

Jace looked up from the sink, taking in her friend's red-and-white, candy-striped sundress and wide-brimmed navy picture hat. "You look patriotic."

"Thank you. You look . . . anti-monarchy," Sabine said, looking at Jace's Sex Pistols T-shirt with "God Save the Queen" sprawled across it.

"It was all I had in red, white, and blue," Jace said, immersing a pan into the sink full of suds.

Sabine spread her arms wide. "This place is so cute! Are you loving it or what?"

Jace nodded as she scrubbed. "Yeah, it's great to be together in the city, and Paloma doesn't have to trip over a roommate's empty beer bottles anymore."

"It's about time you moved out of that sardine can in Hamtramck, too, my dear," Sabine said, picking up a dish towel. "How's cohabitating going?"

Jace's first impulse was to keep her answer light and vague, but she really needed some advice. "We weren't here even one day before Paloma talked about getting a dog."

"Oh, wow," Sabine said with a small laugh.

"Then she asked if I wanted to have a baby with her," she added, rinsing the pan and handing it off to Sabine.

Sabine's mouth fell open. "Double wow. What did you say?"

"That we'd talk about it later."

"And has 'later' happened yet?"

"No. She hasn't brought it up again, and I sure as hell don't intend to."

Sabine set the pan down and frowned at her friend. "Oh my God, Jace, you're impossible."

"What do you mean? She's the one springing all this on me before we even unpacked a box."

"What I mean is, this is great news! Paloma is envisioning your future together. She's mapping out the next phase of her adult life and wants you to be a part of it. You've got to talk to her about it."

"I know," Jace said, drying her hands. "Thing is, she also said something about maybe not being in the music business forever, and that spooked me. I've spent months setting up a string of gigs up and down the West Coast, and there's a promoter from Seattle who just emailed me about going there in October. Should I even be doing all this if she doesn't want to go the distance?"

Sabine's finely etched eyebrows went up. "Don't ask me. Ask your girlfriend."

Jace was so invested in creating a perfect comeback, she jumped when Colin came in from the back door, looking for a lighter. After he left, lighter in hand, Sabine said, "I hope to God he's just lighting up a joint. You can still see the scorch mark on the left corner of the Artemis marquee from his last experiment with fireworks."

Jace sighed as she tossed some silverware into the suds. "Look, I've never dated anyone for more than a few weeks, much less fallen in love before. I'm terrified that if we don't agree on big stuff like this, it'll all be over."

"Yeah, that could happen. But isn't it better to know that sooner rather than later so you can move on if you have to?"

Jace focused on shining every tine of a dinner fork so she wouldn't have to look Sabine in the eye. "Actually, I'd rather not know. At least not now. Not yet."

Sabine looked toward the ceiling with an *ugh!* "Jace, do you hear yourself? You are the best person I know when it comes to getting things done. No matter how puny the budget or ridiculous the request, you plan and you follow through, and it turns out great. But what's your plan for your own life, apart from work?"

"Hey, you are the last person to talk to me about a life apart from work, Miss Galanis. You practically sleep under your desk."

"Well, maybe I'm speaking from bitter experience, then," Sabine said, rising to her full height. "I made all the mistakes so you don't have to."

Jace leaned against the island in the middle of the kitchen and wearily folded her arms. "From the time we were little, my sister knew she wanted to have children. By now, she's no longer interested in getting married, but she has not given up on being a mother, and she's trying to find an adoption agency that'll work with single parents. But me? I've never had that innate desire. I like kids, but being a parent is something I've never considered, especially now that I'm working in the music world."

Sabine stood across from her, her eyes level with Jace's. "Well, if she's asking about babies, it sounds like Paloma is considering it. What are you going to do?"

Jace wilted. "I need to talk to her."

"Yes, you do." Sabine put her towel on the counter then hugged her friend. "I gotta go. We've got a double bill tonight, and Clem will crumble into dust if I don't get back soon. Thank you for hosting a great party, sweetie." She took Jace's hands in hers and took a step back, like she was sizing her up. "So you're in love with Paloma?"

"Yes," she said without a doubt in her mind.

"She's a talented gal, but from what you've told me, she has a big, gnawing hole in her self-esteem. Just make sure she doesn't drag you down when she starts doubting herself. You're her girlfriend and her manager, not her fairy godmother. Keep some wishes for yourself, okay?"

"Of course," Jace replied with certainty, knowing that her biggest wish was to make Paloma successful and happy.

Sabine left through the front door, and Jace returned to the backyard. As she fished for a beer in a cooler half full of icy water, Paloma waved her over to join the group, which was in the midst of trading war stories from performances past.

"Babe, help me out," Paloma asked. "What was that guy's name who owned that bar in Chicago where we played after that show at Northwestern?"

"Vonn?" Jace said as she popped the cap off a Labatt's.

Paloma squealed with laughter. "Yes, Vonn! Oh my God, he was a wreck! When we got there for sound check, he told us we had to wait for him to sweep the rat shit off the stage first. Mary almost threw up."

Jace shuddered for theatrical effect as she sat down. "I was jumpy the whole night. I thought rats were going to overrun the place."

"They wouldn't have been able to squeeze in there," Paloma explained to the folks sitting around them. "The whole bar could fit in this yard, and it was packed."

"Beyond 'packed.' It was illegal." Jace took a gulp of her beer as she adjusted to being the center of attention for once. "When Paloma had gotten some radio airplay, ticket sales went through the roof. Vonn lost track of how many he sold, though, so the patrons stood asses to elbows right up to the lip of the stage. Not a square inch of visible floor space; you'd have to crowd surf to get to the bathroom. And then the fire marshal showed up."

To Jace's pleasant surprise, the group reacted with hoots and groans. Paloma picked up the storyline. "I'm in the middle of singing a number, and this guy in a fireman's helmet with a bullhorn appears at the back of the house. For a second, I thought it was Vonn, since it wasn't that long after Halloween. Then there's a brain-melting squawk from the bullhorn, and at full volume, the guy yells, 'This event is officially over, by order of the Fire Marshal. Everyone must leave now.'" Paloma looked gleefully at Jace. "And did they?"

"Of course they didn't," Jace said, jumping back in. "The crowd started chanting, 'Fuck you, Fire Marshal!' and 'FU, FD!' and descended on the guy. He got spooked and hightailed it out of the bar, and everybody cheered until they heard the sirens go off outside. Turns out the Fire Marshal had called his buddies from the police department for backup. They'd surrounded the building and were planning to ticket every last person in the venue."

"Then it became full-on chaos!" Paloma interjected. "People were running for the exits. Some guys grabbed liquor bottles off the bar before they took off!"

"Then I see that Paloma had gotten trapped behind a bank of speakers," Jace said, shaping the scene with her hands. "I'm practically swimming toward her, elbowing through the crowd until I could grab her and make for the exit."

"Which was blocked by the biggest cop I've ever seen!" Paloma exclaimed.

"There I was, calmly telling him we had nothing to do with the riot or the overcrowding, while Paloma had her hands up and was babbling, 'Please, officer! You've got to save my guitar!' And damned if he didn't go inside and bring it out to her, handing it to her like it was a lost puppy."

Their friends guffawed, and Jace took Paloma's hand and kissed it. Paloma gazed at her with so much affection and a dash of lust, Jace could swear her eyes were throwing off sparks. Jace was happier than she'd ever felt, and surer than she'd ever been.

This is who I'm going to spend the rest of my life with, she thought. *Things will work themselves out on their own, I know it.*

8

NOT LONG AGO

MAY 15, 2023

"Why didn't you tell me you were in a documentary, Aunt Jace?" Livvy asked, clearly miffed.

"Because I wasn't," Jace said as she turned down the volume on her cell phone to quiet her niece and closed her office door.

She'd been coming into the Function Fest workspace in Ferndale every day to rally her staff's morale post–Adoption Academy. Their remaining clients still depended on them to provide the services they'd paid for, and their pipeline of potential new clients needed to be cultivated to make up the revenue they'd lost. But mostly, she wanted her team to have faith that their business could recover. "We all have to stay focused," she'd told them. "It only takes one call to turn things around. Then we'll be back in the black and ready to do even more."

Given her speechifying, Jace figured it would be bad form if they overheard the boss rehashing her past glory with Livvy—or finding out that she was producing a fundraising concert that wasn't going to make the company one thin dime.

"Well, I just saw footage of you and Paloma all over this film called *Cut to the Chorus* that came out ten years ago about the indie music of

Detroit in the 1990s," Livvy said. "Pretty much any musician who ever grabbed a slice at the Garden Bowl is in it. And a good chunk of it was about Paloma Doralle. You sure you don't know about it?"

Jace's blood ran cold. "Oh. *That* documentary."

"So you *do* know about this," Livvy said, still sounding annoyed. "Why didn't you tell me?"

Jace hesitated. "I knew it was in the works, but the director never interviewed me or asked me for any input. I've never seen it." She didn't say that Sabine had gotten her tickets to the premiere, but the thought of being in a packed house of her former colleagues watching the best years of her life pass her by again had kept her home. "Did you watch it?"

"Yes, and I think you should, too. There are clips from performances at the Artemis that we might want to have looping on screens before the show starts, for one thing."

"That makes sense," Jace said, her pulse readjusting. "I'll put you in touch with Rennie. They'll be handling the social media and could use that material for promotion for groups that'll be playing the concert."

"Rennie is a media company?"

"No, Rennie works for Sabine. They/them pronouns."

"Copy that." Livvy took a small pause. "Aunt Jace, um—well, I hate to tell you this, but you're going to need to hear what some of these musicians said about you before you approach them to be in the benefit."

Her pulse bumped upward again. "Meaning?"

"They didn't all appreciate how you managed Paloma's career."

"What did they say?"

"That you may have driven her out of the business." Livvy *tsk*ed into the phone. "Shit, I have to get this other call. I'll send you a link so you can watch it, then we can talk."

Jace's heart migrated to her throat. "Wait—are you still planning to come out here Memorial Day weekend? Maybe we can watch it together."

"Sounds good; gotta go. Love you."

"Love—" The call dropped before Jace could finish.

She sat for a couple of moments, parsing what the interviewees could have possibly said about her. She knew all too well that their mutual friends had taken sides after their breakup. She'd gotten Sabine, Mo, and Louis in the divorce, so to speak. Others in their circle had kept their distance, probably hoping to stay in the good graces of a famous person who might help their own careers one day. But what Livvy intimated sounded way worse. Fellow artists, people who Jace had assumed respected her as a businesswoman and a friend, had gone on camera to say the opposite.

Why would they do that? Jace wondered. Paloma had left her, after all. She was the one who couldn't believe in herself without Jace's help. She was the one who never told Jace what was wrong, leaving Jace to try to do whatever she could to keep them both afloat. Jace wasn't the bad guy.

Was she?

9

NOT LONG AGO

MAY 26, 2023

About two weeks later, Jace sat across from Livvy at the beer pub in downtown Clawson, polishing off a fried chicken sandwich and a local IPA. The evening sky was still light, and the place was full of families grabbing dinner ahead of the long weekend that kicked off the summer. For Jace and her niece, though, it was a business meeting.

"Have you set a date for the concert yet?" Livvy asked as she took another bite of her turkey burger.

"Saturday, September ninth."

"That's kind of soon, isn't it?"

"Sabine's bank will only wait so long," Jace huffed. "That was a conversation I never thought I'd have: talking about the monetary value of garage music fans' nostalgia with a bunch of loan officers. Luckily someone's kid watched *Olympia, California* and is dying to see Paloma Doralle in person, so they agreed to work with us."

"Any word from Paloma's brother?"

"Nope, and before you ask, I did search for his phone number online and came up empty," Jace said. "I'll email Dustin again this weekend. Have you found anything online?"

Livvy tutted. "I've found a ton of stuff online, but it's mostly junk: blurry photos of supposed sightings, blog posts from fans, conspiracy theories. My favorite rumor is that Paloma, Chrissie Hynde, and Shirley Manson founded a women's commune in Vancouver. May I have your pickle?"

Jace pushed her plate over with a fond smile.

"She has no social media accounts of her own—no surprise there," Livvy went on. "There are a lot of TikToks using 'Heart Fire' as a soundtrack, though, and I mean a *lot*. Do you get any payout from that?"

"I wish, but Paloma owns the rights to all her material," Jace said. Then something occurred to her. "That means Paloma ought to have had a bump in royalties lately. Could you track her financials somehow?"

Livvy's brows knitted. "I'm a web-savvy copywriter and true crime enthusiast, not a hacker. Besides, that would be intensely illegal, Auntie."

Jace dragged the last shards of her French fries through a pool of ketchup. "I'm staking this whole concert on not only finding her but also convincing her to get back on stage after all this time. What was I thinking? Oh, now I remember: I'm Sabine's only hope, and if Paloma ever wanted to pay off her karmic debt, now is the time."

"I put together a list of all the musicians Paloma played with during her career," Livvy said. "We can go through and decide who to contact first."

Jace sighed. "And we can cross off anyone who thought I ruined her career." She drained her beer and caught the eye of the server to signal for the bill. "Speaking of those people, we have a documentary to watch. You about ready?"

Livvy nodded, and in a few minutes they were walking through the tree-lined neighborhood back to Jace's house.

Once home, Jace brought two bowls of ice cream into the living room, handing one to Livvy before sitting next to her on the couch. She didn't want to admit it, but she was glad her niece was there to supply some much-needed moral support. And technical assistance.

"You know you can access the internet through your TV, right?" Livvy said, picking up a remote. "We don't have to huddle around your laptop."

"Of course I knew that," Jace fibbed, closing her computer.

With a few clicks, the *Cut to the Chorus* title card appeared on screen as the Zoodiac song "Why Am I Here?" swelled in the background. The opening graphics wrapped with a grainy clip of the band: lead singer and guitarist Gemi Twin commanding the microphone with gauze pads over her nipples and a length of orange fringe barely hiding her cooch from the camera; bassist Air Ram wearing nothing but purple micro-shorts that matched his eye makeup; and Lee Scales, bashing the drums in a leather bikini. They always put on a full-throttle performance, Jace remembered; she could practically feel the sweat of the crowd brushing her skin as she watched now from her couch.

Livvy pointed at the screen. "Wait, the bassist: His real name is Jerry Cooke. He was in the Pump Ups, too, right?"

"Yup."

"Two points for me," Livvy said, patting herself on the back. "Did you know him?"

Jace nodded. "Everybody knew everybody back then."

It quickly became clear that the documentary was made for an audience that had little idea of what had been going on in the upper Midwest during the twentieth century. The first part of the film set up Detroit's backstory, hitting a lot of familiar visual signposts: Henry Ford's assembly lines; Detroit as the "Arsenal of Democracy" during World War II; racial segregation and police harassment leading up to the deadly 1967 uprising; streets riddled with empty storefronts and abandoned houses; the skeletal shell of the Michigan Central railroad depot looming over Corktown, its windows broken and encrusted with graffiti. Next up was concert footage of well-known Detroit-born or -based musical icons from jazz, blues, the

Motown era, and the hard rock and proto-punk of the late '60s and early '70s.

"But if that's all you know about Detroit—about the music of Detroit—then you're an idiot," the voiceover scoffed. "Let me take you to the garage."

"Who is narrating this?" Jace asked. "That voice sounds familiar."

"Jerome Brinkley," Livvy said after a quick search on her phone. "He directed it, too."

Jace put her head in her hands. "Oh God . . . Jerome."

"You know him?"

Jace looked up. "I fired him. He was Paloma's bassist when we first met. I told her she deserved better."

"That explains why he found people to talk trash about you later on," Livvy said. "He was a disgruntled employee."

The film sped through footage of seminal local bands, with Paloma featured last. Then it cut to Jerome himself, sporting a goatee, wearing a black DETROIT VS. EVERYBODY T-shirt under his black bomber jacket.

"What is a Detroit garage band?" Jerome asked. "Well, it isn't as simple as the fact that the musicians are from Detroit or that they played in Detroit. And I'll bet most of those guys and gals didn't start their bands in a garage."

But Jace was less focused on Jerome than on the text at the bottom of the screen that read: *Jerome Brinkley, Former Bassist for Paloma Doralle/Blogger.*

"Pretentious bastard," Jace said. "He played a total of three dates with Paloma, and now he's building his whole reputation around it."

"Glad to see he's self-confident enough to admit he's a blogger," Livvy deadpanned.

Jerome continued to opine. "It didn't matter if they could sing or play an instrument; they'd figure out enough to get by. They could groove on any genre: punk, hard core, indie, roots, honky-tonk, a mash-up of all of that, or something else completely. What qualified them for Detroit Garage Band status is what they put *into* the music:

the unironic authenticity, the tenacity, the no-holds-barred energy that came from people who didn't know how to sit idle and created something that belongs to them, belongs to Detroit—and belongs to anyone who'll listen."

"That's awfully romantic," Livvy said archly. "Maybe he should have been a songwriter."

Jace was nonplussed. "Anything other than a bassist."

Jerome went on as clips of stock footage and home movies illustrated what he was saying.

"By the nineties, with Detroit being treated like a ghost town from the Wild, Wild West, we were ready to make our own music out of a crazy quilt of the colorful past. Play the bootleg cassettes and demos from back then, and watch the shaky handheld videos. You'll hear the ramrod conviction of an industrial city that people wrote off to rust and ruin. And that thrill could be yours anytime you put on your headphones."

Jace could barely watch, pulling away from the screen like it stank. "Oh my GOD!"

Livvy stopped the video. "What's wrong now?"

Jace gesticulated toward the screen. "Who appointed him the historian of all things Detroit music? He talks like every band from the nineties was on some mutually agreed-upon crusade to redefine all of popular music, which is bullshit. And while there were folks who moved to Detroit because they wanted a cheap place to live while they made music, it's not like the city was empty and silent until the guys from the suburbs showed up." She took a hot breath before finishing with, "And, Jesus, does that guy love the sound of his own voice."

Livvy snorted. "Tell me how you really feel about him."

"Plus he doesn't even know what a 'garage band' even is. Poser."

"Well, what is a 'garage band,' Aunt Jace?" Livvy asked with a good dose of side-eye.

"I am so glad you asked," she replied with a smirk. "The term doesn't apply to every indie band out there, and the genre certainly didn't start in the nineties. In the 1960s, a lot of guys—probably mere seconds after the Beatles took their last bow on *The Ed Sullivan Show*—started bands with no musical training or experience. On top of that, they couldn't always afford good equipment, and they couldn't access a proper studio crew to produce a polished sound. But they forged ahead anyway, and it was catchy and fresh. Analog, lo-fi, lots of distortion, great to dance to: That's a garage band's stock in trade."

Livvy nodded. "Songs that sound like they actually were recorded in a garage."

"Exactly," Jace said. "A lot of musicians I ran with were trying to emulate that DIY ethos from the sixties. Once certain bands started getting known around town, other bands took inspiration from *them,* and soon you had enough going on to say there was a Detroit garage scene. And once the big music execs flew here expecting to discover the 'next Seattle' after grunge was winding down, everything got tagged as 'Detroit garage' even if it didn't sound anything like it."

Livvy considered this for a moment. "Kind of ironic that the bands that got the biggest press were the ones that sounded the least like garage bands. Like Paloma Doralle."

Jace exhaled. "Yep."

Livvy leaned in. "So why didn't you join a band?"

Jace laughed. "Because I had utterly no talent."

Livvy pointed to the TV screen. "According to Jerome here, that could have been an asset."

"I was wired to be a fan," Jace said with a shrug. "During high school I spent most nights and weekends watching MTV and memorizing your grandparents' massive record collection. Then I met Sabine and got to know actual musicians at the Artemis. Suddenly, I had friends to dissect liner notes with and trade obscure albums with. We could see three shows in one night then play gin rummy until dawn while lobbing music trivia questions at each other."

"You found your people," Livvy said affectionately.

Jace nodded. “I found my people.”

They went back to watching the documentary, which moved away from Jerome’s purple prose toward interviews with a variety of the musicians who’d been active in Paloma’s heyday. Livvy stopped and started frequently to ask Jace if she had stayed in touch with any of them and whether they still played the clubs. Jace would call out any time she saw footage of the Artemis, and Livvy wrote down the time codes so they could use the clip for promotion and during the pre-show. Jace found Sabine in the background of a couple of shots, too, looking sleek in a variety of black ensembles as she chatted with some of the patrons Jace remembered as being in the audience pretty much every night; some of them were better known by the crowd than the musicians they had all come out to see.

Livvy turned to her. “Okay, we’re getting up to the part focusing on Paloma. You ready?”

“Yes,” Jace said firmly, hoping she really was.

It began with a montage of musicians each saying one word—*PALOMA*—then segued into a close-up of the singer. The sight of Paloma’s face millimeters away from the microphone, her eyes green as absinthe, hit Jace in the gut. She recognized the show instantly. It was the night Bob Sarkisian told Paloma that she had an edge over the other acts he’d recorded because of her distinctive style: In a genre full of screamers, a talented singer-songwriter stood out. Paloma was so excited by the prospect of recording in a professional studio with an actual producer, she couldn’t keep her hands off Jace as they drove back to her apartment. They were approaching the first summit of the rock-and-roll roller coaster that night, hand in hand.

There were more clips of other Detroit performances from 1997 to 1999, each of which took up shelf space in Jace’s brain. The gig when Britt Ney opened for them at The Shelter and played backup for Paloma for a howling cover of “Ain’t Too Proud to Beg.” That night at the Magic Stick when an unwell gentleman in the audience got on stage in between acts to demand that everyone vote for Gordie Howe in the next election. The Fourth of July right after they'd moved into their own place when they'd hosted a barbecue and dropped by the Artemis later to watch from the audience, but the Queenlords pulled Paloma on stage to do vocals on one of their numbers. She looked like she was having the time of her life.

The videos flickered by as unseen male and female voices reminisced.

> *"Paloma got her start in Ann Arbor and Ypsi. When she came to Detroit, she caught fire fast. She brought a new kind of energy. You couldn't take your eyes off of her."*
>
> *"Her lyrics actually meant something, for one thing, and she could also shred."*
>
> *"She loved being part of the gang. When she wasn't on stage, she was in the audience cheering us on."*
>
> *"If all these other bands defined what the Detroit garage sound was at the end of the twentieth century, Paloma showed what it could become in the twenty-first."*

Then Jerome returned to the screen.

"Paloma, Paloma, Paloma," the former bassist said. "She was the rising star with international aspirations who never reached back to take any of us with her as she ascended. But if you knew her like I did, that wasn't what Paloma wanted. That was her manager-slash-girlfriend Jace Randolph's doing—and it's likely that it was Paloma's *un*doing, too."

A still of Paloma and Jace filled the screen, seemingly at a party given that Paloma was in a pink cocktail dress and Jace was in a navy-blue tux. Jace's face was caught mid-argument, with her mouth half open, her brows furrowed, and her hand raised like she was about to smack the photographer. Paloma was standing just behind

Jace looking stunned, her pupils reduced to pinpricks by the camera flash.

"Wow, it looks you're deep into something there," Livvy said. "Do you remember when this was taken?" Jace didn't answer, feeling like she'd been elbowed in the chest.

Jerome appeared on screen, sitting in a recording studio across from a lanky gentleman in a cowboy hat and a Western-style plaid shirt with mother-of-pearl snaps down the front. His name appeared in the lower third of the screen: *Tex Mechs, Singer/Guitarist, The Moo-Town Spurs.* Jace searched her memory and recalled he'd been in a honky-tonk band around the time when Paloma started to tour, then got cast in a big-budget movie about singing cowboys and left for LA.

"Paloma was a lovely gal," Tex told Jerome. "We knew a lot of the same people and played on the same bill at the Ferndale Family Fair one summer. Sweet, sweet gal. So generous. She let us use her amp when ours broke."

"And we never got it back," Jace muttered from the couch.

"Did you ever tour with her?" Jerome asked.

Tex shook his Stetson-clad head. "Paloma's opening acts were from other parts of the US."

"Being a music booker familiar with Detroit bands, you'd think that Jace would have brought along some of the performers from back home," Jerome said, his eyes intense. "Why do you think she didn't?"

Tex hesitated before answering. "Jace was a businesswoman first and foremost. She wanted Paloma to be taken seriously as a national artist, and that meant pairing her with bands from bigger cities to build her reputation. I understand where she was coming from."

"He seems to be an ally," Livvy commented, writing his name in her notes. More clips of Paloma in performance played as other voices came and went.

"While there were a lot of women making a name for themselves in Detroit, and frankly no one cared if you were gay or straight or in between, the national music industry was very male and very straight. Misogyny and homophobia—that had to be a lot to deal with."

"No one understood how hard it was for Paloma to be so public, under so much scrutiny. She didn't ask to be a role model. All she wanted was to play music with her friends back home."

"She got popular so fast, maybe she felt like she wasn't in control anymore."

"Sometimes I wondered if Jace was the one who wanted to be famous, and she kept pushing Paloma higher to live her own dream."

Three photos appeared one after the other: Paloma playing at the 1999 Glastonbury Festival in England, sweaty and fierce; Paloma in a dazzling blue satin gown singing in front of a symphony orchestra at the Millennium New Year's Eve Concert at London's Royal Albert Hall; and Paloma flanked by Mary and Colin on the Ed Sullivan Theater stage, her silver-spangled halter dress dazzling in the TV lights with the *Late Show with David Letterman* logo at the bottom corner of the screen.

The musical soundtrack halted abruptly, and the last photo began to darken as Jerome intoned, "Then, she disappeared and hasn't been seen since."

The action returned to Jerome and Tex in the recording studio.

"What do you think happened?" Jerome asked.

Tex looked down, shaking his head. "I can't speak for Paloma, or Jace, although I'm guessing a lot of other folks are happy to speculate. All I can say is, it's hard to be the symbol of other people's aspirations. It means you aren't in charge of your own dreams anymore, and that is a sad and lonely place to be."

There were a few more clips of Paloma, grinning on stage as fans reached toward her from the floor. In the voiceover, commenters added their two cents.

"Maybe it was drugs or booze. If that's what happened to her, she wouldn't be the first musician to have addiction issues. Shit, I hope she's not dead!"

"Look, 'Heart Fire' was a monumental hit. That might have freaked her out creatively, like she was afraid that lightning couldn't strike twice."

"No one knows where she went after she did Letterman. And I respect that. She got all she wanted out of her career and just stopped. That takes integrity."

"Maybe the music business broke her heart—her screaming, tender heart. I guess we'll never know."

"Aunt Jace? Are you okay?"

It took a couple of seconds for Jace to realize that the movie had stopped and Livvy was shaking her shoulder and offering her a tissue. She'd been hit by a cyclone of memories and a tornado of questions, and she was going to have to pick through the damage to figure out how she could possibly produce this benefit with Paloma as a part of it.

She was going to have to muscle through the next few months and make it all work, no matter how she felt.

"I'm fine," Jace said quickly, surreptitiously wiping her eyes. "All I'm going to say is, all those people who were happy to share their anonymous opinions? They weren't in the room with me and Paloma those last few months before she left. She wasn't happy but wouldn't tell me why. She wouldn't level with me. I'd set up dream bookings—the ones she'd been chasing all her life—and after an amazing show,

I'd find her backstage crying, like she'd bombed. She pulled away from her friends, she'd hole up in the hotel and refuse to go out until it was showtime. Toward the end, she couldn't stand to be in the same room with me. And so many times, I'd ask her what I'd done, or what I could do to make things right, and she couldn't come up with an answer. Shit, if all these other people want to find out from Paloma what happened, they're gonna have to line up behind me."

Livvy put her hand on Jace's and squeezed it. "So let's go find her."

10

WAY BACK WHEN

FEBRUARY 13, 1999

Jace lay in bed, eyes firmly shut. She needed whatever rest she could get before the day started, especially after a night of little sleep with anxiety and excitement pumping through her system in equal measures. After a few minutes, though, she opened one eye and looked toward her clock radio: 6:01 A.M.

Time to give up and get up.

Paloma's major label record release party was taking place at the Artemis Club that evening, and if Jace didn't handle every tiny detail perfectly, she could totally derail the whole night. The reps from Seal-Eye Records were flying in from Los Angeles that afternoon, and she needed to re-reconfirm their flights, limo service, and rooms at the Townsend Hotel up in Birmingham plus ensure the restaurant where they and the band were having dinner beforehand would honor the food preference info she'd sent to the executive chef earlier in the week. Mid-afternoon, she'd meet with Mo and Louis for tech rehearsal and sound check. Then she had to review the comp list with the box office and ensure the catering and liquor orders were still on track.

Once onsite, she also needed to make sure the hair and makeup area was organized backstage, the public bathrooms had been thoroughly scrubbed, and no one had carved obscene graffiti into the freshly painted stall doors. Sabine had promised to tidy up her office in case the Seal-Eye reps needed to take a call. Mary had been fighting a cold on and off for weeks, so Jace would have to set up a supply of cough drops and hot water, honey, and lemon. Colin had promised to hit the laundromat before dinner, but Jace was going to have a clean pair of jeans and a T-shirt backstage just in case.

Jace gently rolled into an upright position and looked down at Paloma's sleeping form, relieved that she hadn't woken her girlfriend. Last night, they'd rented a movie, kept the lights low, burned candles, and drank herbal tea in an effort to stave off the stage fright and general giddiness around hosting a massive event with hundreds of friends, fans, reporters, and VIPs. None of that worked, though, and they'd tossed and turned until a couple of hours ago. At least now Paloma could sleep as long as she needed to. Her people could handle the rest. Well, her *person.* Jace would take it from here.

The record release had been a long time coming, yet at the same time it felt like it had all happened in a flash. The *Grit-o-Matic* EP had been playing on alternative radio stations and available in stores nationwide for months; Jace had taken photos of Paloma holding copies and pointing to prominent displays at every Tower Records they could find out on tour. Somehow, the EP had gotten into the hands of an A&R rep at Seal-Eye, who came to see the show in LA and offered Paloma a record deal the next day. He'd been so enthusiastic, Jace immediately assumed they were being swindled. Thankfully, she knew a keyboard player who was also a lawyer, and he assured her the offer was legit and solid.

But even though this was a major milestone, there was one hitch: Mary and Colin weren't part of the deal. "You'll be marketed as a solo artist. Anyone else on stage or in the studio is your employee," the A&R rep had told Paloma and Jace over the phone before they flew to LA to sign her contract.

"We've been humping around the country together for a year,

Jace," Paloma had said heatedly once they hung up. "Mary and Colin have earned their stripes. We're a band."

"Look, I cold-called some of the musicians they represent to get their unvarnished opinions of Seal-Eye," Jace said. "To a person they said the label is going to treat you all fairly. Mary and Colin will get market-rate session fees, and you will be able to keep your publishing rights. This is a good deal; you should take it."

Paloma shook her head. "They should be equal partners here. I wouldn't be getting this deal at all if it weren't for them."

"I know this feels like a betrayal, and your loyalty is something I love about you," Jace said. "But the truth is that you're the sole songwriter. You're the lead singer and guitarist. You're why people show up for concerts, and you're why they'll buy the record. With this deal, you'll be able to pay Mary and Colin more than they've ever made. And no need to feel guilty about it. Think about it: If Mary got this deal without you and Colin, she'd sign the second she got it." She put her hand over Paloma's. "You earned this. You know that, right?"

Paloma took a beat before replying with a coquettish grin. "If you say so."

"Of course I say so," Jace said, following up with a peck on her cheek.

Besides, as Jace reiterated over the intervening weeks, in many ways the record deal was better for Mary and Colin financially than it was for Paloma since they'd gotten paid up front by the label. Jace kept Paloma's modest advance under lock and key, since they'd have to live off that money while they put the album together, and she wouldn't start collecting royalties until after the advance and the label's marketing expenses had been earned back, which could take months or even years. On top of that, the label did not budget for a music video, even though Jace was certain that would be key to promoting the album; if they wanted one, Paloma and Jace would have to pay for it out of pocket. Determined to make it happen, Jace tapped into every contact she had, from the club owners and musicians they'd met on tour to the kids in the AV club from her high school days, and they'd been able to pull off a pretty great video on the cheap.

With all that promotion and a bit of luck, Paloma could clear the debt with Seal-Eye, start making money, and maybe, just maybe, have an even more successful follow-up album in a year or two. But for now, Jace was spending a lot of sleepless nights ruminating over the finances, sometimes even wondering if it would have been better to just keep recording with Bob Sarkisian and handling the distribution themselves.

Hence the insomnia.

Jace put her flannel robe over her T-shirt and tiptoed toward the kitchen in stocking feet. The plumbing made enough noise to wake Paloma out of a sound sleep *without* the water running, so Jace decided to wait on taking a shower until a slightly more decent hour. She grabbed her notebook from her backpack and sat at the head of the table, figuring she could get some cereal and coffee into her system then re-review her to-do list for the day. The coffee maker had barely started to burble before Jace felt a gentle hand on her shoulder.

"Hey, babe."

Jace stretched up to meet Paloma's kiss. "I'm sorry I woke you up."

"Not your fault; I wasn't really asleep." Paloma sat in the chair next to her, wearing an ancient pair of gym shorts and a frayed henley shirt, her blond curls compressed around her face. With no makeup on, Jace could see the handful of freckles speckling Paloma's nose. She loved being one of the few people on earth who was allowed to see them.

"Want some coffee?" Jace asked.

"Desperately."

Jace poured out two mugs' worth and came back to the table. "So, Record Release Day . . . how are you feeling?"

Paloma took a large slurp of coffee. "Tired. Hungry. A little chilly. You paid the heating bill, right?"

"Ha, ha," Jace said. "What I meant was, how are you feeling about this ginormous achievement of yours?"

She rolled her eyes with a blasé smile. "Oh. That."

Jace was determined to overwhelm her with glee. "I, for one, am so stoked! When I met you for the first time in that rasty bar in Ann Arbor two years ago, you thought playing the Artemis was going to be your biggest gig ever, and now look at you! You're about to conquer the East Coast before taking over England and Scotland! And *Cutie Pie*! It's a mass-produced, nationally distributed album with shrink wrap and liner notes and a logo instead of being a cheap-ass CD we copied off a laptop with your name written on it in Sharpie. I'm so proud of you!"

Paloma chuckled. "Well, I have to admit, I'm proud of me, too." She sat low in the wooden chair, her legs extended and her arms folded across her stomach. "It's weird, though. When you've longed for something this big and impossible for so long and it finally happens, it doesn't even make sense anymore."

"What do you mean?" Jace asked.

"We know so many musicians who have been hacking away in this business for a lot longer than I have. They're more groundbreaking than I am, have better licks, a cooler vibe. Only a couple of them ever got this far."

"I know some of this is because you were in the right place at the right time," Jace said. "That doesn't mean you don't deserve it. You believe me, right?"

"I'm lucky you love me," Paloma said, sharing a sloe-eyed smile. "Because I would not want to do this without you. Any of it."

Jace sat with this, joy glowing like a jewel within her chest. "I wouldn't have wanted to do anything else."

Paloma sat up and pulled Jace's left foot into her lap, removing her slouchy sock before starting a massage. "You mean to tell me this is a dream come true for you, too? Like, ever since you were a little girl, you wanted to be the business manager for a singer-songwriter from Taylor, Michigan?"

"No, I wanted to be Wonder Woman," Jace said, a pleasant shiver spreading through her nervous system as Paloma's hands stroked down the top of her foot and back up underneath. "I used to wear my red-and-blue bathing suit and rain boots with a jump rope taped to my side and run around outside looking for bad guys."

"Oh my God, that is so adorable!" Paloma said with genuine delight.

"I was only five but had a huge crush on Lynda Carter. I didn't know what to do with that, so I decided I should *be* her instead."

"You kind of are," Paloma said, gazing at Jace. "My one-woman Justice League. And you look like her, too."

"You're shitting me."

"You've got the dark, wavy hair, the blue eyes, the perfect skin."

"I can't hold up the eagle breastplate," Jace joked, waving her hands in front of her minimal boobs.

Paloma halted the foot massage, her expression crafty. "Do you have the costume somewhere? Because if you put it on, I will definitely make it worth your while."

Jace laughed. "Anyway, I know I wouldn't have become a talent manager if I hadn't seen you perform that night in Ann Arbor."

"I was such a mess, and you're such a perfectionist, you couldn't stand by and let me screw up," Paloma said with a sultry wink.

Jace grunted as Paloma's thumb pushed into the arch of her foot. "I'll never forget watching you on stage for the first time. It wasn't just that you could break out of the Midwest and be known nationwide, which I knew as soon as you started playing. You were exceptional. Like one of those storms that charges the atmosphere; you changed the air I breathed."

"Wow," Paloma said, reddening a little. "That's deep."

"Honestly. I couldn't believe you'd want to talk to me, much less make out in the car after I drove you home."

"You don't give yourself enough credit," Paloma purred. "For one thing, you've never been on the receiving end of one of your smiles."

"Like this one?" Jace said, pouring all she had into what she hoped was a flirty grin.

"Ooh, just like that: going from low beam to high beam. I won't be able to stand up now. And you have sexy wrists."

"I . . . what?"

"Strong yet sensitive, like you could throw a punch just as easily as you could hand me a bouquet of flowers." Paloma kissed the top of Jace's left foot before moving it off her lap to pick up the right one. "You also have this way of standing that says you had everything under control and no one is going to mess with you or anyone you're with. Confidence is such a turn-on." She ran her fingernails lightly across the back of Jace's naked calf then stroked the back of her knee.

"That feels nice," Jace said on a sigh. She watched as Paloma kissed her way up her shin.

She looked up at Jace with hooded eyes before licking the inside of her thigh. "I want to see what you've got under that robe," she murmured, "even if it's not a Wonder Woman costume."

Jace's mouth opened, but no words came out. She stood and led Paloma back to the bedroom, their fingers laced together.

Jace wondered if there was enough time in the universe to spend with Paloma. She wanted all of everything. To see her on stage. To gossip over coffee. To hear her snore and be happy that she was finally able to fall asleep.

To watch Paloma slip her clothes off before giving Jace a little push onto the bed, telling her to lie back and relax because she was in good hands.

Later that night, Jace was in her spot next to Louis at the back of the Artemis Club, her palms slightly damp as the opening notes of "Detroit Dancing Days" played and the crowd noise went up a few notches. The regulars knew that was the signal the show was about to start. Jace looked over to the space they'd cordoned off for the Seal-Eye reps, with high-top tables and a minibar, hoping they appreciated the effort. She scanned the space to see if any of the typical problems had started to surface, like drunken spats over who claimed what part of the standing room, drug dealing in the wings, or people being assholes for no good reason. So far, so good.

Sabine sidled up to her in the near darkness. "Have a good show, Jace."

"Thanks," Jace said automatically, her eyes fixed on the screen that was taking up the majority of the stage.

The song faded, and the room went dark, prompting cheers and whistles as the screen blazed with white light, and a block of black text appeared in the bottom left corner:

Paloma Doralle
"Wreckage"
Cutie Pie
Seal-Eye Records

A churning guitar riff played as the light faded and a tight shot of Paloma's face sharpened into focus. She'd been reluctant to have the camera come in that close, sure that her pores would look like craters, but she shouldn't have worried. Even without any extreme makeup, she looked extraordinary, like a haunted porcelain doll with her wide cheekbones and full lips taking up almost the entire screen, her eyes enormous and chilly. She lip-synched the first verse, her voice wary:

I can't have friends
And that's okay.
I'm all I have.
That's all I need.
So don't get close.
Just run away.
Can't help myself.
I'll make you bleed.

The camera pulled back to reveal Paloma playing her guitar in front of Mary and Colin, all of them dressed in industrial black clothing roped with chains that glinted in the lights as they thrashed through the song. The backdrop was the interior of what was left of Detroit's Michigan Theater. If Miss Havisham from *Great Expectations* could be a building, this would be it. Once an opulent movie house seating more than 4,000 in the 1920s, it fell out of favor and had its last gasp as a rock-and-roll venue in the '70s as the Michigan Palace before being slated for demolition. In a quirk of architecture that seemed like it could only happen in the Motor City, the owners weren't able to tear it down to install a parking lot because the theater's walls were essential to the structure of an adjoining building. Instead, the seats were ripped out, the auditorium gutted, and the chandeliers evicted to turn the formerly grandiose space into a parking deck. The ornate ceilings and plasterwork were left to degrade, their bright colors clogged by exhaust; the elegant archways and vaulted stairways led to hallways tangled with rebar and blocked by broken bricks. The site was gorgeous and ghastly at the same time: a haunted house that was once the temple of the American Dream.

At least that's how the director had explained his vision for the music video, which meshed well with Paloma's chorus:

You'll be lost in the wreckage
Broken in bone,
Crushed by a heart
That's made out of stone.
Lost in the wreck
Of a life on my own.
Lost.

Intercut with the images of the band performing were shots of Paloma against the crumbling walls of the structure, her pale eyes looking skyward. Details from the aging trim in the corners of the garage—children dancing, a face jutting out of a sconce—conveyed an overwhelming sense of loss. Views through the arches out toward the street, cluttered with cars and melting snow, made Paloma look even more trapped.

Jace had been on set when the video was recorded as the crew rushed to complete all the shots during the one night they could afford to pay for the garage to stay closed. Since she had only done live shows, where the sound was more important than the staging, Paloma had needed several takes before she could relax into the style the director needed for the camera. The whole evening, Jace had a sinking feeling that there were too many takes, too many moving parts, and was certain that the video was going to be a jumble of artsy ideas that did nothing to promote Paloma or her single. Watching now as the song moved into the second verse, though, Jace couldn't believe how wrong she'd been. The gritty visuals added heft and context to Paloma's spare lyrics and aggressive tempo while revealing a vulnerability that she'd never shown to audiences before. It was cinematic and personal.

Paloma was in close-up again for the final frames, singing the last lines of the chorus as the blinding white light enveloped the screen once again.

I want you here with me.
I'm scared on my own.
Lost . . . so lost.

The last note sounded, and the Artemis went utterly bonkers. This wasn't just a friendly crowd cheering on a local favorite. They were yelling, stomping, calling Paloma's name. Jace's heart swelled into her throat, relieved and proud that all that work, and money, had paid off. She caught a glimpse of the Seal-Eye guys, who were grinning and nodding their heads, before Sabine hugged her around the shoulders and kissed her cheek.

"She did it!" she yelled. "You both did!"

A couple of stagehands raced to take the screen away, revealing the drum kit, bass, and a black-and-white Stratocaster at the ready.

The cheering rebounded as Mary and Colin took their places, and it scaled to new heights as Paloma made her entrance. She wore an oversize black T-shirt belted like a dress and emblazoned with a full-color print of the album cover art, which had *Paloma Doralle* and *Cutie Pie* arching over a photo of the back end of a turquoise 1959 Cadillac Series 62 Coupe with fins like missile launchers and a Michigan license plate saying DEEETRT. Silver lace tights peeked out above her white go-go boots, and her blond hair, sporting an intentional stripe of dark roots, was pulled off her face with an accordion headband.

Paloma looped her guitar strap over her head and slung the instrument across her hips. "Thanks, everyone. Thank you so much!" She motioned for them to quiet. "We're going to play you some highlights from our new album, after which we'll all wanna get shit-faced, so I want to do my thank-yous now. First, thanks to Mary and Colin here for being the best rhythm section ever invented." They waved from their spots on stage, and once the applause crested, she pointed toward the back corner of the room. "Thank you to my label, Seal-Eye Records, and the crew at Sound City for bringing *Cutie Pie* to life. You guys are the best." The reps clapped and saluted her.

"We also have Rich Feldman, our incredible video director, in the house with some of his crew. Get a good look at them now before they win an Oscar, folks!"

Paloma grinned as the team waved awkwardly, then she continued. "For everything you're doing tonight—and with apologies for what you'll have to clean up later—thank you to the entire Artemis Club staff and their queen, Sabine Galanis. Take a bow!" Led by Mo, the bartenders and security folks whistled and hooted, and Sabine stepped out from the corner where she'd been sitting with the Seal-Eye reps, holding her tiered black lace skirt out as she curtseyed like she did back in her ballet days.

Then Paloma searched the room, looking over hundreds of heads in the dark until her eyes fell on Jace. She smiled wide without her usual attempt to hide the gap between her front teeth. "There you are," she said softly into the microphone before addressing the audience. "My biggest thanks go out to my manager who put me on tour, the businesswoman who got me this record deal, and the hostess behind this amazing party tonight, with an open bar no less. She is all that and more. I'm talking about Jace Randolph! Come out here so everyone can see you!"

As she moved into the light at the edge of the audience, Jace looked over to the Seal-Eye table at one particular executive, wondering if he caught the subtext of what Paloma was saying about the two of them, recalling what had gone down during final contract negotiations a few months prior.

"Gay content is rare in indie music," the exec had said to Paloma. "Rare for Detroit, too, right? I mean, are there any other gay or lesbian musicians in Detroit?"

"Well, I haven't slept with everyone, so I'm not completely sure," Paloma said with a campy wink.

"We at Seal-Eye want you to be authentically yourself, on stage and off. None of us here care who you sleep with."

"Whew!" Paloma said, wiping her forehead melodramatically.

He'd taken a long drag on his clove cigarette, a puff of spicy smoke hissing through his teeth. "But here's the thing. When it comes to songwriting, the more your lyrics are open to interpretation, the bigger the market for your record."

"I'm not sure I know what you mean," Jace said, even though she had a pretty good idea. She needed to hear him say it.

He looked at the ceiling. "Oh, like describing situations that don't depend on a specific place or time . . . or leaving the gender of the other person in your love songs unsaid."

"You mean making people think I'm singing to a guy, right?" Paloma said. Her voice was light, but her eyes were telling a different story.

"All I'm saying is it's hard enough getting airplay as a female musician. Being labeled a 'lesbian musician' can really limit your reach at stores and radio stations."

"Bisexual," Paloma corrected.

"Which most people think is you denying the fact you're a lesbian," he said, stubbing out his cigarette in a large crystal ashtray. "Look, I'm simply suggesting that, since this is your first national release, you focus on reaching as broad an audience as possible. That way you remove some of the risk here, for you and for us. And you keep your personal life, well, personal."

At this point, Paloma was squeezing Jace's hand so tightly she could barely feel her fingers. "Could we have a couple of minutes, please?" Jace asked.

"Of course."

The door closed, and Paloma finally let go of Jace's hand and her own self-restraint.

"What a fucking hypocrite," she said through gritted teeth. "We should leave."

"He's not wrong," Jace said quickly, her hand on Paloma's shoulder guiding her to sit back down. "You're not just playing for our friends and college kids anymore. You're introducing a unique sound to a general audience, and since you're talented enough to write songs that can appeal to anyone—gay men, gay women, the straights, and everyone else—why not do that?"

Paloma's mouth fell open. "You want me to sign with a label that wants me to censor my own material?"

"That's not what this has to be about," Jace said as levelly as she could, desperate to preserve the deal that she'd worked so hard to hammer out. "You've told me you want to do so much more than play the same little clubs over and over again. That's what this contract will do for you. And if you don't sign, remember that opportunities like this come only once, and news travels fast; other labels may not be that eager to meet with someone who doesn't want to take their advice."

Paloma slumped in her chair, her bravado deflating. "So integrity means nothing?"

Jace sat back as well. "Integrity means picking your battles, babe.

And sometimes it's easier to win those battles from the inside. Once you're more established and earning big piles of money for them, then you can push the envelope again. I promise."

When the exec came back a moment later, Paloma had smiled and signed and shaken his hand.

Now, as Paloma and the crowd at the Artemis applauded her, Jace realized the exec from Seal-Eye wasn't even looking at her or Paloma, as if they weren't even in the same room. Relieved, she took a brief bow and returned to the sound board, and Paloma turned her attention toward the audience once more.

"And finally, thank you all for coming. I've seen so many of you at shows at the Artemis and anywhere I've toured, and I've had the honor to play with a lot of you, too. I would not be up here if you weren't here with me. I appreciate that more than you can know." She applauded with her arms extended, moving back and forth to include everyone in the venue. Then she adjusted her guitar, checked with her rhythm section, and grabbed the mic. "All right, are you ready to hear some tunes from the new album?"

Paloma went through five of the strongest cuts on *Cutie Pie* and played several more from her typical touring set before telling the crowd, "Well, friends, Sabine told me to wrap up the concert before eleven-thirty so we can get the party going. Does that work for everyone?"

It did, and Paloma brought Mary and Colin forward for a bow before exiting to the wings. The lights came up, and Jace bolted toward the area where the label reps were seated to find the space empty, save for soggy cocktail napkins and empty glasses strewn across the tables. At first, she thought they'd already merged with the rest of the patrons to be first in line for the food, but looking around, her heart sank. They'd left.

Jace wove through the crowd in search of Sabine, but ran into Mo first. "Jace," Mo called, stopping her. "Those Seal-Eye guys told me to tell you they had to catch a red-eye. They said it was a great show."

"Do you think they meant it?" Jace asked.

"They seem like the kind of guys who don't have any problem saying they hate something, so yeah, I believed them." Mo clapped Jace on the shoulder. "They invested in Paloma. They believe in her, and you. You did good, pal, so relax."

Taking Mo's advice, Jace moved on to make the rounds and ensure the food, the drinks, and the guests were all being taken care of. When she felt the party could run under its own steam, it was time to make a pit stop in the ladies' room.

She was doing her business when she heard the main door swing open.

". . . and you looked like you were going to put someone's eye out in that video," a woman said.

"Thought about it," another responded.

Jace froze. She knew that voice. It was Mary.

"We were freezing our asses off in that garage for fourteen hours, and we didn't go home until seven A.M.," Mary griped as she settled into the stall to Jace's left. "I've had a fucking cold for two fucking months because of that fucking video."

"Well, at least you're gonna get a wad of cash off the album, right?" Mary's friend asked from the stall on Jace's right.

"Are you kidding? I got a flat fee for doing rehearsals and the recording and will get a teeny-tiny royalty because I played on the record, but that's it."

"But you're a member of the band!" her friend protested.

"Paloma and Jace sure acted like I was when we were on tour, but when the Seal-Eye deal came around, Jace made it clear it was just for Paloma. Colin and I are just session players." There was a flush and a *thud!* as the stall's lock banged against the door frame.

Another flush, another *thud!* from the other stall door as Mary's friend joined her at the sink to wash their hands. "That sucks. Paloma would be nowhere without you."

" 'That's *standard* for a *solo* artist. You *knew that* when you *signed on*,' " Mary said, doing an overly nasal imitation of Jace that made the real one flinch. "Well, when I go solo, Jace'll wish she paid me twice as much." Her voice trailed off as the bathroom door swung open and closed.

Jace had been so focused on eavesdropping, she'd barely taken a breath. Once she was certain they'd left, she washed her hands, muttering, "Shit, Mary, can't you just shut up and enjoy the party?" It was kind of depressing to find out that even with a good deal, one that Jace negotiated for her without asking for a commission, Mary wasn't satisfied or grateful and likely never would be. At least she blamed Jace for this perceived injustice. The last thing Jace wanted was for Mary to take out her grievances on Paloma on stage or elsewhere. They didn't need to be best friends, but they at least needed to stay civil.

Jace dried her hands and rejoined the crowd. She found Paloma at the merchandise table, finishing up taking pictures with fans and autographing CDs.

"I've been waiting for you!" Paloma said once the last fan left for the bar, planting a sloppy kiss on Jace's cheek that perhaps was inspired by a couple of whiskey sours. "Where have you been?"

"Sorry. I had a lot to take care of," Jace said with a chaste hug. "You were amazing tonight."

"Have you met Tex?" Paloma asked, gesturing toward a tall, dark-haired man dressed in a black-and-silver Western-style shirt, Levi's, and, of all things, a white Stetson. "He leads the Moo-Town Spurs."

Jace shook his hand, earning a broad smile of even whiter teeth. "Sabine told me about you guys. You do old-time cowboy songs, right?"

"Modern honky-tonk," he replied blithely. "And you can call me Nolan."

Jace looked at him more closely. "Wait, Nolan Greene of the Greenerators out of Kalamazoo?"

Nolan grinned. "That was a while ago. You've got a good memory."

"You had some kick-ass songs. I like screaming along to them when I'm stuck in traffic." Jace stared at the Stetson. "What possessed you to give up punk for country?"

"I missed being melodic, and country is better on the vocal chords," Tex said, tapping his throat. "Anyway, I was telling Paloma how much we'd love to tour with you if you need an opening act, or an opener to your opener."

Jace hesitated. "I wish I could help you, but our lineup is set for the rest of the year. We'll be playing with other Seal-Eye bands during our US dates; that way the label can promote us all at the same time. I'm sorry."

"I get it. You need to do what your label tells you to right now." Nolan turned to Paloma. "But if you're in town the first weekend in August, maybe you could do a set at the Ferndale Family Fair. It'll be a fundraiser for a bunch of community groups, including gay and lesbian youth outreach programs. I'm sure they'd be thrilled if you could be a part of it."

"Of course," Paloma said without a glance at Jace. "Count me in."

"We'll need to check your tour schedule first," Jace said quickly, feeling a bit miffed that Paloma would agree to do a low-profile benefit in the middle of festival season without talking to her first.

"Fair enough." Nolan fished a business card out of his shirt pocket and handed it to her. "Here's my info; I'll be in touch closer to the time." Nolan tipped his white hat toward them then said, in an accent thick as corn pone, "Congratulations, Miss Paloma. And Miss Jace, thank you for throwing such a first-class shindig."

Finally alone, or as alone as they could be in a crowded room, Jace embraced Paloma, surprised to find herself near tears. "You are a star," she whispered into Paloma's ear. "You're my star."

"And you're my night sky." Paloma pulled back slightly, her fingers brushing Jace's jaw, her mouth soft. Jace wanted this so much—a lover's kiss of victory—but stiffened and stepped back. She noticed something that confirmed she was right to have her guard up.

"Reporters at ten o'clock," Jace whispered as two men in denim jackets approached, one with a mini tape recorder and the other with a camera slung around his neck.

"You have a minute, Paloma?" Tape Recorder Guy asked.

Jace stuck out her hand. "I'm Jace Randolph, Paloma's business manager. Who are you two with?"

"Platter.com," Tape Recorder Guy said with a brief handshake.

Jace and Paloma had talked with Seal-Eye about what press coverage would be the most valuable to them; Platter.com was at the top of their list.

"Wow, I'm glad you guys were able to come out for the show and stay this late to chat," Paloma gushed. "What would you like to know?"

He started his interview with softball questions about the album and the Detroit garage scene, but just as Paloma seemed to be hitting a comfortable stride, he threw a curve ball. "Do you think Detroit bands are superior to what's coming out of the East and West Coasts right now?"

"In terms of what, exactly?" Paloma asked.

"Musicianship. Talent. Something more substantial than just being the next fad the promoters have glommed onto."

Based on his smug expression, Jace could tell this guy had already made up his mind that Detroit was not on that level, and perhaps Paloma was a prime example of why. She was ready to interject that many *important* national music critics had been buzzing about the city for some time, but Paloma answered first.

"Well, this isn't a competition. There's room for all of us. We all have our fans."

"Next question: In your previous EP, your lyrics are overtly homosexual."

"Is that a question?" Paloma's voice was playful, but Jace could see her body tense.

"I thought it was interesting that *Cutie Pie* has none of that," the interviewer said. "Did that change in direction happen because of pressure from the label?"

Jace stood very still. She knew that even after all these months, this was still a sore subject for Paloma, and this guy from Platter.com was already working her nerves.

She kept her cool. "I'm proud to be a Seal-Eye artist, and I hope anyone and everyone will give *Cutie Pie* a listen."

"Do you still consider yourself a lesbian musician?" he asked.

Paloma kept smiling. "I'm a musician."

"A musician who's sold out?"

Jace stepped between them as the camera flashed. "It's been a long night. You can follow up with me later if you need anything else, okay?"

"She didn't answer the question," he retorted.

"She's done. Enjoy your evening." They turned their backs on the two men and headed backstage.

Jace caught up with Paloma in the dressing room. When she touched her shoulder, Jace realized Paloma was shaking. "Hey, don't let that guy ruin your night."

"At least that reporter was straightforward about being an asshole, unlike a lot of our supposed friends," Paloma said as she stepped away from her, her arms folded tightly against her chest. "Colin's brother made a crack about me 'selling out' earlier tonight. I thought he was joking, but thinking about it now, I'm pretty sure he believes I violated some unspoken code of indie ethics by signing with a major label."

"He's probably just jealous."

"And when I went by the bar a while ago, I overheard the drummer from Whistle Rod trashing the video, calling it 'ruin porn' and saying how disgusting it was that we made Detroit look like a wasteland. I mean, are they right?"

"Of course not. You know and I know that's not what anyone thinks when they see your video."

Paloma didn't seem to have heard her. "One guy even yelled at me because our T-shirts sold out. How is that my fault?"

"You should talk to your business manager about that." Paloma's sullen expression told Jace she wasn't ready to joke about anything yet. "Hey, listen to me," Jace said, kissing Paloma's forehead. "That handful of jackasses mean nothing compared to the hundreds of people out there who love you and are thrilled by your success. Think about them instead."

"Maybe we should pull the music video," Paloma said softly.

"Absolutely not," Jace said, hoping she could keep Paloma from falling down an emotional well. "It's cool, it's evocative, and it's gonna help you sell a ton of CDs. It'll make Detroiters proud."

That made Paloma smile a little. "It is cool, isn't it?"

"It really is, babe."

Paloma nodded, but her voice was muted. "I don't know how you can just turn off how you feel when shit like this happens. I sure can't. Maybe I'm in the wrong business."

At this point, Jace was used to Paloma's negative self-talk even in the midst of success. She knew those doubts and fears were real, and persistent, and exhausting. As her manager, and her girlfriend, it was Jace's job to keep them at bay.

She pulled Paloma in for a hug. "You're in the right business, and so am I. Tonight, you concentrate on having fun. Leave the jerks to me. Okay, babe?"

Paloma relaxed into Jace's arms, then they headed back to the party, Jace at the ready to defend her from any of the naysayers, even Paloma herself.

11

NOT LONG AGO

JUNE 1, 2023

Jace was nursing a pint in the Cornucopia brew pub on Canfield, watching the front entrance for Jerome to arrive.

According to Livvy's research, Jerome's career had taken off after *Cut to the Chorus* premiered. He had become a noted concert videographer over the past decade and was the host of a reputable podcast about Detroit's indie and garage history. Given that he'd filmed many of the heavy hitters Jace hoped to book for the September show, he was in a position to put in a good word. Plus, he might have a lead on Paloma's current location, which Jace desperately needed since Dustin had yet to respond to any of her emails. Jace agreed it was worth buying the guy a beer and swallowing her lingering distaste long enough to pump him for information.

And just in case Jerome intended to act like a total prick, Jace had brought backup.

"Thanks for dinner," Rennie said between bites of an artichoke pesto panini. They were wearing a snapback baseball cap and a ringer T-shirt with a cartoon of Detroit Tiger Miguel Cabrera. If they weren't close to six feet tall, Rennie would look like a middle schooler on a field trip to Comerica Park.

"My pleasure," Jace responded. "I figured you can talk to Jerome about how we're staging the event in case he needs more details, and besides, I wanted to see where you are with our social media plan, so—why are you looking at me like that?"

"Sorry!" Rennie said, dropping their moony-eyed gaze. "I'm just amazed that I'm actually sitting here, talking to you. You're a legend."

"You're kidding," Jace said with an astonished laugh.

"Sabine's told me all about how you put Paloma Doralle on the map," Rennie said. "You took a queer, female guitarist from Detroit and made her into an inspiration and an icon for all of us next-gen queer musicians."

Jace felt her face pinking up. "That's really nice of you to say."

"Plus, you managed Bitemother. BITEMOTHER!"

Jace was caught completely off guard. "You know Bitemother?"

"Oh my God, they are the absolute shit!" Rennie said, their face lighting up. "I watched them a bazillion times on YouTube. Amazing energy, those guys. So much confidence and badassery. I wish I could have seen them play live, but they broke up before I was in kindergarten. And you made them possible, too! Like I said—*legend*!"

"Uh, thanks." Jace had never had a fan before and wasn't sure what was expected of her, so she reverted to the business at hand. "Can I see what you've worked up?"

"Sure thing," Rennie said, wiping olive oil off their fingers and pulling their laptop out of their shoulder bag. They opened a series of images, sized for posters and social media sites, each in a different neon shade and headed by the same title in black block letters: **SAVE THE ARTEMIS & SAVE THE WORLD.**

"That's quite a statement," Jace said, pointing at the screen.

"The Artemis Club has been a lifesaver and lifeline for musicians, for fans, and the city of Detroit for decades," Rennie said eagerly. "We all need to come together and help her, so we're sounding the call."

Jace smiled. "I like it."

"What do you think of the rest?"

An outline of the Goddess of the Moon and the Hunt statue stood at the left of the design, gazing toward a column of sans-serif text listing the handful of bands that had already committed.

"Purple Betty is on the roster?" Jace asked.

"Sabine insisted," Rennie replied. "I am, shall we say, stoked and honored to share a stage with the titans of the industry."

"Congratulations," Jace said, knowing full well she was not going to dissuade Sabine from giving her protégé a spot on the bill, whether or not they'd learned how to tune their guitar. Moving on, she asked, "Are the online updates ready to go?"

"Yes," Rennie said, opening a tab on the Artemis website. "I've already beefed up the Our Story page with more photos and an updated history of the club, and if you click here—there you go—you'll get a comprehensive list of who performed on what date, along with a prompt for people to add their memories of the shows for me to turn into posts for our Instagram account. And when we're ready to start promoting the benefit, this page will go live along with the 'Click here to donate' button going to the Artemis Reconstruction Fund." The concert info filled the screen, listing the range of ticket prices and guest experiences Jace had hammered out with Sabine.

"And are the announcements mocked up?"

"I'll send those to you later so you have more time to read and approve," Rennie said. "Don't want to rush and miss something."

Jace was impressed. Rennie was behaving exactly how she would have with a Function Fest client. "What's your day job?" she asked. "PR? Ad agency?"

Rennie shook their head. "I'm a coder for a web security outfit in Santa Ana. I work remotely."

Jace cocked her head. "And the pay's so low you have to have a second job at the Artemis?"

"Oh, no, I make bank through my regular job. Sabine doesn't pay me. I told her not to."

Jace wondered if Rennie would ever stop surprising her. "Really?"

"Yeah, I love being around the club, and Sabine always needs help doing a bunch of stuff that I'd want to do anyways. And if I ever switch over to playing guitar full-time, I'll have a ton of connections. I'm investing in my future!"

"Well, nice work on the media plan," Jace said, pointing at the computer screen.

"Fantastic!" Rennie gushed. "I am so, so, *so* glad you like it!"

Jace took another look at the poster and whistled. "Wow, this is really happening."

"Yup!" Delighted, Rennie tucked into their sandwich but suddenly stopped mid-chew and pointed toward the entrance. "Is that Jerome?"

A middle-aged guy in black jeans and T-shirt was scanning the restaurant. The years post-documentary had added salt and pepper to his beard and sent his hairline into recession, but his aggrieved expression was the same as when he was in his twenties. Jace waved him over.

"Jace, my God," he said. "How long has it been?"

"A long, long time," Jace said as they exchanged a brief handshake.

"Hey, I'm Rennie," they said with a wave. "I handle promotion for the Artemis Club, and I'll be overseeing the tech for our fundraiser. Good to meet you."

Jace motioned toward the bar. "What can I get you? And Rennie, you want another round?"

Jerome followed Jace to the bar and groused about hitting traffic on his way in from Northville while they waited for their order. Jace nodded and listened, staying on high alert. This was the guy who'd trashed her personal and professional reputation. Who knew where his mind was these days?

They brought their pints back to the table, which had been cleared of dirty dishes. Once they settled in their chairs, Jace raised her glass. "To the Artemis: Long may she live."

Rennie joined the toast with an affable "To the Artemis!"

Jerome clinked glasses with the others then set his beer down. "So your production assistant said you wanted to talk to me about helping you line up talent for a benefit in a few months."

"That's right," Jace said, making a mental note to thank Livvy for making that call. "It's been a while since I worked with some of these musicians, and listening to your podcast, it's clear you've stayed in touch."

"You listen to my podcast?" Jerome said with a note of disbelief.

"I've kept up with your work," Jace said smoothly. "If you're able to put in a good word, that would mean a lot to Sabine, especially since time is tight."

"Why is she holding a fundraiser?" Jerome asked.

"Financial fallout of the pandemic," Jace responded.

"A lot of that going around in the music business," Jerome said with a shrug. "So do you have a list of acts you want me to call or what?"

Reading his body language, Jace saw this could go one of two ways. She could tell him who they were interested in, and he could agree then ghost them and bad-mouth the event. Or, she could offer him a compelling reason to commit to helping her and trust that he'd follow through out of self-interest.

"You must be wondering what's in it for you," Jace said.

"That crossed my mind," Jerome said, sipping his beer.

"What about doing a follow-up to *Cut to the Chorus:* a documentary about the Artemis centered around the benefit concert?"

"That would be so dope," Rennie murmured in awe.

"Mmm, not sure it would be worth it," he said. "Hey, I respect Sabine, and a lot of talent has appeared on that stage, but there's not really a compelling, new story here. Especially if we are looking for more than a local audience."

"Sabine has been a successful female impresario in an industry known for its misogyny and douchebaggery," Jace said. "That's pretty compelling to me."

He shrugged. "I already filmed most of the Detroit acts that were worth anything ten years ago."

Jace leaned in. "What if this time, Paloma Doralle makes a special appearance? Would that change your mind?"

In a way, Jace hoped Jerome would laugh in her face and tell her that he and Paloma were close and he knew for a fact she'd never agree to do this so she'd have someone to blame other than herself if her ambitious fundraiser plans went to hell. Instead, he went still.

"Paloma? You found her after all these years?"

Masking her disappointment, Jace kept her cool. "I thought maybe you'd have a lead we can follow up on."

"So you don't know where she is?"

"We put out a request, but she hasn't confirmed yet," Jace said, not really lying since, while she hadn't received a reply from Dustin, she *had* sent the emails.

"You haven't even talked to her," Jerome stated with a disgusted snort.

"And you haven't, either, I'm guessing?"

"Not since you told me my services as a bassist were no longer needed back in '97." His eyes were like ball bearings, cold and hard. "Do you know how long it's taken me to get a gig since you fired me?"

"No, I'm sorry. I don't know."

"News flash: I'm still waiting!" he snapped. "I haven't been able to book so much as a kid's birthday party since you told me Paloma needed to 'go in a different direction.' Once Paloma's career took off, every other band in the area figured I must be a total loser since I wasn't going along for the ride, so that was the end of my career as a rock-and-roll bass player."

"Ouch," Rennie said. "That's harsh."

Jace knew full well that Jerome's reputation as a lousy bassist was his own damn fault, not hers. But she also knew she wouldn't gain anything by pointing that out or by asking Rennie to stop with the color commentary. "Look, I apologize," she said. "That happened a long time ago, and I'm sure I'd handle things more sensitively if I could do it over again. But hey, you've done so much amazing work since then as a documentarian and historian. That's a lot to be proud of. Not everyone has that kind of talent."

He rolled the pint glass between his palms. "It's still hard to be on the outside looking in after being kicked out, you know?"

"Yeah," Jace said. She knew what he was talking about; it took her three years after Paloma left to be able to go to a concert without starting to bawl when the lights went down.

"Paloma had the kind of success I would have killed for, and she bolted with no explanation," Jerome said plaintively. "I can't say I'm surprised you two aren't in touch. I wasn't the only one who assumed the problem had to be you. What other reason could there have been for her to drop out of sight?"

Jerome's words stung. Over the years, she had comforted herself by thinking Paloma disappearing couldn't really be her fault. Paloma had deep self-esteem issues and childhood traumas she wasn't willing to fully address, and it wasn't hard to believe that she'd cut and run because of that. That assumption had even become a path toward forgiveness in Jace's mind. If Paloma had been so overwhelmed by her past, she might not have had the strength or the tools to cope, no matter how much Jace loved her.

At least that's what she wanted to believe.

"I don't know," Jace finally replied. "I wish I did."

Determined not to start baring her soul to a guy she hadn't quite forgiven, she redirected the conversation back to her sales pitch. "If you can help me locate Paloma, we can both find out what happened, with your cameras rolling to capture it in real time. Just think what you could do with that, Jerome. Film critics love rock docs as much as audiences do. And so do Oscar voters."

At the word "Oscar," Jerome lit up. "Working title: *Pursuing Paloma: Live at the Club*," he said dreamily.

"And a soundtrack album could come out at the same time," Jace offered.

"That would be awesome!" Rennie said.

Jace pressed forward. "Do you know anyone who'd be willing to take my call to help broker a meeting with her?"

He shook his head. "No one comes to mind."

"What about Tex Mechs?" Jace asked.

"Tex Mechs?" Jerome asked back. "You mean Nolan?"

She thought for a second. "Right, Nolan Greene. He was the only one who went on camera to talk about Paloma in your film. Maybe he was more of a friend to her than some of the others."

"I haven't talked to him in years." Jerome finished his pint. "Look, even if Paloma suddenly appeared in a puff of smoke, I don't know if I'd want to make another film. It would be reaching even further back in time than *Cut to the Chorus* did, and a lot of the old gang have moved on. Besides, is there even an audience for this material? I'm not sure anyone is interested anymore."

"Oh, there is plenty of interest," Rennie said, patting their laptop. "With 'Heart Fire' playing all over social media, a lot of content creators are talking about Paloma and the other acts that came up at the same time. New bands are covering their songs; travel influencers are doing pieces about Detroit's musical history. And the nineties are hot! I'm nostalgic for the whole era."

"Were you even born by the nineties?" Jace asked.

"Nah. I'm Gen Z through and through," they replied.

"How can you be nostalgic for a time you didn't experience?" Jace said, amused.

Jerome stared into his empty glass. "Be careful," he said. "Nostalgia can be pretty painful."

12

NOT LONG AGO

JUNE 12, 2023

Jace entered the Function Fest office just before nine A.M. carrying upscale pastries from the patisserie in Birmingham, the ones that looked like artwork and tasted like angel dreams. She placed them just so on the kitchen counter and brewed a fresh pot of coffee. She set out half-and-half and oat milk in silver pitchers. She even fanned out a pile of napkins instead of just plopping them on the counter.

Louis was the first to arrive, wearing a decade-old company polo shirt. He pointed to the platter of goodies and shot Jace a suspicious look. "You're about to ask us a favor, aren't you?"

"Why would you say that?" Jace said, nonchalantly pouring herself a mug of coffee.

"The last time you had this elegant setup, you were looking for volunteers to spend three weeks in Las Vegas to run a poker tournament. In July."

"Did it work?"

"I have a tattoo of a stack of chips that I can't remember getting, so I guess so." Louis took a chocolate croissant and sat across from her. "Do you want to tell me about it before everyone else gets here?"

"That's why I asked you to be here now. The rest of the crew is scheduled to arrive at ten-thirty."

"If you'd wanted my team here for a meeting before noon, you should have had them sleep under their desks."

The front door opened, and a spray of magenta hair and a full-bore smile entered the office.

Jace waved. "Hey, Rennie."

"Howdy!" they said, putting their computer bag down next to a desk.

"Have you ever met Louis?" Jace asked. "He was the master tech and board operator for all of the Artemis shows when Paloma was performing there."

"Don't think I've had the pleasure," Rennie said, shaking his hand.

"When was the last show you worked there?" Jace asked.

Louis furrowed his mustache. "I left in 2002 when you offered me a salary to work here. Besides, I missed you."

"Aw," Jace said.

"I've got your old job these days at the Artemis," Rennie told him.

"Hopefully you don't have to use my old equipment, too," Louis said. "It was from caveman times. You can do more with your cell phone than I could with all the gear I used to use."

"Oh, wow, is that a pistachio chocolate chip?" Rennie asked, walking to the counter and pointing to a spiral-shaped pastry.

"Knock yourself out," Jace said, turning to Louis. "I asked Rennie to join the two of us because they're more familiar with the current setup at the Artemis."

"Sounds intriguing," he said, taking another bite as he followed Jace into her office. "So now are you going to tell me what's going on?"

An hour later, Louis was fully briefed. By ten-thirty, the other Function Fest staffers arrived, grabbed breakfast, and crammed into the conference room, where Rennie had set up their laptop to run a set of slides. Jace stood at the point of the long, oval table to one side of the wide-screen monitor.

"Folks, you may have noticed I've been taking a lot of calls behind closed doors lately, and it's not for any scary reasons, I promise."

"So we're not closing?" a production coordinator asked. "Because that's what all of us assumed since you made all of us come in so early on a Monday."

"We're not closing," Jace said. There were sighs of relief and muttered comments. "I've been developing a proposal for a very high-profile event scheduled for this fall that had to be kept quiet until we confirmed certain details. I've been dying to tell you about it, so let's not wait any longer."

Rennie started the presentation, bringing up the latest iteration of the poster design which, thanks to Jerome putting in a good word, listed several more bands than it had the week before. Jace cleared her throat and began. "Function Fest will produce a benefit concert celebrating Sabine Galanis, the owner of the renowned Cass Corridor rock-and-roll venue the Artemis Club, that's taking place on Saturday, September ninth. As you can see here, we have commitments from a number of bands so far with more to come, and it's likely musicians will be mixing and matching throughout the show as well. All proceeds, minus expenses, will benefit the Artemis Reconstruction Fund, and we are angling to get as many in-kind donations as we can for food and beverage, accommodations for the out-of-town acts, and so on to maximize the total raised."

"It says 'Headliner TBD,'" a lighting tech said, pointing to the screen. "Can you clue us in on who that might be?"

Jace looked around the room. "Before I tell you, please understand this is a benefit to help someone who means a great deal to me and save a venue that's been the backdrop for a big chunk of my personal history. Because of the pandemic and other factors, Sabine barely has the cash on hand to keep the club open, much less pay our typical rates. Frankly, she won't have any money to pay us at all until the donations from the fundraiser have cleared. That's why I'm not assigning anyone to this who can't wait until October to be paid, and

I know that's a big ask since we aren't working as many hours as when Adoption Academy was still our primary client.

"Long story short, I'm doing this job gratis. I don't expect anyone else here to do that, and I'm not telling any of you to participate. But if you are able to contribute any time or services over the next few months, knowing that our pay is contingent on the fundraiser meeting its targets, I think you'll have the most fun you've ever had." Jace paused. "If you are ready to commit to this, please stay in the room so I can fill you in on the headliner and the rest of the details. If not, I have no hard feelings. It will not be held against you, you'll be assigned to other work, and you can beat everyone to the kitchen to get another croissant."

Every person stayed in their seat, and Jace was so relieved, she almost started to cry.

"Now that we've sworn a blood oath, can we find out who the headliner is?" asked the office manager with feigned testiness.

All eyes were on Jace. "This is a work in progress and is completely confidential—and it may or may not work out at all—but the plan is to have Paloma Doralle as the closing act."

The reactions varied from "Paloma who?" to "Oh my God, the 'Heart Fire' singer!" The production coordinator whistled, clearly impressed. "That would be a coup. When was the last time she performed in public?"

"More than twenty years ago," Jace said. "Given her absence and renewed popularity, we're expecting to attract a lot of online interest and national media attention, so we need to bring in some reinforcements. Please say hello to Rennie from the Artemis Club. They'll oversee the graphic design and social media campaign."

Rennie threw up a hand. "Hey! Glad to be working with you!"

"I've also enlisted a PR and media expert who," Jace said, glancing at the door, "is walking in now."

"Sorry I'm late. I forgot it's construction season in Michigan. Hello, everyone, I'm Livvy Randolph," she said as she appeared in the doorway to the conference room. "And before you ask, Jace is my aunt. Nepotism is alive and well when you're asking for people to work for free."

"I just let everyone know we're in the process of confirming Paloma as the headliner," Jace explained as Livvy sat in the open seat next to Rennie. "Anything you'd want the team to know at this point?"

"Other than this is hyper-confidential right now?"

"Other than that."

"Several artists are contributing their time specifically because they want to be on the same bill as Paloma, so there's a risk they might bail if she doesn't agree to this," Livvy said. "We are optimistic we'll be able to confirm her participation shortly, but we can't wait any longer to start advertising the show. I've got Plan A and Plan B ready to go from a promotional standpoint in case she isn't the headliner and other acts drop as a result, and you all may want to do the same from a production standpoint, especially with the documentary crew there, too."

"Documentary crew?" asked a videographer.

Livvy looked toward her aunt. "Want to take that question?"

Jace looked at her video team. "If Paloma agrees to be part of the show, there's a possibility that Jerome Brinkley will be recording the event and taping interviews for a documentary about the Artemis and the acts that performed there."

"Possibility?" the videographer asked.

"He's a 'strong maybe' right now," Jace said even though she feared she was being overly optimistic. Nearly two weeks had passed since she'd met with Jerome, who'd left the brewery without making any commitments, and he hadn't returned her calls or emails about reaching out to Nolan Greene on her behalf, either. No need to freak out her staff at this point, however. "We'll keep you posted. Next slide please, Rennie."

She pointed toward a chart on the screen. "If you've never worked on a concert before, it may seem straightforward: bring one act up, then another, and rinse and repeat until the night's over. Believe me, there are a lot of moving parts, especially if musicians and their teams are traveling to participate. There's hospitality, food and beverage, ground transportation, lodging. We'll have to manage crowd control before, during, and after the event, which could get crazy. It's a circus. Besides, we don't want this to be a run-of-the-mill concert. This will be a homecoming. It's a celebration of the Artemis and its role in promoting the Detroit indie and garage sound. It may be the last time these musicians and bands ever appear on the same bill. And if Jerome does what we think he can do with the footage, we may have a very high-profile documentary come out of this as well. To wrap our heads around all this, we're going to take a fifteen-minute break, and then we're going to play everyone's favorite game, 'Brain Stew!' See you then and be sure to bring your Sharpies and Post-Its."

As the Function Fest folks filed out of the conference room, Jace walked around the table to where her niece was sitting, hammering away at her laptop. "Liv, are you sure you're going to be able to do PR for us while you're doing work for your agency clients?"

"I can wedge this project in around my billable hours for the firm, and I made sure there aren't any conflicts of interest," she replied, not looking up from her screen. "Besides, you remember that guy in Legal?"

"Yeah," Jace said.

"His girlfriend doesn't know that he asked me out. Doesn't know *yet.* So let's just say he owes me a favor. No one at the agency will find out."

"Okay then," Jace said. "Let me introduce you to the social media lead at the Artemis, Rennie . . . I'm sorry. After all this time, I don't know your last name."

Rennie laughed. "No worries! It's Jackson." They turned to Livvy with an extended hand. "But Rennie is all you need to know."

"I'll remember that," Livvy said with a handshake and, to Jace's surprise, an unguarded smile.

The rest of the day flew by. The team started with Jace's Brain

Stew exercise, a half hour of talking about anything other than the upcoming event, focusing instead on what everyone was watching, reading, listening to, fascinated by, laughing at—whatever was grabbing their attention creatively—to prime the pump for the rest of the conversation. Next they focused on the purpose of the event and defined what success looked like for the client, for the talent, and for the audience. With that done, they broke into groups to examine each of those areas and tease out what would make that success possible and memorable. By the end of the afternoon, the team had a solid outline of what they planned to do in pursuit of an amazing show. Breaking everything into smaller tasks and assigning people to complete them would happen tomorrow. By the end of the week, Jace would be able to take Sabine through their plan, and Louis could bring his team to the Artemis for a site visit.

Right now, though, she needed dinner. Livvy did, too, and Jace knew from experience that she wouldn't be willing to wait until she got back to her mother's house, where she was staying. And maybe Rennie would want to tag along, considering they had been hanging on Livvy's every word since she arrived. The three of them were packing up their computers for the night when Jace's cell phone buzzed with an unfamiliar number from a 323 area code: Los Angeles. She walked into her office, and when Rennie and Livvy appeared at the door, she gave them an OK sign to listen in.

Jace put her phone on speaker as she answered, "Hello, this is Jace Randolph."

There were a couple seconds of hesitation. "Uh, Jace? This is Nolan Greene."

"Hey, Nolan!" Jace said, smiling toward the phone. "Thanks so much for calling me."

"Who's Nolan?" Livvy whispered.

"Tex Mechs," Rennie whispered back. "He may know where Paloma is."

Jace mouthed "What the hell?" and put her finger to her lips.

"Jerome gave me your number," Nolan said. "He said he was

going to film this concert in Detroit for a documentary and you might need my help?"

As relieved as she was to hear that Jerome was fully on board, Jace noticed a touch of tension in Nolan's voice that was concerning. Had she done or said something to him years ago that lingered as a slight in his memory? If she had, she couldn't remember anything specific. "Yes, Jerome is right: I'm organizing a benefit on behalf of the Artemis Club that's taking place on September ninth here in Detroit. We're finalizing the lineup and—"

"Thanks," he interrupted, "but if you're asking if I could join you, I'm sorry to say I'll have to decline. I'm a music supervisor these days, and I've got a full plate until early next year."

"Oh, well, I'm disappointed, but I certainly understand," Jace said quickly.

"You didn't want to book Tex Mechs, did you?" Rennie whispered to Jace from the doorway.

Jace's eyes went wide as she mouthed, "SHH!" before looking back at her phone and steeling herself. "There's something else I wanted to ask you about. We're hoping to coax Paloma Doralle out of retirement to return to the Artemis and headline the benefit, but we haven't been able to contact her. I reached out to her brother, Dustin, and haven't heard from him, so I'm—"

"Dustin passed away four years ago," Nolan interrupted. "Cancer."

"Oh, wow. I'm sorry to hear that; he wasn't even fifty," Jace said, commanding herself not to think ill of the dead, no matter how little she liked him. "Since you knew about Dustin's passing, does that mean you're still in contact with Paloma?"

He didn't respond for several moments, and Jace checked her phone to see if the call had dropped. "Nolan, are you there?"

He responded with a long sigh.

Her blood ran cold. "Wait, is Paloma okay? Did something happen to her, too?"

Jace had spent the last few weeks talking about Paloma like she was an abstract concept: the magic formula for saving the Artemis and making all of Sabine's problems go away. But in that instant, she reverted back to full-blown mortality: the achingly beautiful artist Jace had loved like no one else, the woman no other could ever equal. As much as Jace had hated her for leaving, she couldn't imagine life without Paloma still walking the earth.

"Yes, I've stayed in touch," Nolan said at last. "And yes, she's fine."

The pounding in her ears started to subside. "Oh that's good to hear, very good."

"I didn't mean to scare you."

"No, I'm—it's—anyway, would you feel comfortable giving me her contact info so I can invite her to perform?"

"Actually, no."

"Ah. I see." She wasn't really surprised, but disappointment pinged around in her stomach anyway. "Then could you please give her my phone number and ask her to call or text me instead?" When he didn't answer immediately, she started to babble, hoping he wouldn't hang up if she kept talking. "I think she'd want to know that the Artemis is in danger of closing for good. That venue was where her music took off, where she found her voice, where we—where *she* made a lot of friends who became her chosen family. It's still a place for new musicians getting started, and a lot of the Detroit folks she used to play with continue to do gigs there. If she's able to join us, we have a real chance to keep the Artemis alive for future generations of bands and fans . . . and if she can't, I'm not sure it will survive."

"That may be a lot to ask," Nolan said. "For one thing, I know that you two didn't exactly end on the best of terms."

"Yeah, and whose fault is that?" Livvy angrily whispered. With that, Jace shooed her and Rennie out of her office and took the phone off speaker.

"Look, if she doesn't want to talk to me about this, we can work through an intermediary," Jace said, feeling the lifeline to her past unraveling in her hands. "She can dictate the terms for publicity and performance. She never has to see me or be in the same room or—"

"Jace, she dropped out of the public eye for a lot of reasons, some of which had nothing to do with you."

Some of the tension Jace had been feeling eased. "I know," she said. "Her childhood wasn't easy, and I know she struggled with self-doubt and—"

"But," Nolan cut in, "some of the reasons had everything to do with you."

Her words dried up in her mouth. Nolan was confirming what Jerome and all those random voices in the documentary had said, and all her old fears rushed back in: that Jace had driven Paloma away and pushed her too hard. That she'd focused too much on making Paloma a star. That she'd wanted Paloma to be her everything. That Paloma's disappearance was all her fault.

But instead of all this making her feel sad or regretful, it pissed her off.

"I wouldn't know her reasons," Jace said, her voice rising. "She never told me why she left. Not once in more than twenty years. How can I make things right if she won't even agree to talk to me?"

"I'm going to hang up now."

"No, I'm sorry, Nolan. Please don't hang up," she said, ratcheting back her volume and squeezing her eyes shut so she wouldn't cry. "You barely know me, and I don't intend to drag you into this. All I'm asking is that you please give her my phone number and my good faith request that she help me save a piece of Detroit's musical history, which is her history, too. If she says no, I will never try to reach her again. Okay?"

After an agonizing moment of silence, Nolan said, "Let me think about it."

That was better than another no. "Thank you. I really appreciate it. Have a good night."

"You, too, Jace." He hung up, and Jace put her head down on the desk.

Livvy and Rennie popped their heads in the door. "Everything okay, Aunt Jace?" Livvy asked.

Jace stood up and smiled, attempting to shake off the stress that was knotting her shoulders. "Nolan said he'd consider giving Paloma my number, so that's progress, right?"

"Right!" Rennie seconded. "There's still hope!"

Jace reached for her computer bag. "Ready to go eat, and maybe drink?"

"Anytime," Livvy said.

They opted to go to an unpretentious Mexican place on Woodward, and soon they were installed in a wooden booth plowing through chips and salsa and sharing a pitcher of margaritas. Jace rarely went out with anyone more than ten years outside of her age group, so she was glad the alcohol had washed away enough stress for her to enjoy herself, even though she wasn't 100 percent sure about all the slang. At first, she'd assumed that when Livvy said she was going to "get that bag" by starting her own PR firm someday that she meant she wanted to buy an expensive purse. If nothing else, Jace was thrilled to have a conversation about something other than heartbreak and financial peril. Especially since Rennie was eager to hear tales from her concert days.

"What was the craziest shit you've seen happen during a show?" Rennie asked.

"Wow, there's a lot to choose from," Jace said, thinking it through. "Here's one: At the end of Paloma's first show in Boston, she threw one of her guitar picks into the crowd. Two girls dove for it at the same time, crashed skulls, and knocked each other out cold. An EMT was in the audience and hovering over them when they came to. Then one of them realized the other one had the pick, so she jumped up to take a swing at the other girl and clocked the EMT. Law enforcement were involved shortly thereafter."

"Ouch!" Livvy laughed.

"Oh, and then there was this show Paloma did at an outdoor venue just outside of DC in July. They didn't go on until ten, but even at that hour it was hotter than hell and so humid the instruments were going out of tune halfway through each song. And no one had told us it was flying ant season."

"Ewww!" Rennie said, fluttering their hands in front of their face in disgust.

"Swarms of them started flying around the stage lights," Jace continued. "Thing was, Paloma and Mary were performing as if nothing was wrong, but Colin? He didn't see the bugs at first because he was head down in the drums, but when he looked up, he shrieked and ran off stage."

"I don't blame him," Rennie said, sticking out their tongue.

"I remember the weirdest show we went to, Aunt Jace," Livvy chimed in. "You took me to a four-act bill at the Artemis to celebrate my eighteenth birthday, with the Little Vettes going on last. The first band was a bunch of kids who looked younger than I was. One of the guys started hitting on you after they got off stage."

"He just wanted me to buy him a shot of Jäger," Jace said with a grunt. "Then the DJ blew out two of the house speakers playing punk over the PA between sets, so Mo had to run home to get more equipment."

"Right!" Livvy said, bobbing her head. "It was still so noisy, no one noticed there wasn't any background music until someone started singing 'Ninety-Nine Bottles of Beer on the Wall.' We got down to 'two bottles of beer' by the time Mo got the speakers set up ahead of the Little Vettes coming on stage. It was one in the morning by then, and everyone in the room had had plenty of time at the bar, so we were all rarin' to go. Then the lead singer—"

"Cora Vette," Rennie said.

"That's right," Livvy said, lifting her margarita skyward in tribute. "Cora Vette gets up there, dragging on her vape pen, and sings three or four songs. She's chatting with the audience in between numbers and looking fine in a leopard-print getup. Then, in the middle of the next song, she walks off stage mid-lyric. The rest of the band is vamping and cracking jokes, and it's clear they have no idea what the fuck happened to their singer. Cora finally comes back a few minutes later like nothing happened. Then she tells the audience, 'Clearly I'm not as punk rock as I used to be. I don't throw up *on stage* anymore.' "

Rennie guffawed. "I love that! MOTHER!"

Jace nodded, not completely sure what they meant but assuming they were calling her a badass, which Cora Vette most definitely was.

"I wish I could go to more concerts, but no one wants to do them the right way," Livvy said. "I haven't found anyone in Chicago who likes the same music I do who's also willing to stand in line for an hour before doors open and protect our two square feet of standing room for the next four hours to be near the stage but not too close to the speakers, and hang out to chat with the band afterward. Doing all that by yourself is fucking depressing."

"It's hard to be an aesthete," Jace said, smiling into her margarita.

"Do you see many shows these days, Aunt Jace?"

"Not often," she admitted. "Function Fest took over all my free time. I was always prepping for an event, at an event, or recovering from an event. Besides, I don't know anyone with the patience or stamina to deal with general admission; if there isn't seating near a bathroom, they aren't going. So I don't go either because, like you said, Liv, seeing a concert by yourself is fucking depressing."

"Sorry I can't be your Detroit concert buddy," Livvy said, frowning.

"You always have friends at the Artemis," Rennie said.

"Sure, but there's not really anyone to hang with anymore. Sabine has her hands full running the place. Mo rarely stays long because she has to get up early for work. Louis has priced himself out of the Artemis's range and works at the Fox and the Fillmore when he doesn't have an assignment through me. And there's been such a revolving door of bartenders and house staff, I can't keep track of who's who."

Rennie patted Jace's hand reassuringly. "You can always hang out with me, unless I'm on stage. Then you get to be right up front!"

"Thanks," Jace said, appreciating their sincerity.

"Do you miss being part of the scene?" Livvy asked. "Managing a band. Going on the road and being at clubs night after night. Being part of the chaos. It has to be better than the corporate America homophobic bullshit you've had to deal with."

"If I'd had the hits that you did with Paloma, I never would have looked back," Rennie said.

Looking at Livvy and Rennie, Jace realized they were the age she'd been when her burgeoning career and her romantic relationship coalesced into a shimmering, upward arc. At the time, she had been certain that her entire life would be a never-ending series of performances, record deals, and world travel, with her relationship with Paloma at the center of it all. Together, they'd ride the trends from decade to decade. They'd be a power couple within an elite group of rock stars who earned respect and sacks full of cash while maintaining their street cred. They'd beat back lesbian bed death with an optimistic mindset, a stockpile of sex toys, and gallons of K-Y. Their tattoos would never sag with age, and they'd look fierce with gray hair and wrinkles. It had all seemed like a foregone conclusion.

"Sure, I miss it," Jace replied. "How could I not?"

"Would you ever go back?" Livvy asked, her eyes hopeful.

She wasn't going to admit it to her present company, but for the first time in a long time, Jace allowed herself to accept that she'd been thinking about getting back into the whole shebang: the Artemis, talent management, the music biz. "Let me see how this show goes first."

They stayed for another hour, sharing more memories of shows gone by over burritos before going their separate ways. Jace got in her car and plugged in her phone to find a soundtrack for her ride home; after her iPod's demise, she'd uploaded a portion of her music library as a temporary solution. Finding herself in a Little Vette state of mind, she went to search for their debut album when she saw she had a text from an unfamiliar number with a 231 area code. She read the message and immediately felt like she'd plunged through a hole in a frozen pond and came back to the surface, gasping for breath. It said:

> I'd like to talk
>
> Call me tomorrow at noon
>
> P

PALOMA
DISC TWO
DISC TWO

13

WAY, WAY BACK WHEN

FEBRUARY 24, 1986

"Paloma, it's time to get up, hon."

Paloma's eyes flew open in the pitch black. Even after ten days of staying with the Morries, every morning there was a moment of panic before she remembered where she was.

She looked at the clock next to the bed, which read 6:15 A.M. "Thank you," she called back, trying to sound polite even though it was so fucking early. In the darkness, she stared at the ceiling, reorienting herself. It was Monday. That meant she had to go back to school.

Her breathing started to speed up, and her heart began banging against her ribs. She reached for the lamp on the bedside table; it cast a yellow glow across the twin bed, the walls decorated with cheap reproductions of Monet's water lilies, and the black garbage bags of clothes on the floor. The warmth of the light helped her focus her attention on calming down, and she chanted what had become her mantra over the last few days:

Everything will be okay.
You're safe here.
Everything will be okay.

Finally able to get out of bed, Paloma pulled jeans, a floral long-sleeved T-shirt, and underwear out of one of the bags and walked down the hall to the bathroom. Without having to compete with Dustin for the shower, she had plenty of time to wash off the flop sweat of insomnia before starting her day. Still, she was on the Morries' schedule, so she didn't dawdle. In less than twenty minutes, she was clean, dressed, blow-dried, and made up: the perfect image of a typical fifteen-year-old sophomore.

Not that it was going to matter the moment she got to school.

The scent of bacon and coffee drew her toward the kitchen, where Mr. and Mrs. Morrie were bustling. Standing in front of the stove, Mr. Morrie greeted her with a grin. "Look at that. The sun is up!" He worked the afternoon shift at the GM plant. Paloma knew if it wasn't for her, he'd be asleep instead of making her breakfast in his robe and pajamas, his graying short-cropped hair skewed by bed head. He looked down at the frying pan. "Over easy, right?"

"Yes, please." It was a new experience to have someone cook breakfast for her, much less remember how she liked her eggs. Frankly, it was a new experience to have breakfast on the regular; by the time her mom remembered to buy cereal, the milk had usually run out or soured.

Mrs. Morrie was dressed in a navy pantsuit with a blouse the color of pink carnations, her dark brown hair a little lighter than Paloma's and recently permed. Paloma watched as she sliced a tomato and put it into a tiny container before slipping it into a paper bag. Reading her confusion, Mrs. Morrie smiled and explained, "I made you a turkey sandwich, and you can put the tomatoes on right before you eat it so the bread doesn't get soggy. Just bring the Tupperware back, please." She put the sandwich in the bag along with a green apple and a small bag of potato chips and folded the top down twice, neatly creasing it with her fingers before handing it over. "Remind me to give you a buck so you can get a pop at the cafeteria, okay?"

The effortless kindness flowing from both adults almost made

Paloma cry. "You've been so nice, letting me stay with you for so long. You don't have to make me all this food."

Mr. Morrie clucked his tongue as he flipped two eggs at once with a large metal spatula. "You look like you could use all the food you can get, girl. It's my pleasure."

Mrs. Morrie checked the clock and poured three mugs of coffee. "Okay, fifteen minutes to showtime. Let's eat."

After breakfast, after thanking Mr. Morrie one more time, after rechecking her backpack to make sure she had all the homework that Mrs. Morrie had brought home for her to do while she was on suspension, Paloma got into the passenger seat of Mrs. Morrie's Caprice Classic. They pulled out of the garage slowly and wended their way down the suburban streets carefully in case there were patches of black ice. Even with the heat on full blast, Paloma felt ice cold, from her brain to her stomach. She tapped her fingers on the armrest in time to her mantra:

Everything will be okay.
Everything will be okay.

"Are you warm enough? Want me to turn up the heat?"

She didn't want Mrs. Morrie to worry about her; she didn't want to be a burden; she didn't want her to reconsider taking her in. She flashed a smile. "No, I'm fine. Thank you."

Mrs. Morrie kept her eyes on the road as she spoke. "I know today is probably going to be awful. Kids are ignorant and cruel, and so are a lot of educated adults, unfortunately. Just focus on getting to the end of the day, and hopefully, tomorrow will be easier."

Paloma was flooded with embarrassment. Why had she ever thought giving Brenda Finney a Valentine was a good idea in the first place? She should have known that a few stolen kisses underneath the bleachers in the gym weren't going to make Brenda brave enough to admit she liked her, much less stick up for her; besides, she was probably just getting off on the thrill of being reckless and sinful. And Brenda's bitchy friend Jessica was jealous that they had been getting close; she probably couldn't wait to swipe Paloma's pathetic little red-and-pink Walgreens card and run to Principal Tucker's office to rat her out.

Plus, Paloma's parents were already down her throat after finding her diary before Christmas. She'd been careful not to list any of her crushes by name, but her pages of secret longing and adolescent desire were deemed scandalous enough for her father to make a show of ripping it up in front of her and making her throw it in the dumpster outside the building, consigning her dreams and wisps of poetry to the landfill. They'd told her she ought to be grateful for three days without dinner and only her shoeboxes of cassettes being confiscated. She shouldn't have risked getting caught again, especially with another girl involved. She knew they'd be beyond furious.

She hadn't expected them to kick her out of the apartment, though.

After Principal Tucker called to tell them she was suspended for a week for being a "disruptive presence," her father tore around the bedroom stuffing Paloma's clothes into garbage bags and shrieking that they had to get rid of the "filth" she'd brought into his house. Her mother had stood stock-still throughout her father's rampage, her eyes wide with fear. She didn't move until her father threatened to kick her out, too, if she didn't take a stand with him, at which point she unzipped Paloma's backpack, removed her Walkman, and crushed it under her heel.

Terrified and desperate, Paloma's mind had raced through her limited options. Her grandparents lived too far away; her uncles and aunts were even more homophobic than her parents. She had a couple of friends—who were gay themselves, as a matter of fact—but with all the shit going on at school, they weren't about to let Paloma stay with them and put themselves in the crosshairs. She had nowhere to go, no one to stand up for her. According to her parents, not even God wanted her.

They were about to shove her out the door when Paloma begged them to let her call Mrs. Morrie: the only teacher who'd called her folks to share what a wonderful choral student she was; to let them know she was a natural guitar player and could borrow the school instrument any time; to encourage them to come to the school concert even after they said they had to work and didn't like secular music much. Paloma had overheard the ladies at church gossiping with snide voices and raised eyebrows about Mrs. Morrie and her husband taking in "troubled kids" when there was a family crisis, no questions asked.

Paloma's heart had nearly shut off when her dad said no, screaming at her mother and demanding that they teach their daughter a lesson and pitch her out on the street. But then her mother spoke up, telling him that of course she supported his decision, but if Paloma got arrested for vagrancy, people at church would talk about them like they were bad parents. Then she handed Paloma the phone.

The last words her mother had said before Paloma left the apartment were, "If you had kept your feelings to yourself, you'd still have a family."

When Mrs. Morrie slowed for a yield sign, Paloma asked, "Have you heard from my mom?"

The Morries were genuinely considerate and warm, telling her over and over that she could stay as long as she wanted, but it wasn't like she could stay with them forever. And even after all the shit that had gone down, in spite of the heart-racing nightmares fueled by that awful night, she longed to hear her mother's voice. She could live a long life without ever seeing her father again. But her mother? Even if she was angry or hurtful or screaming at her over the phone, it would be better than hearing nothing, because silence meant that, as far as her mother was concerned, Paloma was consigned to hell and no longer her daughter.

"If she doesn't call tonight, we'll give her a ring tomorrow. Just concentrate on getting through today first." The car stopped at a red light about a half mile from school, and Mrs. Morrie kept talking. "My advice is, don't go looking for trouble. No hanging out at Brenda's locker or flipping off Jessica in the halls. Keep your head high and don't feel like you have to explain yourself to anyone. Ignore the gossip and the bullies; they're beneath you. Your real friends will seek you out to see how you're doing."

Paloma wasn't sure if she had any real friends anymore.

Mrs. Morrie kept going with her marching orders. "I have the letter from your folks allowing me to be your temporary guardian, so I'll register that at the front desk when we go in. I'll make it clear to Principal Tucker that I'm supervising your return to classes, and I'll tell Miss Trent you're excused from gym this week because of menstrual cramps—sorry, that was the best I could come up with to keep you out of that snake pit of a locker room—so go to the library during that period. And I'm not saying this will happen, but if you ever feel unsafe, go right to the music room and find me. Got it?"

"Yes, ma'am."

They pulled into the teachers' parking lot, and before opening the car door, Mrs. Morrie turned to face her.

"Paloma, believe me when I tell you you're a good person. You have done nothing wrong and deserve so much better, especially from people who say they care about you. I really hope there'll come a day when you can love who you want to and be loved back, and no one will bat an eye. Until that day comes, I will always be in your corner. Bud, too. Got it?"

Paloma nodded, feeling a tiny bit more confident that she was going to survive this. "Yes, Mrs. Morrie."

The lady chuckled. "I've told you already, that's my name when we're inside this building. But any other time, please call me Bobbie."

14

NOT LONG AGO

JUNE 13, 2023

Paloma stared at the water from her back deck, goose bumps rising on her arms as the breeze came in from the lake. The clouds had rolled in, preventing the sun from peeking out and warming the late morning chill. The coffee in her stoneware mug had gone cold. With only about ten minutes to go till noon, she felt stuck in place. After a lifetime of huge mistakes, had she just made another one by reaching out to Jace?

When Nolan let her know that Jace wanted to pitch a concert opportunity, for a split second it had seemed like old times. Back when she and Jace lived in that cute little house in Woodbridge, Paloma could have been doing anything—wrestling with a lyric, cooking dinner, trying a new yoga routine on a mat in the backyard—when Jace would interrupt her, eyes dancing, rocking up and down on her toes. "You won't believe where you'll be playing next!" she'd announce. At first, it was like she was setting up a bad joke. Since Jace would sign on for any gig that paid enough to cover the gas in order for Paloma to get exposure, they'd ended up in some very unglamorous locations, from the Plumbers Union Hall in Toledo to the Elks Club in Paw Paw. After *Cutie Pie* started to gain traction, the opportunities Jace negotiated became pretty amazing: "The Hideout in Chicago!" "Two nights at the Roseland-fucking-Ballroom in New York!" or "Holy shit, I just got off the phone with the producer of the Millennium New Year's Eve Concert—they want you to play the Royal Albert Hall in London! And they'll pay for the flights and everything!"

The current situation was radically different, of course. It had been more than two decades since Paloma had done a high-profile public performance and even longer since she'd enjoyed doing one. The concert would be in Detroit, a city she'd barely recognize, since it had practically been torn down and reassembled since she'd last set foot there. It was at the Artemis Club, where she'd played so often with so many different configurations of musicians that she had trouble remembering which memory applied to what show. And Jace was asking, not telling, her to do this show, not because it was a step forward in Paloma's career but because it was going to help preserve a part of her past.

Their past. Which by now was long in the past.

Paloma heard her front door swing open. "Hello?"

"Hey!" Turning, Paloma saw Bobbie step into the kitchen and wave. "Ooh, those smell delicious. Mind if I have a scone?"

"Help yourself."

Carrying her pastry in a paper towel, Bobbie came out to the deck and plopped into an Adirondack chair. She was wearing her usual outfit of a long-sleeved T-shirt, fleece jacket, khaki Bermuda shorts, and ancient Birkenstock clogs. Twenty-five years into her retirement, and twenty-two years after Paloma became her next-door neighbor, she had no compunction about dropping by any time she felt like it and saying whatever was on her mind once she arrived.

"What's Bud up to this morning?" Paloma asked, downing the last of her cold coffee.

"He's meeting the guys for lunch over at the Cherry Mill, which ought to keep him out of the house long enough for me to vacuum the living room, thank God. There's a ring of potato chip crumbs around his La-Z-Boy." She tore off a corner of her scone and had it halfway to her mouth before asking, "Has she called?"

"Not yet."

Bobbie's brows arched beneath her freshly permed white bangs. "Is that what you're going to wear?"

Paloma looked down at her ancient black tee and buffalo-check flannel shirt. "Why?"

"Don't you want to show her how well you've been doing since you saw her last instead of looking like a bum?"

Adjusting her faded blue baseball cap with the VISIT THE GREAT LAKES: NO SALT, NO SHARKS, NO PROBLEMS! graphic, Paloma smirked. "This is going to be a phone call. It doesn't matter what I look like."

Bobbie chuckled. "She might FaceTime you. She's got to be curious . . . almost as curious as you."

Paloma's eyes went wide. "Shit. You're right."

She rushed into the house and nearly crashed into her acoustic guitar stand on her way to her bedroom. She cast off her cap, stripped off her shirts, and threw on a cream-colored cotton fisherman's sweater that made her look casually beachy while masking the belly she'd acquired thanks to the one-two punch of quarantine and menopause. Checking herself in the mirror, she fluffed her auburn bob and put on a pair of gold hoop earrings. She didn't have time for full makeup—she barely remembered how to put it on these days anyway—so she squirted some tinted moisturizer into her palm and worked it into her face, hoping it would ease the lines around her eyes and the parentheses framing her mouth. She grinned to make sure she didn't have any bits of blueberry stuck in her teeth, swept on some ultra-moisture lip balm that smelled faintly of honey, and dashed back to the deck to grab her phone. It was 11:59. One minute to spare.

Her phone buzzed in her hand. She stared at it, frozen.

"FaceTime?" Bobbie asked, sounding smug.

Paloma came to. "Yeah."

"Told ya." Bobbie chuckled as Paloma dashed back into the house.

Settling into her office chair, she swiveled so her shelves of vinyl records would be in the background. She held the phone slightly above her so her neck looked its best then answered the call. "Hello, Jace."

"Hey there."

Immediately, Paloma tried to absorb everything she was seeing and hearing. Jace's face was more angular than she remembered. She hadn't dyed her hair, and her salt-and-pepper shag was as wavy and thick as ever. She looked even more intelligent now that she was wearing glasses, and her voice sounded a couple of shades darker than it used to. She must have been doing well financially, since she was sitting in a well-appointed professional office wearing a periwinkle chambray shirt that was expensive but effortless. She looked good—guarded, but good. Paloma hoped Jace thought the same looking at her.

"This is weird," Paloma said.

Jace nodded. "Exceptionally weird. You look great."

She recalled how much Jace hated small talk, so she probably meant what she said, which was satisfying and surprising. "So do you." She was about to ask, "How are you doing?" but didn't. If Jace was doing badly, Paloma would assume that was her fault. And if she was doing just fine, it was in spite of what Paloma did to her. No upside either way.

Since that fateful day in 2001, Paloma had wondered what she'd say if she ever saw Jace again. During the first weeks and months, she wouldn't have said anything; her fight-or-flight response would have kicked in, and Paloma would have literally run away, again, to avoid explaining her actions. A couple of years after she'd left, she was prepared to be curt: "I have nothing to say to you, and what's done is done."

But over the years, as much as Paloma worried about what might happen if Jace ever confronted her, what came to mind more often was the warmth of their past. She found herself having imaginary conversations with Jace when she heard a song playing in a store that caught her ear or saw a news item about changes to the Detroit skyline. When loneliness crept in during the winter while the beach was deserted and the lake was a frozen slab, she'd replay times when she'd share a song she'd written only for Jace to hear, sparking a movie-star smile and a hug that made her feel cherished. When she couldn't sleep at night, her mind inevitably returned to when they were young and unafraid together, chasing across the country not knowing what would happen next, stealing kisses at every opportunity, and letting their hands and mouths roam at the end of a long day. And there were other times when she'd be driving home from a date that didn't end well and find herself yelling at Jace in her mind: "Thanks for setting the bar so goddamned high!"

Jace cleared her throat, snapping Paloma back to the present; she realized neither of them had spoken for several moments. Jace looked off camera before squaring her shoulders and adopting a professional demeanor. "Well," she said, "let me tell you about the benefit concert."

Over the next couple of minutes, Jace laid out the situation: Sabine needed an infusion of cash to keep the club open, a lot of their old friends had expressed interest in participating, Jerome (*that shitty bassist? Unbelievable . . .*) was committed to shooting a documentary of the concert and the history of the Artemis, and so on. The details blurred together as Paloma focused on watching Jace speak. She still had that distinctive cadence to her delivery, like the shuffle groove of a snare played with brushes. She still talked with her hands, and Paloma noticed she was wearing those chunky silver rings she'd bought for her in LA to commemorate signing with Seal-Eye. Her flawless Wonder Woman skin was showing some spots and lines around her startlingly blue eyes: evidence of her being in her fifties. So much the same, so much not.

"That's about it," Jace said at last. "Any questions?"

The novelty of seeing her jilted lover, and her amazement that

Jace wasn't screaming at her for walking out, was starting to recede. Jace had always been able to put her emotions in a box and stick to business. Over the years, Paloma had finally learned to do the same. "If all those musicians are already committed to play, why do you need me?" she asked.

"For a lot of them, their participation hinges on whether or not you agree to appear."

This surprised her, since she hadn't been in contact with any of the old gang in years. "Why would they say that?"

"We all think a 'very special guest' like you could ensure a sold-out event."

"A 'very special guest' like me?" Paloma repeated.

"Sure. I mean, have you looked at your royalty statement lately?" Jace said, her dry humor kicking in at last. "You're every Netflix subscriber's favorite musical artist right now."

That influx of revenue had certainly surprised Paloma. Her catalogue had lain dormant for a long time, despite some songs being picked up for background music in the *CSI* franchises, and, typically, streaming paid artists in pennies. Then the *Olympia, California* season finale aired, and the craziness of internet fame provided her with more than just pocket money. However, that wasn't enough motivation to play a show to satisfy the TikTok generation, along with anyone from the old days who wanted visible proof that she wasn't dead.

"You could bring longtime and brand-new fans together at the Artemis like no one else," Jace added. "And you have to know that people have been curious about what you've been up to all these years."

"Things must be really bad for Sabine and the club right now if you think I'm your only hope," Paloma said with a sideways glance.

Jace didn't flinch. "Things are bad—very bad—but you could make things better."

"Flattery aside, I don't think this is going to work. I haven't had a large-scale public appearance since New York." That's what she'd labeled that harrowing day. Not *when I quit being a rock star* or *when I left my girlfriend of five years with no explanation* or *when I decided to live my life on my own terms, no matter who I hurt.* Just *New York.*

Jace wasn't ready to give up. Paloma knew she wouldn't. "You still play, right? I see your Strat on the stand behind you."

"Yes," Paloma admitted.

"Are you singing?"

"Yes."

"I'm glad to hear it," Jace said, her voice softening. "So music remains an important part of your life. And I know what Detroit meant to you, and all those musicians who were like family would be thrilled to see you again. Plus it's just a few numbers on one night. So let me ask you: What would it take to get you back on stage?"

Paloma recognized Jace's relentless negotiation style and knew she wouldn't stop her pitch until Paloma said yes. For a brief second, she pictured herself on stage at the Artemis, the lights hot on her face and the crowd pressing forward with their hands in the air, and it was enticing. But once Jace found out why Paloma had left all those years ago, there would be no way Jace would ever want to speak to her again, much less have her headline the benefit. The only way to get Jace to give up and move on was using a tactic she wouldn't see coming.

She took a deep breath. "Why don't I tell you tomorrow over lunch at my place?"

By the look on her face, Jace had not expected that at all. "That works," she said, quickly reverting to producer mode. "I'd need to know where you live, though."

"Are you still in Detroit?" Paloma asked, trying to keep her voice level.

"North of the city," she said. "In Clawson."

"I'm in Stone Beach, not far from Traverse City," Paloma said.

Jace's eyebrows shot up. "You live up north?"

Paloma realized Jace hadn't expected to find her at the other end of the state, so far from Detroit yet so close. "I'll text you the address.

It'll take you about four hours to get here. Could you be here by one?"

"Of course," Jace said with the level of enthusiasm that, as Paloma remembered, signaled she thought she was close to closing a deal.

"Great. I assume my curried chicken salad is okay, the one with the slivered almonds and the golden raisins. The one you used to like. You haven't gone vegan or developed a nut allergy, have you?"

Jace chuckled. "I'm the only lesbian I know without special dietary restrictions. The menu sounds great. I'll see you tomorrow."

"See you then."

The phone went dark.

Paloma's mouth had gone dry, so she got a glass of water before returning to the deck. Bobbie was engrossed in a sudoku game on her phone, a crumpled napkin with scone crumbs on the side table. Paloma sat down in the wicker chair next to her, feeling flushed, like a hot flash was coming on.

"Want to give me a recap?" Bobbie asked, not looking up from her phone.

"I invited her to come over for lunch tomorrow."

That got Bobbie's attention. "You did?"

"And she accepted."

"You asked her on a date during your first conversation in twenty-two years?"

"It's not a date!" Paloma protested. "It's a business meeting."

"Are you going to do the concert?" Bobbie asked.

"Once we chat, I'm not sure she'll want me to."

"Would you want to?"

That spark of excitement rekindled, but she snuffed it out with a measured breath. "Even if I did, I don't sound like I used to. I don't play like I used to."

"Of course you don't," Bobbie said. "You're more mature. You've lived a lot more of your life. You bring a different perspective to your material. Plus you're in great voice and your technique has a lot more finesse. It's high time that more people get to experience that than the Friday night crowd at the Cherry Mill." Bobbie stared at Paloma over her wire-rimmed glasses. "You didn't answer my question. Would *you* want to play the Artemis again?"

The thrum in her chest flared up again. "I don't know."

"I think you do know but you're not willing to admit it. Yet." With a shrug, Bobbie turned back to her phone. "How'd she look?"

Paloma chuckled. "Very sure of herself. Just like always."

15

NOT LONG AGO

JUNE 14, 2023

Paloma spent the morning attempting to be calm. She went for a walk on the beach, listened to three different guided meditations, and journaled. When that all failed miserably, she ate half a gummy, trying her damnedest to visualize a positive outcome. Instead, her mind raced through scenarios worthy of a Lifetime melodrama: verbal tirades, buckets of tears, squealing tires as Jace drove away in bitter agony, then took a wrong turn and ended up at the bottom of a gulch, not that there were many gulches in Michigan.

A few minutes ahead of schedule, Jace's black Escalade pulled into her driveway. Paloma stayed seated on her couch, repeating "Stay cool, stay cool, stay cool" in a low, measured voice. Then the doorbell rang, and, much to her dismay, she jumped.

Paloma opened the door to find Jace standing on her porch, holding a brightly colored mixed bouquet and a bottle of wine in a gift bag, as if they were about to have the first date they'd never gotten a chance to experience. Jace's eyes went wide. "Wow," she said. "It's you."

Paloma was caught in the same sense of disbelief, as if a ghost had put a hand on her shoulder. She managed to manufacture a smile and responded at last. "Hi. Come in."

Paloma had coached herself to stay pleasant: nothing more, nothing less. But once Jace entered her home, it was clear it wasn't going to be that easy. Something as simple as thanking her for the flowers and wine needed an extra second of forethought to accomplish. The situation was complicated further by the fact that Jace looked amazing: healthy, fit, and meticulously dressed in an ice-white tee, a sandy cargo jacket, and jet-black jeans. She even smelled fantastic, a combo of herbal bodywash and some sort of citrusy, unisex cologne. She had become the accomplished adult she'd aspired to being in her late twenties, and it suited her. Meanwhile, Paloma's style had devolved from the snug thrift-store finds of her concert days to a closet full of oversize tops, ragged Levi's, and well-worn Vans and Converse: Middle-School Chic. She'd scaled up a notch today, opting for the plum-colored, long-sleeved tee that made her green eyes pop, a pair of white capris, and the bright pink flats that served as her dress shoes.

As they chatted about Jace's drive up from Clawson and the endless construction on Interstate 75, Paloma didn't know where to focus. Looking Jace in the eye was more than she was ready to do quite yet. She busied herself with filling a vase with water.

"I was wondering the whole way up here, *Why Stone Beach?*, and now I see why," Jace said, moving toward the French doors facing the water. "That's some view, and the sound of the waves is so peaceful. Not like the sirens going twenty-four seven in Woodbridge, huh?" She took in the high-ceilinged living room and open-concept kitchen, which Paloma had installed after watching hours of HGTV and spending numerous weekends in Home Depot. "This is a beautiful place, too. How'd you find it?"

"You remember me talking about Bobbie Morrie, my chorus teacher who took me in when my parents kicked me out in high school?"

"Yes."

"She and her husband retired here, and after New York, I came to stay with them for a while. When the house next door to them went up for sale, I decided to live here full-time."

"I see." Jace came over to the kitchen island and stood across from Paloma. "When I was trying to find you after you—after New York—I grilled every one of our friends for leads. I called your parents several times. They never answered the phone, of course, and Dustin finally called back to say he was going to pick up your stuff but wouldn't tell me where you were."

"He didn't know; I didn't tell him."

"Oh. Well, it never occurred to me to look up Mrs. Morrie." She watched as Paloma unwrapped the flowers and began trimming the stems. "I'm sorry about Dustin, by the way."

"Thanks, but we weren't close," she said, placing snapdragons and echinacea into the vase stem by stem.

"Are your parents still living?"

"I don't know." She saw Jace's concern and knew she had to redirect the conversation to save her energy for more important topics. "Do you ever come up north for vacation?"

Jace visibly relaxed. "I used to come up to Petoskey with Joyce and her kids almost every summer when they were growing up. We'd rent a place for a week so the girls could swim and eat their weight in chocolate-covered cherries. She's been talking about us doing a sisters' weekend and going on a wine tour, but I've been so busy."

"With Function Fest?"

Jace smirked. "You've looked me up online."

"I haven't been trolling your Instagram account, if that's what you're wondering. I wanted to see what you've been up to lately, and up popped your website." Paloma finished the arrangement then placed the vase toward the end of the island. "Pretty impressive business you've built for yourself."

"I'm just glad I could find a line of work based on my particular set of skills."

"You didn't want to stay in talent management?"

"I tried for a while, but when your hottest act bails on the entire music industry, it's hard to get anyone to take your calls." Jace quickly changed the subject. "What about you? What are you doing these days to pay for this amazing place, or are you living off your royalties?"

Paloma intuited that Jace was trying hard not to sound bitter. "If I tell you, you have to keep this confidential, no matter what happens with the benefit."

"Of course," Jace said.

"I've been ghostwriting songs for other performers, using an alias."

"Really? What's your pen name?"

"P. D. Smith. People up here call me Petie."

Jace chuckled.

"I have a knack for writing what indie bar bands want to sing on their fifth or sixth albums, and there are a lot of those bands out there. I've had a few songs end up on TV dramas. One of them climbed the country charts, if you can believe it."

"I believe it," Jace said warmly.

Paloma smiled. Now as before, Jace believed in her talent.

"It's nowhere near the money I used to make off of merch and ticket sales, but it keeps the lights on." Paloma took a large, green ceramic bowl of bright yellow curried chicken salad out of the refrigerator and removed a layer of plastic wrap before walking it over to the table opposite the kitchen. "Since it's not pathetic enough to work in one creative industry, I'm working in two. Over the last ten years or so I've also been a freelance columnist and critic, writing concert reviews and articles about music culture." She pointed toward the counter. "I have some ciabatta to go with the chicken salad. Could you put it on a cutting board and get a bread knife out of the block in the corner there, please?"

Jace did as she was told then brought it all over to the table. "You're doing concert reviews? What bands play up here?"

"Who said I have to stay in town? I go to Chicago or the East

Coast for a lot of them, depending on where the magazines send me. What would you like to drink: tap, sparkling, flavored, something stronger?"

"Tap water is fine, with some ice if you have it," she replied. "Back to what you were saying. Magazines: You're doing print journalism?"

"The internet is a hungry beast that needs to be fed regularly. Plus, if the act is popular enough, my editor can scrape together a few hundred bucks to fly me out." She put two glasses of ice water on the island for Jace to set on the table then got a bowl of watermelon and feta salad out of the fridge.

"Do you cover Coachella and Bonnaroo and that sort of thing?" Jace asked.

Paloma brought the melon to the table and sat down. "Nope, I'd had enough of the festival circuit when we were a part of it. I prefer to write about rising acts playing in smaller venues, but even that can be a grind sometimes. The audiences seemed to be more focused on getting photos of themselves at the events than actually listening to the bands."

"I can't believe no one has recognized you," Jace said, sitting across from Paloma.

Paloma *tsk*ed. "Maybe people know my singing voice, but my face?"

"There are so many clips of you online, though."

"Those were from twenty years and twenty pounds ago."

"Before you became a redhead."

"Right."

Jace pointed toward Paloma's face. "And before you closed the gap between your front teeth."

Paloma quickly covered her mouth with her napkin, as if she'd been unmasked. "I finally had time and money for an orthodontist."

"Not because you wanted to eliminate one of your most distinctive facial features?"

Paloma put her napkin back in her lap and smiled without apology. "Let's just say you'd be surprised how little attention you get if you aren't looking for it. Dig in."

Jace took a large bite of chicken salad, closed her eyes, and *mmm*ed. "This is so good."

"I haven't made it in ages. It's one of those recipes that everyone was making for a few years then, suddenly, no one was anymore."

"I remember you being so proud of yourself when you learned how to make this," Jace said, pointing to her plate.

"Now that I've had more time at home, I've figured out how to make a lot of better dishes. I just didn't have time to throw anything else together."

"No worries. You're way ahead of me. I can't do much more than order takeout." Jace smiled, her eyes bright. "You are a woman of many, many talents."

Paloma's defenses went up. She knew Jace well enough to know she was using flattery to test her resolve and see if she'd warmed up to the idea of performing again. She put her fork down and looked straight at Jace.

"Let's cut to the chase. You wanted to know what you'd need to do to get me to perform at your benefit. Honestly, there's nothing you can do, because I don't intend to go back to public life."

"And why is that?" Jace said, not looking away.

"Some of the same reasons why I left after New York."

"You left without telling me what those reasons were," Jace said, her voice controlled. "Could you tell me now?"

"Anxiety, for one thing. I was having panic attacks regularly, starting with Glastonbury."

Jace's eyes widened in surprise. "I never knew you were having panic attacks."

"Remember when we came back from the UK and I set that rule that you couldn't talk to me for an hour ahead of a big show?"

"Yeah."

"That's because I was afraid I'd have an episode in front of you and you'd get mad at me, so I made sure you weren't around in case that happened. Good thing, too, because the attacks got longer and harder the more I performed."

Jace's hand went to her chest, as if she'd taken a punch to the sternum. "Why did you think I'd get mad at you?"

"You were so wound up those last couple of years, putting so much pressure on me and yourself," Paloma said evenly. "You got really short-tempered, complaining about every little thing, getting so frustrated whenever something didn't go the way you wanted—and yelling at me when you couldn't yell at the person who pissed you off."

"I wasn't yelling at you. I was venting," Jace said, looking confused. "I thought you knew that."

Paloma pushed on. "If I'd told you I wanted to cancel a date or take an extended time off, I was sure you were going to get angry, so I shut my mouth and showed up anyway, thinking I could keep the anxiety under control."

"I wouldn't have been angry," Jace said gently. "I would have found you a doctor to prescribe something or helped you get a therapist."

"That's what you'd do now, but it was at a time when we were barely making our expenses on the road. We didn't have insurance, and we sure as hell didn't have enough money for therapists or medication. Besides, I honestly thought it was stage fright: a problem I needed to solve on my own. I thought I was just going to have to toughen up, stop whining, and get over myself."

Jace's right eyebrow went up. "That sounds like your parents talking."

"That sounds like our *friends* talking," Paloma corrected. "Remember when Freida March was diagnosed with depression and had to be hospitalized after opening for me in Chicago? No one would hire her when she got out. Mary used to call her 'Freida Froot Loops' and told everyone she faked the whole episode because she wanted a bigger cut of the door receipts."

"Mary was a great bassist, but shit, was she ever a class-A bitch," Jace said flatly.

That made Paloma smile. "She sure acted like one anyway."

"Are you still getting panic attacks?" Jace asked, concern written across her brow.

Paloma shook her head. "Bobbie convinced me that taking care of my mind was no different than taking care of my body. And I finally had the money to pay for insurance, and medication, and a great therapist . . . one who believes that performing in front of large crowds is a significant trigger for me."

"Is that still true, even after years of treatment and all this time off the circuit?" Jace asked, folding her hands and leaning in.

Paloma hooted. "Wow, you haven't changed a bit. When it comes to putting a show together, you won't take no for an answer."

"When the stakes are high, no, I don't."

"Don't get me wrong. I'm sorry the Artemis has hit hard times, but venues open and close all the time."

"Sabine wants to keep the club going, and if you sign on to the benefit, that'll be possible."

Paloma stayed firm. "Maybe it's better for Sabine to move on."

"Not yet," Jace said. "She needs to keep the place open."

"Is that what Sabine believes, or what you believe? Because this situation seems awfully familiar." When Jace didn't respond, Paloma realized she was just as slow on the uptake as ever, unable to understand a perspective different from her own, and that irked her. "When we first met, I thought that in order to be a successful musician, I had to become a celebrity, which is why I told you I wanted to be famous. You took that as a challenge and threw all your attention and energy into building my popularity, and it was really fun for a while. But you wouldn't stop. Nothing else mattered to you."

"That's not true," Jace interjected.

"Really?" Paloma retorted with a side-eyed look. "After I cut that first album, you pushed me to start the next one. After I played Los Angeles, you insisted we fly right out to New York. We played Roseland, then you pitched me to the Royal Albert Hall. By that point, I had realized I needed more to my life than packing for the next gig or I was going to start self-medicating, but when I tried to tell you about it, you wouldn't take me seriously. You said I had imposter syndrome and that I'd worked hard and earned my celebrity status, so 'don't stop now.' " Paloma hadn't intended to raise her voice, so she sat back in her chair and took a calming breath. "I loved you, and I didn't want to disappoint you. I did whatever you signed me up for, until I just couldn't anymore."

"Until you left, you mean." Jace's eyes were somber, her voice low.

"Yes."

Jace looked away, as if she was processing what she'd heard. "I'm sorry I pressured you. I'm sorry I caused you pain. I'm sorry I didn't understand what you were going through or what you really wanted."

There was a beat of silence. "But . . . ?"

Jace pursed her lips. "Well, I remember things differently."

Paloma gave a mirthless laugh. "You probably thought I was the devil incarnate."

"Not at all," Jace said. "From the first time I met you, I wondered, *How could someone so incredibly confident on stage be so insecure everywhere else?* I mean, it was understandable that you'd have a hard time trusting anyone after your parents rejected you, and on top of that, people lie all the time to get what they want in the entertainment world. But I loved you, I believed in you, and I thought you knew you could trust me. I thought you *did* trust me. I was committed to making up for everyone who ever let you down. I was there to protect you from the assholes. I assured you that you sounded great and looked fantastic because you always did. I helped you build an international fan base that adored you almost as much as I did. And I never lied to you. I honestly thought that after I did all that, you'd finally believe in yourself."

That had been one of the reasons Paloma had fallen for her. Jace had made her feel so safe, dispelling her fears with a smile and a hug. She never considered how hard that had to have been for Jace, though: so much pressure to keep Paloma's fears at bay. "That's really sweet, and noble," she said, catching Jace's earnest gaze. "But you had to have known you couldn't fix me all by yourself, right?"

"I wanted to try," she replied. "You were unspeakably gifted, but over and over again, you'd go down rabbit holes of self-doubt. You thought your music sucked, your playing sucked, your lipstick was stupid, that anyone who thought you were great was stupid, and that only got worse the more praise you got. When you'd tell me you wanted to take a step back, it didn't sound like you were making a thoughtful decision. It sounded desperate, like you were more afraid of success than failure. I thought you wanted me to push you forward because I believed in you so much, and you weren't willing to believe in your own talent."

"And because you were ambitious."

"Ambitious on your behalf," Jace said bluntly.

Paloma couldn't help but be skeptical. "Admit it. You were caught up in all the hype. You loved the travel and the partying and hanging out with brand-name rock stars."

"I didn't want to do any of that without you."

"You needed me to keep getting bigger to build your own career."

"I needed you to talk to me."

"You wouldn't have listened, so I left."

"You left, and my entire life was obliterated." Her words hung in the air for a moment.

Here we go.

Paloma remembered that when Jace got mad during a negotiation, she didn't yell. Instead, she spoke very precisely at moderate volume, and she typically had a lot of points to cover. There was no use in trying to interrupt or correct her. Jace was relentless when she was angry, and Paloma could tell she had plenty more to say. Paloma focused on her breathing. She didn't want Jace to gain any satisfaction from seeing how her words were affecting her.

"I had to clean up so much shit after you disappeared," Jace said, each consonant slicing the air. "I had to cancel a year's worth of show dates and pay thousands in cancellation fees, and the promoters made it clear they'd never book one of my acts again. I had to return your advance and tell the A&M manager at Seal-Eye you weren't going to fulfill your contract for the next album. That asshole literally laughed at me. He told me to go back to bartending in 'the slums of Detroit' and leave talent management to 'the experts in LA.' Mary and Colin bad-mouthed me from one end of the country to the other, and the bands that were supposed to open for you that summer did the same, so no musicians with any future in this industry wanted to work with me. The media practically stalked me to find out what had happened to you, and even though I put out an official statement that you were taking a break, they figured out real quick that you had gone AWOL and I hadn't seen it coming. And all this was going on while I was barely able to function, because the love of my life had vanished without explanation."

Jace went quiet. She looked hollowed out, like expelling all that hurt and rage at once had left a crater in her chest. Paloma was overwhelmed, not by anger or stress or anxiety, but with consummate sorrow. Ever since New York, she had consciously avoided thinking about the depth of destruction she'd left in her wake, how she'd wrecked Jace's business and reputation as well as her heart. Now, all the damage had been laid at her feet.

"I'm sorry," Paloma said, feeling ashamed of herself. "I never should have left you like I did, no matter how I justified it at the time. You deserved so much better."

"Well, you deserved better, too," Jace replied with a wan smile. "I should have realized that."

They sat in silence for a few moments. The conversation Paloma had dreaded was over, but surprisingly, she wished it could continue. Even though Jace was obviously much more comfortable talking business than talking about her feelings, and even though they'd hashed out some heavy shit, they were connecting in a way they hadn't when they were younger. Jace had changed since their earlier days. Instead of maintaining her reputation for staying in control by minimizing the problem at hand, Jace had just admitted how confused and hurt she'd been. After a five-year relationship based on Jace's "don't worry, keep going, everything will be fine" attitude, this burst of unedited honesty was refreshing. It made Paloma wonder what else they could discover about each other if they could just keep talking.

Then Jace stood up, and her professional demeanor had returned. "I'd better get going. Thank you for lunch."

Deflated, Paloma realized that since she'd turned down playing the benefit, Jace had no further reason to stay. She hid her disappointment by bringing her plate into the kitchen, her food barely touched. "By the time you hit Flint, it'll be rush hour."

"Oh, I'm not going back to Clawson. I booked a hotel room in Traverse City for tonight."

Paloma was both relieved and curious. "How long are you planning to stay up here and badger me about doing this gig?"

"How long will it take?" Jace asked with a disarming smile that quickly faded. "Actually, I didn't want to have to drive up and back on the same day, and I have work to do for the benefit before I leave."

Paloma came out of the kitchen, following Jace as she headed toward the front door. "Hang on, Jace. Please wait."

Jace stopped for a moment to gaze at Paloma, as if she was trying to record every detail. "I promise I'll leave you alone," Jace said.

Then she was gone.

16

WAY BACK WHEN

AUGUST 7, 1999

By the time Paloma parked the car, she was regretting not wearing shorts. Although it was close to sunset, it was still in the high eighties, and she was going to have to drag a flatbed of equipment for several blocks on her own while carrying her Strat on her back. That was one of the downsides of playing a solo gig when Jace was out of town: She had to schlep everything by herself.

Paloma hadn't run her own gig since she met Jace two years ago, and despite sweating like a farmhand, it felt freeing. She knew Jace hadn't wanted her to do a street fair, even in support of The Community. She wouldn't come out and say she thought it was beneath them, but Paloma knew Jace had her sights set on bigger crowds in larger cities. For months, though, Paloma had longed to see some familiar faces and reconnect with her musician buddies after so many strangers had been up in her personal space before and after shows, demanding autographs and passes and acting as if they were longtime friends just because they'd gotten bootlegs of her earlier concerts.

Even though Paloma had committed to do the gig months ago during the release party, Jace still planned her business trip to happen at the same time, which irked her even more. Why would a trip that she could take any time be more important than something close to home?

Walking past the Ferndale Family Fair signs, she cut over to 9 Mile Road. Tents were lined up for blocks and spilled over on the side streets as well, showcasing small businesses, artists, social organizations, and more than a few gay and lesbian groups. The richly charred aroma from the Middle Eastern food trucks made her tummy growl, but she figured it would be better to wait until after her set to dive into food that was delicious but might make her sweat garlic for hours. Apologizing every few steps for nearly running over a baby stroller or a small dog on a leash, Paloma snaked her way through the throng toward the main stage. There was a crowd of about a hundred folks watching a three-piece ska group pogo and shriek through a goofy number that had parents dancing with their little kids. They wrapped their set as Paloma approached, announcing, "We're the Punkins, and you're the best!"

The band came off stage just as Paloma found a place to park her cart behind the structure, and right when she was about to tell them, "Great set!" they turned and went back on stage, not to do an encore but to collect their gear. "Well, Nolan warned me this would be very DIY," she mumbled, sliding her guitar case strap off her shoulders. She wiped her forehead with the back of her hand and searched for a crew member to tell her what to do next.

A man dressed in a black T-shirt and cargo shorts whooshed by her, speaking into a walkie-talkie. Paloma trotted behind him for a few steps. "Excuse me, are you working the mainstage show?"

The man stopped, looking annoyed. "Why?"

For a second, Paloma was surprised he didn't recognize who she was, which was humbling. She offered up her best "We're all friends here" expression anyway. "I'm one of the acts. I'm supposed to go on at eight, and I'm not sure if I'm supposed to check in with someone or—"

"Not me," he said, speeding off.

She knew Jace would have been seething if this had happened to her, but then again, it *wouldn't* have happened to her; she would have arrived a lot earlier with a clipboard full of notes and maps and contingency plans. Paloma hadn't had to keep track of so much as a guitar pick since Jace had become her manager, and she realized she hadn't appreciated all Jace did so Paloma could solely focus on the music part of the music business. Maybe that was why Jace had gone out of town this weekend: to remind Paloma to be a little more grateful.

Paloma moved down the block to the edge of the backstage area, dragging the flatbed and laughing at the absurdity of the situation. Like many events that were long on good intentions but short on infrastructure, no one else walked by who looked like they knew what they were doing. Paloma wished she had put Nolan's phone number into her cellular phone; she was never sure if it was worth the trouble since there were only so many people she knew who bothered to take their phones with them all the time. She looked down the street and scanned the crowd, hoping to spot a white Stetson rising above the fray.

Finally, a tall guy in a black-and-silver Western jacket, spotless black 501s, and pointy-toed cowboy boots walked up to her.

"Paloma?" he asked with a smile so white it seemed to be glowing.

"Nolan! Thank God!"

"I was wondering where you were," he said, enveloping her in a hug.

"I should have figured out the logistics before I left the house," she said, pointing to her equipment. "I've been relying on Jace so long, I forgot how to hustle."

"She's not here?" he asked. "I don't think I've ever seen you two more than a few feet apart from each other."

Paloma knew he was being good-natured, but given how cranky she was at Jace at the moment, she didn't feel like joking. "I mean, I do things on my own sometimes."

Nolan's expression turned awkward. "Of course you do."

"She had a trip planned for this weekend that was too important for her to change," Paloma explained.

"Where did she go?"

"Indio, California, east of Palm Springs. She's meeting with the organizers of some new festival this October. Coach . . . Coachella."

"Coachella? Never heard of it."

"The promoter was passing around flyers backstage when I played Glastonbury. He told Jace his vision is to feature a bunch of cool bands that aren't super well known over a weekend this fall at some polo club out in the California desert." She continued with an exasperated eye roll. "And Jace is all about expanding my reach."

Nolan seemed impressed. "Well, it sounds like a good chance for you to perform for a totally different audience."

"Sounds like a hot box of chaos to me," she said flatly. "I mean, have you done any festivals?"

"Nothing more complicated than this," Nolan said, turning in a circle to take in the Ferndale passersby.

"You're smart then. It was a good business decision to do Glastonbury, but . . ." She trailed off.

"Did you feel like you got lost in the lineup?"

"Actually, the opposite. We had a huge audience, which surprised me since I didn't think anyone outside of the US knew who we were. That was fucking surreal."

"People know awesome when they hear it," Nolan said, delighted. "But even with that, you didn't like the experience?"

"I just—" She paused, her throat going dry.

"I bet it was a lot to deal with all at once," Nolan said, filling the silence and finishing her thought. "So many people, so much noise."

She nodded. "Exactly. I tried to explain that to someone once, and they thought I was crazy. Like, '*Why would you go into rock and roll if you don't like the crowds?*'" She didn't say that the someone had been herself.

A burst of memories overwhelmed her. How her heart started to pound when she looked out at an endless sea of people milling around the Glastonbury grounds. How she started to sweat and the insides of her lungs felt stuck together so she couldn't breathe. How for several terrifying seconds, every lyric she'd ever known had flown out of her head. How Jace hadn't noticed that it had taken forever for her to pick up her guitar and take center stage, probably because she'd managed to snap out of it and put in a great performance. Paloma didn't say anything at the time because, once the show was over, they got swept up in the swirl of the festival, seeing other acts and chatting with producers and promoters. By the time she and Jace got around to sightseeing, she felt like herself again, so she assumed the episode was the growing pains of being an up-and-coming artist. Maybe she just had to get used to it. And with the uptick in CD sales and interviews once they were back in the states, Jace was so, so pleased, so why question success?

"It's tough to be an introvert in the music business," Nolan said. "That's why I left punk for this oddball, alt-country outfit: smaller, more appreciative audiences and a lot less bullshit."

"Yeah," she said, amazed that she wasn't the only musician who felt that way. She looked at her watch. "I'm supposed to go on in a few minutes and need to set up, maybe do a mic check. Do you know who I need to talk to?"

"I'll find Byron; he'll take care of you." He looked at her flatbed overflowing with cables, pedals, equipment, and milk crates full of pieces and parts. "How many of you are going to be on stage?"

Paloma felt like a dope. "Just me; I'm a solo act tonight. Jace warned me that whatever I didn't bring would be the one thing I needed most, so I packed everything."

"Jace knows what she's talking about, but I don't think you'll need this unless you're playing bass, too," he said as he picked up an amp. "May I borrow this? Stuart's fell out of the van when we were unloading."

"Sure," she said, tamping down Jace's typical response: *Neither a borrower nor a lender be.* Jace said it was a quote from Shakespeare.

Obviously, Shakespeare had gotten shafted by musicians who stole his gear.

"Thanks a million," he said, taking his cellular phone out of his jacket pocket. "If we don't connect later tonight, I want to make sure I get it back to you. What's your number?" She told him, and immediately she heard the electronic tootling of her own phone in her bag. He shared another blazing-white smile, this one revealing a dimple in his left cheek. "Of course, I hope you'll stay for our set. You're welcome to join us if you have a country number up your sleeve, too. Always great to play with friends."

Paloma had gotten used to other people asking to join her sets, but Nolan asking her to join him, not knowing if she knew Dolly Parton from the Dalai Lama, was flattering. "Thanks. I'll think about it."

Nolan looked over her shoulder and cupped his hands around his mouth. "Hey, Byron! Could you come over here?" he yelled.

A stocky guy with blond curls stepped out of the flow of people and dipped under a stanchion to join them. Nolan pointed to Paloma. "Can you help this rock star, please? I found her wandering the streets looking for a roadie."

"Sure thing," Byron replied.

"You're in good hands," Nolan told her. "Now, before I leave you to do your magic, just a heads-up that I'll be introducing you. Anything in particular you want me to say?"

"Just my name is fine."

"No, it's not," he said with a raffish shake of his head. "You've been places! You've done things! You deserve a proper intro, girl!"

She smiled, her cheeks reddening. "Whatever you want to say, but leave the 'rock star' part out, please."

"Got it. I need to go get my hat. See you in a few."

Soon, Byron got her gear on stage and did a sound check, giving her a thumbs-up as he climbed down to where she was waiting. She was so focused on reviewing her set list and mentally running through her lyrics, she didn't notice that Nolan had taken the stage until she heard his voice rolling over the crowd.

"Hello, pardners, and thank you for joining us for the third annual Ferndale Family Fair! It's wonderful to see so many kids here, and I have to thank you for letting your parents come, too. My name is Tex Mechs, and my band the Moo-town Spurs will be playing in a little bit, but only if we can possibly follow the incredible musician you're about to hear. She's a hometown gal with an international following. She's a singer-songwriter who just got back from the Glastonbury Festival in England. And you kids in the audience will be able to tell *your* kids that you got to see her play live, and they are going to be so jealous. Folks, I am proud to introduce my friend, Paloma Doralle."

Paloma walked up the metal stairs at the left of the stage and looked out over the audience. Tiny children clapped as they sat on their parents' shoulders; teenagers in eyeliner and shredded jeans were waving their hands in the air; a range of adults, from hippie to alt-new wave, were all smiles. Even though the crowd had grown to fill the block, she wasn't intimidated or nervous in the slightest. And for once she didn't have to deal with Mary's demands or Colin's erratic behavior. There was no pressure to be anyone but herself here, and that felt amazing.

Nolan walked over to her, his Stetson practically glowing in the stage lights. He gave her a quick hug and whispered, "Have fun!" before exiting stage right. She slipped her guitar strap over her shoulder and stepped behind the microphone stand.

"Hello, Ferndale!" she said, waving to the crowd and prompting another round of cheers. "Let me tell you that this has to be the cutest audience I've ever seen. You're worth giving up swearing for a night, let me tell you." She played a couple of chords to ensure everything was ready to go then grinned into the mic. "Are you all ready to stay up past your bedtimes?"

"YES!" responded a choir of voices, ranging from high to low.

She'd never been so charmed. "Good, because so am I! Okay, kids, let's play."

17

NOT LONG AGO

JUNE 14, 2023

The sky was still light at eight P.M. when Paloma took the stage at the Cherry Mill Bar & Grill. Even though she was still a little tender after seeing Jace earlier that day, she had a gig to do.

When she started signing up to play a few years after moving to Stone Beach, Paloma knew full well the majority of the patrons were not coming for the music. The stage was just a platform inside a wooden gazebo, constructed in a corner of the corral-style railings running along three sides of the outdoor seating area that was the real draw for the 1970s-era family restaurant. It could accommodate tipsy batches of bachelorettes, sunburned little kids who might explode if they couldn't get dinosaur-shaped chicken nuggets within five minutes of ordering, and anyone who wanted to sit alone at the bar and savor a Jack and Coke after one too many days of a family vacation. It was also the only place in town with a liquor license, so there would always be people year-round at the Cherry Mill.

The day had been warm, but the evening breeze off the lake was chilly at its core, so Paloma was glad she'd brought her black motorcycle jacket to wear over her faded orange Faygo T-shirt. She looked to her right to check in with Kevin, a retired firefighter who played keyboards when he wasn't out fishing, wearing a short-sleeved white dress shirt and a checkered skinny tie. He gave her a nod, so she looked back at Tony seated at the drum kit, his gray hair pulled into a long ponytail and his black T-shirt barely stretching over his belly. When he raised his drumsticks in salute, Paloma adjusted her bill cap, assumed her spot behind the microphone, and settled her red Rickenbacker across her hips, her trademark black-and-white Stratocaster hidden at home. She smiled at the thirty-odd people sitting on the patio, munching on burgers, downing bottles of beer, and giving her utterly no never mind, before diving in.

"Good evening, tourists and townies. Thanks for joining us tonight at the Cherry Mill. I'm P. D. Smith, and me and my friends Tony and Kevin are looking forward to playing for you tonight. We're gonna start with a song that's kind of a credo for me—and feel free to sing along if the spirit moves you."

As she kicked off the opening riff for Tom Strager's "Rock and Roll Is My Life," some of the customers took notice. She got through the first verse, and she was pleased to see that most of the crowd had looked up from their baskets of fries and were smiling toward the stage, with some even bobbing their heads. Maybe they were surprised at how tight the trio was, or how they brought something new to a familiar tune from a Detroit favorite son. Maybe they just liked hearing a song they knew and would have been okay with a boring cover version. And as their attention drifted back to their drinks and table conversations, Paloma didn't mind. She'd connected with them, human to human, music lover to music lover, even it had only been for a split second.

She and the guys rolled through a song list of tunes that Boomers and Xers knew in their bones that wouldn't make the younger crowd cringe. She liked it when she saw someone's head jerk up in surprise when they heard an indie tune most cover bands would never touch. Some nights, when she was killing herself up there to no applause, she'd rip through "Dick or Dildo" by Fellowchick. Even if the owner took her aside for a sober talking-to afterward, the reactions on the faces of the patrons made the transgression worthwhile.

After an hour of watching the crowd shift and waitstaff haul trays of deep-fried food back and forth, it was time to end their set the same way they'd begun it: with another Strager tune, this time, "Rocky and Rolly." The final chorus wrapped as Paloma strummed the last chord, Tony crashed the cymbals, and Kevin ran his finger up and down the Yamaha keyboard, and they were greeted with a level of applause that was, at best, polite.

A far cry from her nights at the Artemis.

She hadn't thought of this gig in those terms for a long time, and now that's all she could think about. She had to admit: the Cherry Mill was a major step backward from the earlier part of her career.

Paloma put on a practiced smile. "Thanks so much. I'm P. D. Smith, and on behalf of these two fine gentlemen and myself, have a great night." The sound system immediately switched to a top 100 satellite radio station, as if all the work Paloma had put into selecting the eclectic set list and delivering the lyrics meant nothing. She unplugged her guitar and walked down the wooden stairs, feeling out of sorts.

She shouldered her guitar case and was walking past the seating area toward the parking lot when she spotted Jace sitting alone at a back table, staring down at her phone, an empty salad bowl in front of her. She hadn't alerted the staff that she'd be there or cheered loud enough for Paloma to hear her from the stage. She was simply a presence in the rear of the venue, like she'd been so many times at so many of Paloma's concerts. It was almost uncanny.

Instead of heading for her car as part of her wanted to, Paloma walked over to the table, relieved to see that Jace hadn't been so mad at her that she'd driven into a gulch. "This is a long way to come for a second-rate salad," she said.

Pleasantly startled, Jace slid her phone in her jacket pocket. "Well, I heard there was a fantastic musician who was worth the drive from Traverse City." Her expression shifted from breezy to concerned. "Look, I hope this is okay with you. I saw the P. D. Smith sign on the restaurant as I was leaving town this afternoon and thought it would be really lovely to see you perform after all this time. I promise, I'm not stalking you."

"It's okay," Paloma said, choosing to believe her.

Jace gestured to an empty chair. "May I buy you a drink?"

"Sure, but drinks are on the house," Paloma said as she set her guitar on the floor and sat across from her. "That's one of the few perks of playing at the Cherry Mill." She hailed a server, and they placed their order for a couple of pints.

"Free drinks for the talent? Sabine would be shocked," Jace said with a familiar laugh.

"How is Sabine anyway? You sounded really concerned about her. Is she sick?"

"Other than a knee that flares up if she's been on her feet too long, she's healthy as ever. It's just that she got herself in a terrible financial situation during the pandemic, and the last thing I want is for her to lose everything she's worked for her entire career. That club is truly her life."

"Does she have any family? A girlfriend?"

"Chosen family? Yes. Girlfriend? No."

Paloma pondered this. "You mean she and Mo aren't together? I thought they were a couple from the moment I first saw them."

"You aren't the only one," Jace said. "To catch you up, Mo left bartending to become a physical therapist in the early 2000s and fell in love with an RN at her hospital. They were together until Gabby got breast cancer and died in 2018. Sabine was a saint, staying with Gabby whenever Mo needed a break, bringing food over, taking calls all hours of the night from Mo after Gabby was gone. Eventually Mo made her way back to the club to pitch in on her days off, and they socialize a lot after hours, too. They both swear they're just good friends, so we'll just have to take their word for it."

"Do you go to the Artemis often?"

Jace sighed. "Not as much as I'd like, and that bugs me. There are only so many people I know who want to go see live music, and I lost my best concert buddy when Livvy moved to Chicago. It's such a drag to go by myself."

Paloma took this as confirmation that Jace was single. She reminded herself that she shouldn't care about this and kept the conversation going.

"It sounds like you'd see Sabine and Mo whenever you go to the Artemis."

"It's not the same. They have to work the shows, and I'm a civilian now. And if I go to another venue, I'm on my own. Plus, and do not tell anyone this: I'm physically unable to stand for hours in general admission anymore. My feet hurt, my back hurts, my ears ring, and I feel it for days afterward. My mind does not accept that my body is well over fifty. It's depressing."

"You're not a crazy baby anymore," Paloma said. "I'm no better. I had to think through what I have to do tomorrow before ordering a beer tonight."

"No more whiskey sours?"

"Between the alcohol content and the sugar, I can't sleep, and they make my teeth feel mossy." She had to smile, though. "I know what you mean; getting older is a lot to accept."

Jace nodded. "Besides, I don't go out much because I do events for a living, which means I work long hours and a lot of nights and weekends. By the time I have an evening free, I just want to stay home."

"You run your own business," Paloma countered. "If you really wanted more time off, couldn't you cut back?"

"You're sounding like the sensible person I am not."

The beers arrived. As they made small talk about how many brew pubs had sprouted up lately, Paloma wondered why Jace hadn't come right out and asked if she was seeing anyone. This was fine by her. In the past twenty years there'd been two men, three women, no cohabitation, and little to look back on with fondness, which was as embarrassing as it was sad. It seemed like there was no one out there now who made her happy just to wake up beside them day after day.

No one who meant as much to her as Jace had, once upon a time.

Before she embarrassed herself by asking Jace about her recent love life, Paloma got back to the topic at hand. "Well, I'm sorry that Sabine has had to deal with this, but then again, there is life beyond indie music."

Jace chuckled. "No, there isn't. You just proved that to me tonight."

"What do you mean?"

She rested an arm on the back of her chair and casually crossed her legs. "Tom Strager covers? Oldie sing-alongs? In broad daylight?"

"It's what the audience likes," Paloma said defensively.

"Screw the audience. You should be playing what *you* like. Otherwise, why bother?"

"Who says I don't like it?"

"You're not playing your own songs."

"I don't play my own songs in case some tourist in an Artemis Club T-shirt figures out who I am," she hissed.

"Why do you care anymore?" Jace asked dismissively. "You are punching way below your weight here. You ought to be performing your own material instead of selling your songs to other musicians. You ought to be playing to a full house in an actual concert hall, not a half-empty restaurant. So many people want to see you, Paloma. They love your work." She leaned closer. "They love you."

Hearing Jace say "love you" while looking straight into her striking blue eyes hit Paloma hot and hard, like she'd been zapped by an electric fence. She was mystified that Jace could still devastate her like that.

Looking down at her hands wrapped around her pint glass, she sighed. "I have my reasons."

Jace shared a crooked smile, her voice a whisper. "It's been over twenty years. Whatever mistakes you made, you are forgiven."

Paloma looked up, certain that if Jace knew the truth—knew the complete backstory for why she left—she wouldn't be so ready to forgive.

Jace sat back, confident and cocky. "I have three reasons why you should do this benefit," she said, ticking them off with her fingers. "One, you can come out of hiding. No more P. D. Smith. You can be Paloma Doralle, the legendary singer-songwriter-guitarist–international phenomenon again. I mean, it must have been stressful over all these years, worrying that someone was going to blow your cover. If you blow your own cover, you're free. Am I right?"

Paloma had to admit that Jace was right. All these years in, she was tired of looking over her shoulder, tired of her Stone Beach friends not knowing her real name. "Point taken. What's number two?"

"Two, you can inspire the next wave of musicians, especially the queer ones. Those poor souls are trying to make their mark in a world that sees their music as content, not an artist's blood and guts. You were a trailblazer in your heyday, and they can learn something from you now."

"I'm not sure I want to be a role model. I'm a mess."

That prompted one of Jace's megawatt smiles. "I'll bet more than one musician will be glad to see they can be their messy selves, too."

Paloma hadn't considered that there might be an aspect of being famous that wasn't toxic. Being able to pay it forward felt hopeful and redemptive, and that intrigued her. "And number three?"

Jace raised a third finger. "Reclaim your legacy. After New York, all these other shit stirrers—reporters, bloggers, former colleagues—co-opted your narrative because you weren't there to stop them. Now that 'Heart Fire' is everywhere, it's happening again. Back in the nineties, you hated being forced into being someone you weren't. If you do this concert, you can return to the limelight on your own terms and correct the record. Otherwise, the lies are going to outlive you."

Now that Jace had made her case, Paloma had to level with herself. She was so sick of hiding and subverting her own music to play things safe. And talking to an older-and-wiser Jace who seemed like she was willing to listen in a way she hadn't before made Paloma realize how lonely and isolated she'd been for way too long, and how that needed to change.

"Think about it, okay?" Jace took a twenty out of her wallet and set it on the table. "Thanks for making sure our server gets this. I have to get back to Traverse City."

She'd barely gotten to her feet before Paloma was standing in front of her, as if she'd been pushed by an irresistible force. "I'll do it," she said.

For a moment, Jace was sputtering with delight, moving in for a possible hug then pulling back, her words tripping over each other. "Oh, this is great! This means so much to me—to everyone—me included! I'll call you in the morning to give you more details, okay?"

"Actually, I'm tied up over the next few days. Could we talk Monday?"

"Monday it is, then. Oh my God, this is going to be . . . ooh!" Smiling too wide to finish her thought with mere words, Jace hugged her quickly and tightly then practically skipped toward the parking lot. Paloma watched the Escalade pull out into the street before heading to her own car, her nerves buzzing between conviction that she'd done the right thing and dread that she might have actually made things worse.

Bobbie was walking her bulldog mix past Paloma's house when she pulled up. "Hey there!" her neighbor called out. "How'd things go with Jace?"

"I agreed to do the benefit," she replied, each word feeling strange to say out loud.

"Good for you!" Bobbie said, patting Paloma on the arm. "I'm glad you two cleared the air and worked things out the way you wanted."

"I guess so," Paloma hedged.

The dog gave a gruff bark, pulling Bobbie's attention down to ground level. "Are you ready for bed, Buford? I know I sure am." Giving the leash a gentle tug, she and Buford walked home as she singsonged, "Good niiiiight."

Paloma looked up at the night sky, took a long inhale, and groaned.

She went into the house, locked the front door, and was on her way to putting her guitar in her office when she saw a familiar sight: a lanky young man in a blue hoodie and frayed jeans sitting on her couch, hunched over his phone and bopping his dark, curly head along to whatever music was blasting through his earbuds. He looked up and smiled.

She set her guitar down. “Hey, Kaden,” she said.

“Hey, Mom.”

18

NOT LONG AGO

JUNE 14, 2023

Kaden put his phone down and took his earbuds out. "I hope it's okay I came up early. I need to finish packing before Cindi gets here."

Honestly, it was not okay. Paloma wanted nothing more than to pace around her house, without her son and his girlfriend in earshot, so she could yell at herself for agreeing to do a show produced by her ex. An ex who was relentless about achieving her business goals at the expense of everything else. An ex who was willing to put aside the fact that Paloma had broken her heart into a billion pieces in order to get what she wanted, for the Artemis and herself. An ex who'd somehow read Paloma's mind and knew how much she wanted to perform her own music again after laying low in Stone Beach for so, so long.

An ex whose smile could still turn her bones to melted butter and send her libido skyrocketing.

Paloma pushed all of her angst down deep, far away from her son. "You're living here for another forty-eight hours," she told Kaden. "You don't need permission to come home."

"It looked like you might have plans. I saw all that chicken salad in the fridge and wondered if you had houseguests or something." As she put her guitar away, he added, "I ate some of it. Hope that's okay, too."

She reentered the living room. "Show me what you're planning to get rid of. I want to make sure you're not throwing out a family heirloom."

The state of Kaden's bedroom was somewhere between an intolerable mess and a FEMA-worthy disaster. Plastic bins half filled with winter clothes, comic books, LEGO collectibles, and random boy crap took up most of the floor space. His bureau drawers were hanging out, and his closet door was propped open by a pile of long, skinny sneakers and various boots. While one wall was bare, the others still sported posters of *Star Wars,* Iron Man, and Sleeping Bear Dunes National Park.

"Packing is going well, I see," Paloma deadpanned.

"Don't worry, I have all day tomorrow." He carefully stepped over a cardboard box marked "PlayStation shit" to reach the closet. "These, I wouldn't wear again even if they still fit," he said, removing several button-down shirts and pairs of khakis that had been standard dress for his many years of high school orchestra concerts where he dutifully stood in the percussion section behind the ensemble, bored out of his mind between snare cues, itching to ditch the Sousa marches and get back to wailing his way through a Nirvana set.

Next, he handed her a couple of well-worn parkas. "I won't need these or the gloves or snow boots in LA."

"Want me to save them for when you visit at Christmas?"

"Good idea."

Paloma was secretly glad to hear that he still intended to come home. Once he got used to the California warmth and sunshine, and lack of maternal supervision, she was afraid he'd change his mind.

He motioned toward the shelves on one wall packed with baseball trophies and plaques from band competitions and honor societies. "I don't want to take these, but I don't want you to get rid of them, either. I worked hard for them."

"Yes, you did," she said, a thousand images of her son's childhood and adolescence flipping through her mind.

"Just don't leave them out when you turn this into a guest room. People will think your son was a nerd who peaked in high school."

"Okay. Box them up, and I'll store them in the basement."

Kaden pointed at the desk. "There's a bunch of computer cables and gaming mice we can toss, and some dead iPods, too. The Apple Store won't give you any money for them now that they're discontinued, but they might be able to recycle them."

Paloma's stomach dipped. "Do you have my iPod? The one I used to use?"

He picked his way over to the desk and rifled through the box. "Here you go."

"I wish this still worked," she said softly.

"All of those songs are on your laptop and an external drive, and I have everything uploaded to my cloud account, too. You can listen to any of them anytime you want. You don't need that relic anymore."

She cradled the device in her palm. Locked away in its impenetrable innards were thousands of songs that Jace had carefully curated for her during their relationship with an attention to detail that bordered on obsessive. After New York, this was the one relic Paloma hung on to. Although most of the material made her dreadfully sad post-breakup, she couldn't bear to part with it, even if it was only a hunk of dead hardware.

She slipped the iPod into her back pocket. "Anything else?"

"I have some dorm furniture and junk from my apartment we'll take to Goodwill tomorrow. We'll buy everything new once we find a place. Dad said he'll take us to IKEA."

"Got it," she said, trying not to grind her molars at the thought of how much she'd spent on all the household items he needed during his four years at University of Michigan, only to have them cast aside and replaced by new and shiny things from Nolan in

LA. She tried not to think that she was one of those replaceable things, too.

He followed her as she walked toward the kitchen. “How was the gig tonight?”

“I’d barely call it a gig,” Paloma said, getting a sparkling water out of the fridge. “The usual uninterested crowd, the usual drunk guys trying to drown me out.”

He shook his head, accepting the Coke Zero that Paloma handed to him. “I don’t know why you bother. They pay you shit.”

“It keeps my chops up.”

“What for?” he asked with a light laugh. “You planning a world tour with Tony and Kevin?”

“Actually, I’ve been asked to be part of a benefit in Detroit this fall.”

“Oh, that’s cool,” he said with a good-natured nod.

“And I need to talk to you about it,” she said, using her tone of voice that meant business, and maybe some bad news.

“Oh, okay,” Kaden said, arranging himself against the arm of the couch so he could prop his skinny, sock-clad feet on the table. “What’s up?”

Sitting at the other end of the couch, she looked at her son, his dark brows framing the green eyes she’d bequeathed to him and his sharp jaw shaded with a couple days’ worth of scruff à la his dad. She wished she could summon a time machine and change how she’d mothered him over the last couple of decades so she wouldn’t have to explain so much in so little time. “You know how I used to live in Detroit before I moved here when I was pregnant with you?”

“Yeah, so I could have a boring life.”

“A *better* life.”

“Call it what you want, Mom. Nothing happens up here. Never did, and never will, not even during tourist season. No wonder Dad didn’t want to move here to be with us.”

“Is that what he’s told you?” Paloma asked, wondering what else Nolan had been telling him about her motives.

"He always says what you've always said. The two of you were in bands in Detroit and crossed paths, you got together for a hot minute, you both wanted to have a kid but neither of you wanted a long-term relationship, he had a job in California and you wanted to live in a small town . . . blah-de-blah-de-blah. Why are you bringing this up?"

"The truth is, I was in a relationship with someone else when I got pregnant."

"Oh?"

"A woman."

"Oh!" Kaden said, his deep voice lifting in surprise. "So obviously, she knew she wasn't the father."

"She didn't even know I was pregnant. I left her before she found out."

"Okay . . . so?"

Paloma exhaled. "We'd been together for several years. She was my business manager, too."

"You had a business manager?" Kaden asked, a mixture of disbelief and suspicion in his voice. "Why? You told me you just played a few clubs in Detroit and Ann Arbor."

Paloma pressed her lips together. "I actually had a pretty high-profile career from the late nineties to 2001."

She saw the wheels turning in his head. "The year I was born."

"Yes."

"How high profile?"

"Headlining national tours. Some international dates. Glastonbury Festival. TV appearances."

She saw the confusion creep across his face. "And you gave all that up because of me?"

"No, K," she said gently. "I wasn't giving up anything I wanted to keep. I had never wanted that kind of nonstop pressure, and, for a lot of reasons, my girlfriend and I weren't on the same page about my music career or our non-musical life, for that matter.

What I did know was that I wanted you. I wanted to be a much better parent than my parents had been, and I wanted you to be surrounded by people who cared about you: Aunt Bobbie and Uncle Bud, the friends we've made through school, and all the other folks up here."

"And Dad," he added pointedly.

"Yes, of course—your father, too. I wanted you to feel loved and safe. That was all I wanted."

"Are you telling me all this because I'm moving?" he asked with a note of amused confusion. "Is this some sort of empty-nester love dump?"

"Ugh, sorry. I'm giving you a long-winded explanation for why I needed to talk to you about this benefit in Detroit. Have you heard the song 'Heart Fire,' maybe on Netflix or TikTok?"

"Cindi's obsessed with that song." From what she'd observed over the three years they'd been dating, Kaden's girlfriend Cindi was obsessed with a lot of things: lifestyle influencers, *Friends* reruns, poke bowls, baby goat videos. She was also obsessed with Kaden in a caring, mutually beneficial way that made Paloma feel better about the two of them moving across the country together. "Why?" Kaden asked, his eyes narrowed.

"Well, 'Heart Fire' is my song."

"You mean you wrote it for Paloma Doralle?"

"I mean, I'm not P. D. Smith. I'm Paloma Doralle."

Kaden stared at her momentarily before muttering, "Cindi called it. I am such an idiot."

Now it was Paloma's turn to be surprised. "What do you mean?"

"Cindi knew that was you, and I wouldn't believe her!" he said. "She kept saying, 'That sounds a lot like your mom.' She found other Paloma Doralle songs online and said the same thing. She even showed me online photos of Paloma Doralle and said it was obviously you with a bleach job and no dental work." His voice went hard. "Even though all that evidence was right there in front of me, I refused to believe it, because I knew you wouldn't have kept this a secret from me." He retreated into the corner of the couch, his arms folded protectively across his chest. "Why didn't you tell me about this sooner?"

"Because I was—I am—ashamed of what I'd done," she said, relieved she'd finally said the words aloud. "Instead of breaking up with my girlfriend and wrapping up my career like an adult, I left her without any explanation and reneged on my tour commitments and my album contract. I dropped completely out of sight and came here to hide under Aunt Bobbie's wing."

"Hold on. Your ex didn't know you were pregnant? Did Dad know?"

"Yes."

Kaden looked stricken. "Did he not want you to have me?"

"Oh my God, sweetheart, he wanted you," she said immediately. "He wanted you just as much as I did. But like we've told you, we weren't a couple, and I didn't want to move to LA, and he couldn't work in Michigan, so we developed our own custody arrangement. I wanted to keep our lives private, so he helped me find a lawyer to set up an LLC so my royalties and performance rights are controlled by me but not as Paloma Doralle."

"So you started using a fake name."

"An alias—'aka P. D. Smith,'" she confirmed with air quotes around the legalese.

"Using your real initials."

"Yes."

His brows furrowed. "You always told me you were named P. D. to honor members of your family."

"Technically, that's true," she mumbled.

He thought for a moment. "So that's why you got all weird when we went to the Secretary of State to get my driver's license and wouldn't let me touch my birth certificate before you handed it over to the clerk: You didn't want me to see your real name on the document. Unbelievable."

Kaden went quiet, staring at a point on the floor. She wished he'd say something, or yell, or walk away. Finally, the silence got to be too much for her.

"I know it was wrong for me to wait this long to tell you. The more time passed, the more it seemed like a non-issue because 'Paloma Doralle' was pretty much forgotten. But because this old song of mine is suddenly crazy popular, I got asked to do this benefit, and I knew I couldn't hide much longer."

He looked unsympathetic. "All this time you were lying to me and everyone we know, pretending to be someone else."

"I wasn't pretending to be someone else," she protested. "I've always been me. I wanted to put distance between my current life and my prior career, and I couldn't do that unless I changed my location and my name."

He glowered at her. "This is the exact opposite of what you taught me. Own up to your mistakes. Apologize right away and make things right."

"I know. I wanted you to do better than I had done, so I drilled that into you."

He shut his eyes in exasperation. "It's not like you robbed a bank, Mom! You got pregnant and wanted a job change. So what? Why all the drama?"

"I knew my girlfriend—Jace—was going to be devastated whether I stayed or left," she blurted. "I took off so I wouldn't have to look her in the eye and break her heart."

His volume ratcheted up over hers. "But if you hadn't gotten pregnant, I wouldn't be here, so you can see why I'm not exactly caring about what this Jace person might have thought about it."

Paloma powered on. "Well, now we're back in touch. She's the one organizing the benefit in Detroit I told you about. She's raising money to save the club where I got my start. Your father talked to her and gave me her phone number. And she came up here and met with me today."

His face darkened. "So that's why you finally decided to tell me that you've been living a lie my entire life and forced me to grow up in this broke-ass town: because your ex finally caught up with you."

Paloma inwardly flinched. He wasn't entirely wrong, but he wasn't completely right, either. "I always meant to tell you, but when you were younger, I didn't want you to accidentally slip up and tell someone. When you were older, I couldn't figure out the best way to bring it up, so I'd put it off again and again."

"So you *weren't* going to tell me! Just like you weren't ever going to tell that Jace person. This makes no sense. Why were you so afraid?"

The words spilled out before she could stop herself. "I learned at a young age that revealing a secret makes the people you love turn against you. I've told you that when I was in high school and my parents found out I was bisexual, they kicked me out of the house, turned my brother against me, and never spoke to me again. I didn't think I could survive being abandoned like that again. Not by my girlfriend, and certainly not by my son."

"So them being raging homophobes and terrible parents justifies you running out on this Jace person and lying to me?" he shot back. "Do you understand how messed up this is, Mom?"

Her chest started to tighten. "I should never have talked to Jace or agreed to do this benefit. Forget it; I'm not going through with it."

"*Mom!* Listen to yourself!" he scolded. "You're trying to run away from the consequences of your decisions. *Again!* At least have the guts to follow through this time." He got up from the couch and walked toward his bedroom.

Paloma hurried after him. "I was trying to protect you. I—"

He turned to face her. "Bullshit! You were trying to protect yourself, and you dragged me along with you. I can't tell you how glad I am that I'll never set foot in Stone Beach again."

He slammed the door behind him. Paloma was certain he was crouching on the edge of his bed, texting Cindi, bringing her into the circle of shame his mother built so many years ago. As awful as it had been to watch, she knew he had every right to be angry, and all she could do right now was hope that they'd find some way to reconcile.

She went to her bedroom and lay on her bed, staring at the ceiling as her own mother's final words blinked on and off in her brain like a neon sign:

If you had kept your feelings to yourself, you'd still have a family.

19

WAY BACK WHEN

APRIL 12, 2000

Around four A.M. when they finally got to their suite at the InterContinental, Paloma was so full of champagne and birthday cake, she couldn't move. She had just enough energy to sprawl across the couch, the glitter from her HAPPY 30TH! sash embedded in the tulle of her Betsey Johnson tutu, her tiara digging into her scalp along with the bobby pins holding up the remains of her ersatz bouffant. Through her half-closed eyelids, she spied the huge floral arrangements from Ticketmaster and the editors of *Rolling Stone* and *SPIN*. Earlier, she'd tripped into a stack of unopened presents that would have to be repackaged and shipped back to Detroit. By their size and weight, she assumed most of them were cases of high-end booze or extravagant items like martini shakers or crystal decanters sent by liquor brands that wanted to sponsor a future tour. There was nothing personal or thoughtful at all.

Jace was changing into her sleep duds and prepping for bed as if it were any old Wednesday night back at the house. As usual, she'd had no more than two cocktails and kept moving throughout the evening, sipping club soda and squiring Paloma around to meet the industry folks she needed to kiss up to. Thankfully, a few people they'd met during their Chicago gigs had swung by; even so, Paloma felt like she was the entertainment at a convention instead of the guest of honor.

That was the downside of having a milestone birthday in the middle of a tour: She'd celebrated with the people footing the bill, not her friends.

"Do you want to sleep there tonight?" Jace asked as she brushed her teeth.

"Nungh," Paloma replied as a stiletto slipped off her foot and hit the floor.

"Does that mean you *do* want to sleep on the couch?"

"No, I'm coming to bed," she said, carefully rolling into an upright position and kicking off her other shoe before walking barefoot toward the bathroom. She turned her back to Jace, who slipped the sash over her head before unzipping her dress.

"I got us late checkout; we don't have to be out of here before two," Jace said.

"Thanks." Paloma stepped out of the frock and left it in a fluffy pile on the carpet, not wanting to risk what might happen to her digestive tract if she bent down to pick it up. She stood behind Jace to look in the mirror and reared back when she saw the flaky black rings around her eyes. "Why didn't you tell me my mascara looked like shit?"

"You've done it that way on purpose before," Jace said, rinsing her toothbrush and putting it into her travel kit.

"I look like a raccoon after a bar fight."

"You always look beautiful to me," Jace said with a twinkle in her eye before kissing Paloma's bare shoulder.

Paloma tried to lift the tiara off her head and yelped. "Can you get this off of me? I think the hair stylist used staples."

"Sure. Sit down."

She sat on the toilet seat in her bandeau and underpants, the weariness of playing a concert then partying for hours settling in. "I'm really looking forward to being off the road for the summer. Aren't you?"

"Sure," Jace said as she worked the tiara free. "I have to get back to the sound engineer, check on your royalty statement . . ."

"And see your brand-new nieces."

"They're not so new," Jace joked. "They're four and seven."

"New to your family. What's the latest from Joyce?"

She placed a bobby pin on the counter. "She called this afternoon during sound check. She said the girls are finally getting used to sleeping in their own beds. The first two weeks, she'd find them curled around each other on the floor in a puddle of blankets."

Paloma flashed on her first few nights at Bobbie and Bud's, huddled in a corner fully dressed, terrified that her parents would break down the bedroom door and throw her out on the street. "It's going to take a lot of time and love before they'll be able to trust her."

"Joyce said the social worker told her that a huge part of being a successful adoptive parent is physically being there. The girls have been in the foster system for a long time and don't expect anyone they love to stick around. Seeing that she's there when they go to bed and when they wake up will go a long way." Jace gently pulled the tiara free. "Joyce is already in love with them; I can hear it in her voice. She's wanted to be a mom forever, and she's going to do great."

"I know how much you wanted to be at the adoption hearing."

"Well, we were on the other side of the country, and the judge moved up the date."

"You excited to meet them?"

Jace smiled. "Yeah, I'm looking forward to being the 'cool aunt,' taking them to the playground or going to a concert when they're old enough. It'll be fun."

"Could I go with you when you meet them?"

Jace dropped a handful of pins onto the counter. "Let me check with Joyce."

Paloma froze. "Does she not think of us as a couple yet? We've been together three years."

"That's not what I meant."

"Is she nervous about having the queers around her kids?"

"Oh my God, no! That's not it at all," Jace replied. "I want to check with Joyce about when's a good time for us to visit. She said she's trying to get them used to a routine before bringing people over. She likes you. She likes us being together."

As Jace brushed the hair spray out of her hair, Paloma's scalp tingled. "So you do like kids. I wasn't sure."

"Yeah, I like kids. I was a great day camp counselor in high school. I babysat a little boy on my block for a few years. Kids are fun. Of course, it helped that I was getting paid and I could send them back to their parents at the end of the day."

With her Big 3-0 birthday looming, Paloma had planned to have this conversation for months and hadn't found the right time or place. Now it was coming up at four in the morning, and since she was too tired and residually drunk to stop herself, Paloma dove in. "I really want to be a mother. Soon."

The brush hit a bobby pin. "Oh?"

"Being thirty is young enough for me to have the energy to play with our kids but old enough to have my shit together and be an adult."

Jace hooted. "We're in rock and roll! We're more like eternal teenagers: playing music too loud, drinking too much, staying out really late, and sleeping most of the day."

"That can change. I can change."

"If you want to end your career, sure."

"Lots of female rock stars have kids. Pat Benatar. Nancy Wilson."

"When's the last time they've had a hit?"

"Melissa Etheridge has two kids."

"She didn't get pregnant. Julie did."

"If they could figure out how to have babies and a music career, so could we."

Jace snorted. "Well, I'm sure as hell not getting pregnant."

"I'm not asking you to!"

Jace stood in front of Paloma and gently cupped her face in her hands. "Babe, I love you," she said tenderly. "I love us. I love that you're finally getting the attention you've deserved all along and your career is in a really good place. So many doors are opening right now, based on all the work you're putting in. This isn't exactly the perfect time to have a baby."

"There's never a perfect time to have a baby."

"And there's no magic age to have one, either. We've got some time yet. Let's get through the summer, get your album done, and we can talk more about this."

We. That gave Paloma hope. Besides, she was too tired to talk much longer.

"Okay."

Jace's fingers roamed over Paloma's scalp. "That should be all of them."

Paloma stood and gave Jace a peck on the lips. "Thank you. I'm taking a shower."

Jace kissed her back. "That's a birthday gift for both of us."

Once she'd successfully dissolved the layers of makeup and hair spray and downed a bottle of water and a couple of Tylenol, she slid into bed next to Jace, trying not to wake her but nudging her out of a doze anyway.

"Did you enjoy your party?" Jace whispered.

"It was *a* party; I'm not sure if it was *my* party," Paloma replied.

Jace put her arm around her and kissed her brow. "Do you want your present now or in the morning?"

Paloma snuggled in. "The morning."

Jace chuckled. "Well, it is morning."

Paloma didn't answer. Within seconds, she was asleep.

She regained consciousness just before noon. Jace was huddled over the desk, talking on her cell phone in low tones. Figuring it was a business call, Paloma went into the bathroom to get dressed and made up before saying hello. By the time she came out, Jace was off the phone. She took one look at Paloma and beamed. "Who is this sexy, mature woman I see before me?"

She snickered. "I'm only ten months older than you."

Jace wouldn't let up. "You're dating a girl in her twenties, Mrs. Robinson."

"Shut up and get me some coffee, youngster."

"Want to go out or have room service?"

"I'm making room-service-level money now?"

"The suite is on Seal-Eye's tab. That's what you get for your birthday when you close a deal for your third album."

"And you're sure they aren't going to charge this back to us?"

"I have an email saying they're covering all expenses, so you've got the green light to order whatever you want, babe."

Soon, they were sitting at the dining room table in their suite tearing into surf and turf, giddily feeding each other forkfuls of heavily buttered mashed potatoes and sipping out of each other's champagne flutes. Paloma picked up a lobster tail by the fin and looked at it from every angle, perplexed. "How do you get the meat out of this thing?"

"Here, let me show you." Jace put the tail in her left hand. "You take this weird-looking little fork and slide it in here under the shell and pull it out." Mission accomplished, she put the lobster meat on Paloma's plate next to her filet.

"How did you learn how to do that?" Paloma asked.

"We went to Maine when I was a kid," Jace said, wiping her hands with a massive cloth napkin. "They had instructions on the placemats."

"See, I knew you grew up rich," Paloma said. "I've never eaten lobster before."

Jace looked confused. "We only went that one time, and—wait, you mean you never went to Red Lobster?"

"We couldn't afford it when I was growing up. Besides, my parents thought eating out was 'sinful spending' and yelled at me and Dustin if we asked to go to McDonald's." She looked at her plate. "Now what?"

"Cut off a piece, dip it into that bowl of melted butter, and enjoy. Oh, and you can use your regular fork now."

She did so. "Oh my God."

"Good, huh?"

"This must be what being a princess tastes like."

Jace laughed. "Rich, sweet, and salty?"

"Yep."

Jace leaned closer. "Wait until you have French food."

Paloma waved a bite of lobster on her fork like a baton. "I dunno. This will be hard to beat."

"Well, you'll find out in a few weeks."

"What do you mean?"

Jace was so excited, her words cascaded over each other. "I've booked you a summer European tour, babe. We're going to Paris. And Amsterdam, and Berlin, and a bunch of other places. Happy birthday!"

Paloma put her fork down. "Wait, another tour? When?"

"In a couple of months. The headliner dropped out, and the promoter reached out to ask if you could fill in. It's an insane opportunity. There's lots of love for American indie music over there, and we'd get to see more of the world together!"

"I thought we were going to stay home for the summer. Rest and relax for a few months."

Jace's smile dimmed a few watts. "We'll do that when we get back."

Paloma's heart rate felt like it had doubled in a matter of seconds. "And by then you will have booked another batch of gigs."

Jace looked puzzled. "Well, that's what you do for a living."

"I make more in album sales than concerts. The new record will be out this fall, and we can live off the advance until then. We don't need to tour again so soon."

"I can't believe I'm saying this, but unless we are really frugal, you may not make back the advance this time."

That was unexpected. "Why? Do you think the songs suck?"

"God, no! Why do you automatically assume I'm criticizing you?

Your material is fantastic, but that's not the issue here. You've heard of Napster, right?"

"Yeah. Nerds downloading songs onto their computers."

"But then they can send those songs to their friends or post them on a website without buying a record in the first place. Nothing's stopping them from stealing and sharing your music, and you're not getting a dime. And it's not just nerds using it anymore. Just about every high school and college kid in America has a Napster account these days."

Paloma's palms started to get clammy. "They can't keep this up. The labels will go to court to shut it down."

Jace sighed uneasily. "The genie's out of the bottle, babe. Once folks realize they don't have to buy a whole album to get the one song they like, they aren't going to shell out fifteen bucks for the CD. And if they're getting it for free, they won't even have to pay for the single." Jace put her hand over Paloma's. "Look, don't worry about this. I'm making sure you're going to be okay, even if record sales take a dip. And this European tour couldn't have come at a better time. You can tease the new album and boost sales for your current catalogue while getting your cut of ticket and merch sales that Napster can't touch. We'll be fine. *You'll* be fine."

Paloma took her hand back. "But you promised we'd stay home for the summer."

"I know you're tired right now, but we'll have two whole months before this happens. You can rest up."

"I have to finish writing the songs, then I'm going to be in the studio. None of that is relaxing. Plus, I want a life beyond just being on the road all the time."

"It sounds like a lot, but if we can just—"

"You promised, Jace!" she shouted. "You said we'd be home for the summer, maybe the rest of the year!"

"Okay, okay," Jace said, her hands up as if she was trying to calm a growling dog. "I'm sorry."

Hot tears were trailing down Paloma's cheeks. "Why won't you listen to me? It's my career. It's my life!"

"It's *our* life," Jace blurted.

"I can't believe you're making this about you!"

"I'm not! I honestly thought you'd want to go to Paris."

"To work?"

"Yes, work would be a piece of it, but you'd told me you'd always wanted to see the Eiffel Tower, and I wanted to surprise you for your big birthday." Jace sounded crestfallen. "I thought you'd be thrilled."

Paloma wiped her tears with the back of her hand. She felt like she'd been thrown in the ocean and had to thrash her way back to shore. Jace was so good at remembering dates, names, conversations. She knew the business end of their partnership so well. Why was she often so blind to what Paloma really wanted and needed?

Then again, what kind of idiot would turn down a trip to Paris? Jace was right: Paloma had always wanted to go there, especially on the arm of someone she loved. And if doing a few dates would help weather the financial storms Jace saw on the horizon, why not just do them? What was wrong with that? What was wrong with *her*?

Paloma took a couple of breaths to steady herself. *"I'm* sorry. You found this amazing, romantic opportunity, and I shit all over it." She paused, thinking about Napster. "Do you really think CDs are on their way out?"

Jace shrugged. "I don't know for sure. There's always some new technology out there that'll make the current one obsolete. But seeing live music? That's something no computer can replicate, and people will always pay for concert tickets because they know if they don't, they may miss the experience of a lifetime. Especially if you're the one they're coming to see."

"I'm not sure I can keep living up to the hype, though," Paloma said with a sniffle, fiddling with the napkin in her lap. "All of those people will get tired of me, maybe sooner rather than later. Tastes change so fast. I can count on one hand the indie bands that are around a year after they break through."

Jace shook her head. "You're not just any indie band. I've seen a lot of them, and I've never seen anyone better than you. Last night's show was maybe the best one you've ever done, and your next show will be even more fantastic. Believe me."

Paloma looked at Jace, with her beautiful eyes and serious expression. This was the first woman she'd ever dated, the first person who she'd ever wanted to make a life with, the first professional to believe in her talent and range. She was sincere, she was loyal. She adored the large gesture and the finer details. She made Paloma laugh. She made Paloma feel safe and protected. Jace was her first love, and Paloma would do anything to keep her by her side. If she did anything to make Jace leave, Paloma didn't think she would survive. Plastering a smile over all her fears, Paloma said, "Okay, I'll do the tour."

"Really? You will? So you forgive me?" Jace said, crying and laughing at once.

"What is there to forgive?" Paloma replied, hoping her tears looked like joy.

Jace pulled her to her feet to share a kiss. Paloma relaxed in her arms, wishing with all her might that she could power through the European dates and return home with her nerves intact, for Jace's sake . . . and the sake of their relationship.

The clock ticking toward checkout, they finished their elaborate meal, even though it had grown cold. Jace was about to pack her laptop when she asked, "Do you want to check your email before we go to the airport? See who's wishing you happy birthday?"

"Sure." Paloma logged into her AOL account and scanned her inbox, which was overflowing with messages from her friends waiting for her in Detroit, sending love and promises to get together and celebrate her birthday once she was back.

Including one from Nolan. They'd run into each other at shows around Detroit a few times since the festival in Ferndale the previous summer, and they'd grabbed lunch together a few weeks earlier to check in on each other, musician to musician. His email said:

Howdy, birthday girl!

I'm sure all of Chicago was at your feet last night. I know how hard touring is for you, and I know how much you're looking forward to a nice, long break back home. You've earned it, superstar!

Hope you saved me a slice of cake. See you soon.

XO

20

NOT LONG AGO

JUNE 15, 2023

Paloma sat on her deck with her Strat on her lap and a glass of pinot grigio on the table, staring out across the lake. The sun cast a fiery glaze over the waves and onto the gray shingles on the back of her house. She'd finished the last of the chicken salad for dinner, but it wasn't sitting well. She wondered if it was cursed.

She took an ample sip of wine and strummed through a melody that had been itching in the back of her mind for several days. She was paid to invest her creativity into her songwriting gig to the point that she'd finish a day of contract work feeling like a husk. Since she was between assignments, it would have made sense for her to do anything else: watch a cooking show, visit the winery up the road to breathe in the spiky scent of the grape leaves and chat up the owner over a rosé slushie, or even play Scrabble with Bobbie and Bud. But during this liminal time between her argument with her son and when his flight landed in Los Angeles, it was as if her electric guitar had called to her. It was a lot like when the Morries had given her the Stratocaster as a sixteenth birthday present: Whenever Paloma couldn't figure out her feelings, she'd plug in and go.

She couldn't believe that once again, she was forced to choose between Jace and Kaden. Why was it that whenever she considered strutting back on stage in a miniskirt with a playlist of Paloma Doralle songs, she imagined him judging her for all the wrong decisions she'd made as a mother? And when she reminded herself that she had Kaden's best interests at heart when she left show business, why could she hear Jace telling her that she was smothering her talent? Why did the two of them continue to cancel each other out?

Her guitar buzzed against her pelvis as she strummed, singing a fragment of a lyric she wanted to get to the next stage of development:

I hit a tripwire, and my heart exploded.
You roll in with rifles loaded.
Put 'em down, girl, and have a seat
Cuz I have a lot of explaining to do.

She swiped her notebook off the table and scribbled her lyrics and chords, knowing that if she didn't document them, they'd be gone forever. She repeated the lyric, substituting *boy* for *girl* in case it was going to be a better fit for her family dilemma instead of her romantic angst. Looking at the horizon line, she decided it would be about romance. Children were supposed to grow up and move away and clash with their parents, but if there was love in the relationship, they'd usually find a way back home at some point. There was a lot more potential for failure with a lover, hoping all could be forgiven by saying the right thing or singing the right song.

She wouldn't be in this mess if Jace hadn't been so . . . Jace. Driven. Slyly funny and charming. Turning Paloma's unspoken longing to be more than the star of Stone Beach into a hero's journey back to the spotlight. That was brilliant and manipulative, and so seductive. Was Paloma right to think there might be a mutual glimmer of attraction between them still? Or was she being snowed over again, like all those times when they'd decided to ignore their problems instead of bringing them out into the open and solving them?

After a while, she realized she was played out and put the Strat away. She turned her attention to her handwritten list of the tasks to get ready for the benefit. After their argument the night before, she begrudgingly agreed with Kaden: She had to follow through on her commitment, and with that in mind, she had a lot to do in the next three months to prepare. Some tasks were pretty easy: booking a soundproof practice room at the local high school where she could work up the louder songs in her repertory without aggravating her neighbors; identifying an outfit that made her look as awesome as possible without tipping over into ridiculousness; finding a stylist who could bring her hair back to presentability after two decades of do-it-yourself dye jobs and trims while she was incognito.

The other tasks were more involved. First and foremost was to finalize her set. As the closing act, she was expected to play three of her own songs then lead the rest of the bands in an all-hands jam as a tribute to the Artemis, using a tune that anyone who'd played in Detroit for any length of time would know well enough to sing or play along. Jace offered her the opportunity to select that final song with one caveat: no Tom Strager. No shade to him, but selecting one of his well-known songs would be too simple, too reductive, too stereotypical. Besides, Jerome had told Jace the rights would be too expensive to secure for the documentary.

She couldn't get over the fact that Jerome was a respected documentarian. The three months she knew him back in 1997, he was completely insufferable and utterly unwilling to chip in for gas and food, even though he was coasting off his dad's executive salary from Ford, to the point where she and Jace used to refer to him as His Ass-Holiness. Once it was public that Paloma had joined the lineup, she'd have to schedule an interview with him and maybe ask him to pay her the twenty dollars he still owed her.

Next on the list: hiring a rhythm section that could help her recapture her trademark rough-around-the-edges sound. At the Cherry Mill, Kevin had covered the bass part on his synth since there wasn't a decent bassist within twenty miles of Stone Beach who didn't have a curfew, so she had no local favorites. Given what Jace had told her about the post–New York fallout, Mary would probably laugh in her face. Still, Paloma worried that if she didn't give her the right of first refusal, she'd go back to bad-mouthing her yet again, and she didn't want to undermine the benefit from the get-go. Hopefully Mary would decline anyway, seeing that she was never one to forget a grudge. Paloma would have to ask Jace if she had any backup recommendations.

And on drums? As with Mary, Colin ought to be asked first, but Paloma couldn't find his contact information anywhere, and his social media trail went cold after 2002. She considered checking police records but figured Jace might have suggestions here, too.

Besides, she knew which drummer she wanted to sit in with her, but he wasn't taking her calls.

Yesterday, Kaden had stayed in his room with the door shut, unwilling to answer when she knocked and asked that they clear the air before he flew out. Cindi arrived mid-morning and, following an awkward hello, lured him out to ship boxes and run errands ahead of their cross-country move. Paloma's offer to take them to dinner went unanswered, and they didn't come back until after she'd fallen asleep. Earlier that morning, the three of them had driven to the Traverse City airport in sullen silence. When Paloma went to hug Kaden goodbye, he turned and entered the terminal without looking back. She returned to Stone Beach alone, mad at herself and miserable.

She checked the time. Kaden and Cindi should have landed at LAX a while ago, yet he hadn't called or texted to let her know they were safely on the ground and on their way to his father's as he'd done after every other flight. She emptied her wineglass and was on her way inside for a refill when her FaceTime chime rang.

"You could have given me a heads-up before you let Kaden in on our big little lie," Nolan snapped before she could say hello.

Since relocating from Detroit in 2001, Nolan had become one of those Californian men who had enough self-discipline and money to be scrupulous about diet and exercise, and he was even more sharply handsome at sixty than he had been in his late thirties. His silver-spangled, close-cropped hair and beard were never unkempt, and his horn-rims were never smudged. Being a twice-divorced music supervisor who surfed on a daily basis definitely agreed with him.

Over the years they'd worked hard to stay on the same page when it came to parenting decisions. As Kaden had gotten older, their interactions had gone from talking daily about all the glorious things their child was discovering to texting when necessary about the logistics of long-distance parenting: setting visitation schedules, confirming tuition payments, strategizing when Kaden was having trouble in school, sharing suggestions for Mother's and Father's Day presents. By the scowl on Nolan's face, it was clear this was not going to be a friendly chat.

She plopped into her office chair. "I didn't plan it out; it just happened. And by the way, I texted you yesterday and this morning to call me."

"I was on location until I went to the airport this afternoon," he said. "We didn't get home until a few minutes ago." Paloma could see he was in his den, given the framed movie posters and the gold records on the walls he'd moved from his studio office during the Covid lockdown. "You didn't tell me it was important."

"I said, *We really need to talk about Kaden!* With an exclamation point."

"Fine; my bad. You wanted to talk, and we're talking now."

Paloma was about to make a crack about how the *women* she dated would have called her right away, but didn't. "How's he doing? Is he still mad at me?"

"He is beyond mad at both of us," Nolan said. "He let me have it from the moment I picked him up at the airport. 'Why didn't you tell me? Why would you support Mom lying to me? How could you let me grow up in that sand dune of a town?' I wasn't about to go into everything in front of Cindi, and that poor girl didn't know if she was supposed to stick up for him or referee, so when both failed she stared out of the window. I ended up taking them to In-N-Out Burger to get them something to eat so he'd shut up for five minutes, like I did when he was in grade school."

"Did it work?" she asked, smiling in spite of the situation.

"It bought me time until we got home and I could talk to him alone, which is when I found out he didn't know about our NDA, either."

"Shit." Paloma's stomach dropped to her shoes. "I can't believe I forgot to tell him about that. Our conversation went sideways, and I wasn't thinking clearly, then he refused to talk to me. I'm sorry."

He winced, hissing in frustration. "Paloma, you've had *decades* to work out how you were going to tell him."

"The NDA is a moot point now anyway. It expired when he turned twenty-one last fall."

He leveled his gaze. "Sure, there's nothing that legally prevents us from revealing his name and our identity as his parents. But do you really want to do that without his approval?"

"Of course not."

"Well, what are you going to do when it's public knowledge that you're coming back from your 'hiatus' for the concert? It's only a matter of time before you're being interviewed and a reporter squeezes the truth out of you."

"I won't let that happen," she countered. "I'm going to focus on music and my history at the Artemis when I talk to the press, and if they start asking questions about my personal life, I'll figure out a polite way to say, 'Go fuck yourself.' "

"How punk rock of you. Good luck with that," he said, his voice dripping with disdain.

"Kaden has never come up in *your* interviews."

"It's not the same situation and you know it!" Nolan retorted. "I'm just a guy with a guitar and a cowboy hat, but you were this shooting star that crashed somewhere on earth, and once your location is revealed, there will be a lot of people who won't quit until they find out every detail about why you disappeared. Kaden is central to that story, and it's only a matter of time before he's pulled into the spotlight, no matter what you do."

"You're right, you're right," she muttered.

"You know, when we created this wall of documents to shield you, I supported it because I thought it would be temporary. You'd been through a lot of stress with Jace and the record label, and you wanted to focus on motherhood without anyone invading your space. But the longer it went on, the more ridiculous it got."

"Yes, you've told me that many times," she said tersely. "Is that why you gave me Jace's message about the Artemis? To get me interested in getting back on stage and goad me into telling him? Like when you did that interview for that documentary ten years ago?"

"Maybe," he said, folding his arms. "Then again, I didn't expect you to sign on to perform before you talked to Kaden. Or me."

"As God is my witness, that's why I texted you earlier: so the three of us could work this through together. Can you convince Kaden to talk to me?"

"He's made it perfectly clear it'll only be when he's ready and on his own terms, and I don't know how long that will take." Nolan's expression shifted, as if he'd just remembered something else she'd done wrong. "Hang on. When you told Jace you'd do the show, did you tell her about Kaden?"

She hoped he couldn't see her face flush with embarrassment. "No. I didn't tell her."

He sat back and smirked. "I guess you should be glad that some things never change."

By mid-July, it was getting harder and harder for the "Keep Jace in the dark" task to remain on Paloma's punch list. They'd chatted quite a few times since Jace's second trip to Stone Beach to review the appearance agreement, stage setup, hotel, and various other details. And even with a staff of people handling all the logistics, Jace would somehow find a reason to text or call her nearly every day. It wasn't always about the event, either. Sometimes, she'd text her *Good morning,* and that brief exchange would extend itself until they were texting each other *Good night.* Paloma found herself looking forward to their interactions: cracking jokes, getting fresh gossip about their musician friends, watching Jace's brilliant organizational mind at work once more. It was familiar and brand-new at the same time. Paloma was amazed by how nice and effortless it all was.

But the only response she'd gotten from Kaden after daily calls and texts was silence. As she'd told Nolan, she didn't feel comfortable telling anyone about him without his permission. His silence meant she was going to put off having *that* talk with Jace.

Having a semi-legit reason not to come clean just yet should have been a relief. Instead, Paloma was worn out. She'd spent almost half her life burying her creativity and her autonomy to keep her presence small to protect herself and her child, but now she and Kaden both wanted something bigger. She'd severed her relationship with the woman she'd loved because she'd been too scared to be honest, well before she got pregnant. Over the last few weeks, she'd gotten a taste of what she once had, and she hadn't realized how much good she'd left behind when she ran from the bad.

With all this on her mind, Paloma drove south on 75 toward Clawson, determined to stay up in the air, walking the tightrope between what she'd always done and what she wanted and needed to do, for a while longer.

Jace had offered to take her on a driving tour of Detroit so Paloma could get reacclimated after so many years away. They were also slated to drop by the Artemis so she could get her bearings well before the show in September. Since the press release announcing Paloma's return hadn't gone out yet, they'd keep everything on the QT. No one would even know she'd come back to town.

Jace's neighborhood was walkable and welcoming, featuring a variety of brick and clapboard cottages with large trees and green lawns occasionally disrupted by a two-story modern house crammed into a tiny lot. Her house was gray stucco with dark red trim and black shutters. Her front yard had a Japanese maple surrounded by a ring of stones painted white, and there was a mammoth oak in the backyard that shaded part of her roof. Each bed of hostas and impatiens was well tended and weed-free. Clearly Jace was just as meticulous about managing her property as she had been about managing her musicians.

Jace greeted her at the door with a grin and a hug, looking relaxed in a black-and-gold athletic polo and shorts set. Paloma idly wondered if she'd played a few rounds of pickleball before she'd arrived; Jace was clearly doing something to keep her arms as toned and her body as compact as it had been half a lifetime ago. Jace ushered her into a tastefully modern living room with oyster-white walls, a steel-and-glass coffee table, and a long, black leather couch: the opposite of their shabby, comfy decor when they lived in Woodbridge.

"I brought you this," Paloma said, handing over a substantial gift basket. Along with two bottles of wine from Suttons Bay, it was crammed full of Michigan-made cheeses, crackers, dried cherries, and other refined snacks.

"You didn't have to do this," Jace said, eyeing the contents. "Thank you."

"It's the least I could do," Paloma said. "There's a specialty food shop on the main block of Stone Beach called Motor City Finest. They sell the full line of 'Jam Band' jellies and preserves. I thought you'd appreciate it."

Jace peeled back some of the cellophane and pulled out a stout white jar of tangerine marmalade. "Ooh, my favorite. Thanks for remembering."

"You practically cleared out the jam shelf at Harrods when we were in London. How could I forget?"

They held each other's gaze for a split second before Jace put the basket in the kitchen. "Want some coffee before we head out?"

"Yes, thanks," Paloma said.

Paloma took a seat in her kitchen, which had a bay window overlooking a well-manicured backyard where a couple of black squirrels were munching on the birdseed under the feeder. Jace set up her coffee maker. “So what’s been going on with your day jobs lately?”

“I’ve been heads down all week trying to finish a song I owe this guy. You ever hear of Treat Dawson?”

“No.”

“He does *Austin City Limits,* tools around Nashville, has a solid but unremarkable career,” she explained. “He charted with a song of mine last year and wants an even bigger hit this time around, but there are only so many rhymes for ‘truck’ that I can use without him getting bleeped. I’m glad you called. I needed a break.”

“Happy to help,” Jace said, scooping dark roast into the filter.

“How’s the benefit shaping up?”

“We’re deep into the logistics right now,” Jace replied, the coffee maker burbling as she sat down across from Paloma. “I wanted to talk about who’s playing bass and drums for you. Mary reached out to me. She has no idea you’re on the bill, by the way.”

“Oh? What did she say?”

“She assumed I wanted to book her since she’s a Detroit garage legend. She also said she’d email me her rider.”

Paloma snickered. “Of course she did: Mary has to be Mary. Had you even asked her to play?”

“No, I hadn’t. She doesn’t have to play with you if you don’t want her to.”

“Honestly, I don’t have anyone else in mind. She’s available, she knows the material. And for all her attitude issues, she really is the best bassist I ever worked with. But if she’s not worth the hassle, I think there’s a sophomore at Stone Beach High who’s teachable.”

Jace grinned. “I’ll talk her down. Don’t worry; I’ve got this.”

Paloma knew she did. The negotiation table was Jace’s happy place, and she admired her for it. “Have you heard from Colin? I called the last number I had for him, but it was disconnected.”

“Oh, that’s because he’s a monk now,” Jace said.

Paloma wasn't sure she heard this correctly. "Do you literally mean he's a monk, or is he just hard to reach?"

"He is a bona fide Benedictine monk," Jace replied. "Sabine tried to track him down when a couple of drummers got Covid a couple of years ago, and his brother told her that living through the pandemic gave Colin a chance to sit still for the first time in years, and it was a revelation. He lives in a cloistered order in Oklahoma. Apparently, he's quite content."

"Good for him," Paloma said.

"Is there another drummer you'd like to bring in?" Jace asked.

Don't say Kaden, she told herself.

"Let me know if you have suggestions," she said instead.

"I dunno. It's getting harder to find people who are willing to play for free. I'm calling in every favor I can to keep the production costs low so Sabine's overall take is as large as possible."

"I'm sure you'll make it work," she said. "You made sure your clients made oodles of money from their fundraisers. Especially that adoption agency. Wasn't that the one Joyce used?"

Jace frowned. "Yeah."

"You don't sound too happy."

"I lost them as a client a few months ago."

"Oh no! Did they have trouble after the pandemic?"

"No, they didn't like that I shut up an asshole megadonor at their black tie event."

Paloma was intrigued. "What was he saying?"

"He was on stage making a lot of noise about who 'deserves' to have children, and according to him, it wasn't single people or queer folks. That pissed me off on behalf of Joyce and all the other nontraditional parents I know, so I turned off his mic."

Paloma wondered if she could segue into talking about having Kaden, damn the consequences. Instead, she said, "Sounds like you did the right thing."

"Thanks. Someone had to." The coffee maker dinged, and Jace went to the counter, returning with a creamer and sugar bowl set in one hand and a mug of coffee in the other. "And maybe I did it because I was trying to make up for being such a coward for so many years."

"What do you mean?"

Jace came back to the table with her own mug. "I knew I was a lesbian by the time I hit high school, but I was so scared to own my identity. Maybe it was because of that bully in middle school, or internalized homophobia; I don't know. But I look back at when we were together, and there were so many times when my fears drove me to push you away. Not allowing us to hold hands or kiss in public. Telling people I was your 'business partner' instead of your 'girlfriend.' That must have made you feel like I didn't care about you. I'm sorry about that."

The earnestness in Jace's gaze was touching. "It wasn't always safe for us to be out in the open," Paloma said. "You were protecting yourself and me. It's okay."

"It's more than that, though," Jace said. "I still think about when you wanted to walk out on the Seal-Eye deal for *Cutie Pie* and I talked you out of it. If that happened today, I promise you I'd open the door and follow you out, right after I flipped the guy off."

"I appreciate that." Paloma smiled in wonder. Vulnerability wasn't something she'd ever associated with Jace during their relationship, and she could only imagine how much work this no-nonsense businesswoman had done to be able to open up like this. That was sweet to see. "So you can say 'queer' now without flinching. I'm proud of you!"

"Yes, I've matured." Jace chuckled. "And losing half my business gave me a reason to reassess what's important to me at this point in my life. How to live my life on purpose."

"What have you come up with?" Paloma asked, genuinely curious.

"Not being a workaholic, for one thing."

"By the time stamps on your texts, you have a way to go."

"Progress is better than perfection," Jace said with a sly smirk.

"Then I thought it would involve getting back out on the dating scene—nothing serious, just for fun—but that crashed and burned pretty quickly."

That was welcome news. "Really?"

"I don't know if you've been dating lately, but surveys are required these days."

Paloma had no idea what she was talking about. "I'll take your word for it."

Jace nonchalantly raised her mug to her lips. "Have you been seeing anyone?"

She didn't mind answering. "Not for a long time, and whenever I was with someone, it didn't last very long."

"That's tough."

Paloma appreciated her sincerity. "Well, Stone Beach is a really small town, so I ran through all the good prospects pretty fast. And when you're unwilling to talk about any part of your life that happened more than twenty years ago, it makes intimacy impossible."

Paloma expected Jace to say something snarky, like, *Well, that was your choice.* Instead, she said, "I didn't think, with all my friends and my sister and nieces, I'd still feel so lonely sometimes—a lot of the time, actually. It's nothing like living with someone you're in love with."

"I know what you mean," Paloma said. "Having that center to your life. Knowing even on your worst days, they'll still be there."

"Even when the truth is hard to talk about."

"Or hard to accept."

They held each other's gaze, the cicadas buzzing in endless cycles, the air between them charged and intoxicating. Paloma wanted to pull Jace close, weave her fingers into Jace's thick hair, press into her, kiss her until she moaned. And all Paloma had to do was reach out.

Then she remembered that she'd need to tell Jace about Kaden first, and that wasn't going to happen.

Paloma looked away. The spell was broken.

Jace managed a self-conscious laugh. "I'm sorry. I didn't mean to turn this into a therapy session. We should get on the road soon if you plan to get home before dark. Want a travel cup for your coffee?"

Paloma pushed herself to smile. "Yes, please. Where's your bathroom?"

"End of the hall."

After she finished her business, Paloma was walking back to the living room when a large poster hanging in a bedroom caught her eye. She went in to confirm her suspicions: Yes, it was the broadsheet from the Royal Albert Hall's Millennium New Year's Eve concert. Along the bottom of the midnight blue design with the year 2000 spelled out in stars was a row of black-and-white stills of the performers. Among the opera singers and titans of twentieth-century classical music were the rock and pop vocalists who were meant to represent the sound of the twenty-first: all men, all Brits . . . except for Paloma Doralle. Strangely, the organizers had not wanted them to sing their own material. Instead, they'd been asked to perform holiday songs, with Paloma being assigned a Christmas ballad, "When the Lights are Brightest." She'd never felt so elegant as when she stood on that stage, looking out at the lush seats, the swell of a full orchestra behind her. It was so grand compared to the grind of the concert circuit, such a bonkers fairy princess moment, she hadn't been nervous for a second. It had felt as natural as singing in Mrs. Morrie's annual holiday concert, just with the queen seated in a box seat instead of the school principal sitting in a folding chair.

Jace came to stand behind her, and Paloma pointed at her photo. "One of these things is definitely not like the others."

"Yeah, you were a better vocalist than any of the rest of them. And less drunk."

Paloma turned to her. "I'm surprised you kept this after we broke up. If you'd have thrown it and all the other souvenirs on a pile and set them on fire, I would have completely understood."

"I'll admit, it's been in storage for a long, long time," Jace said.

"But lately, I like to look at it. It represents a fantastic accomplishment of ours that I never want to forget."

Before Paloma could respond, Jace was walking toward her front door, keys in hand.

After grabbing a couple of sandwiches at a shop near Jace's house, they spent the afternoon driving through the streets of Detroit. To Paloma, they looked more like a film set than the hungry and hollow-eyed city she'd left in 2001. The cluster of sports stadiums, the renovated palatial theaters, and the high-end restaurants and hotels that studded Woodward down to Jefferson Avenue were astounding. The train station in Corktown that had been a windowless shell of Detroit's former glory was under construction to become a jewel of the city once more. Even the old landmarks—Rodin's bronze "Thinker" at the white-stepped entrance to the Detroit Institute of Arts, the Art Deco tower of the Fisher Building—seemed burnished and hopeful. Paloma had read articles about the city's recovery, but seeing it in person was astonishing.

When Jace asked if she wanted to drive by their former house in Woodbridge, though, Paloma declined. Some parts of her past were better kept out of sight and out of mind.

They arrived at the Artemis in late afternoon and found a parking place out front. "You ready for this?" Jace asked, putting a reassuring hand on Paloma's shoulder.

"Is Sabine here?"

"No. She and the staff don't arrive for a couple of hours. We'll have the place to ourselves."

"How is she taking the news that I'm doing the show?" Paloma asked, bracing herself for the answer.

Jace looked at her sheepishly. "I'm not gonna lie. She's not been your biggest fan since you left me. She's a loyal friend, and she wasn't crazy about me reaching out to you. But I told her that you apologized and we've cleared the air, so she seems to have changed her tune."

Paloma knew full well they hadn't completely cleared the air, and Sabine would hate her even more if she found out she was still holding something back, but she brushed that aside for the moment. "Good to know."

Getting out of the car, Paloma noticed a battered slab of concrete next to the venue entrance with exposed bolts at the corners and gasped.

"Oh no! Where's the Goddess of the Moon and the Hunt? Did she finally fall apart?"

"No, we sent her to a spa," Jace said with a grin. "There's a statue repair place out in Romulus that's fixing her up. She'll be back." Then she unlocked the front door.

When she stepped in, Paloma was broadsided by an immense wave of nostalgia. Even with new floors, a refurbished bar, and smoke-free air, the place remained a shrine to her youthful dreams and ambition. It was as jarring to see it now, far more pristine than when she'd known it, as it was looking in the mirror at the lines time had etched into her own face.

"Let me give you the nickel tour," Jace offered.

She flipped on the work lights and led Paloma across the main floor to backstage. Memories pursued her like ghosts: the ebb and flow of crowd noise, the rubbery smell of newly printed T-shirts at the merch table, the sweet-tart taste of cheap whiskey sour mix. So much of the life she'd loved, and had spent so much energy suppressing, had taken place in this building.

"You'll see that the dressing rooms have been upgraded," Jace said, gesturing toward the banks of lighted mirrors. "There are two full-service bathrooms now, so you don't have to drive back to Hamtramck before you take a shower anymore."

Paloma could practically hear the walls giggle, given how many times they'd seen Jace and Paloma nab a quickie between sets.

"And here's the green room, which will be where you can hang out and grab snacks and beverages during the benefit, unless you want to be backstage to watch the other acts, which is totally understandable."

"No more bringing our own water bottles in a picnic cooler, huh?" Paloma said.

"Nope, Sabine has made this an honest-to-God professional venue." Jace cocked her head. "Want to go on stage?"

Paloma froze momentarily, as if she'd encountered a force field. Then, with a small inhale, she walked to the center.

What she'd always loved about playing the Artemis was how it brought the performers and the audience together. The arch of the ceiling flowed into the sides of the proscenium, and the floor was more of a horseshoe than a square with its feet at the stage and the curve toward the exits. Even when it was full to bursting, she could see every single face in the crowd if the lighting was right. And, just like always, the tech board was in the back, with room for Jace to stand next to the engineers and watch the show with hearts in her eyes.

"I've missed this place," Paloma said quietly.

Jace stayed in the wings as Paloma walked from side to side, reorienting herself with the grooves in the flooring and marks for the microphones. After a few minutes, she looked over her shoulder. "I'm good."

"Do you want to know what we're thinking about for lights, or the running order, or anything?"

"No, I can wait until rehearsal. Let's go."

They chatted a bit as they drove back to Clawson, but Paloma appreciated the moments of silence so she could watch the streets roll by. She wondered whether she could fit in here if she decided to return, or if Jace wanted her back. Paloma was beginning to hope so. Reconnecting with Jace over the past few weeks had rekindled the spark Paloma had hidden in the back of her heart, but at the same time, the more time she spent with her, the rawer she felt. Because Jace wanted honesty from her this time around, and Paloma couldn't bear to give that to her.

Jace parked in her driveway, but as she walked toward her front door, Paloma didn't follow her.

"Are you leaving?" Jace asked, sounding surprised.

"Yes, I need to get back on the road," she hedged.

"Shoot," Jace said. "I was going to order some dinner. Want to eat before you go?"

"No, I'll get something on the way."

Jace stepped closer. "You're welcome to stay here. My guest room is made up and ready to go."

She wanted to touch Jace so badly she wanted to cry, but she kept her arms at her sides. "No, I need to go home and rehearse. Thanks for taking me around town."

"Glad to," Jace said, smiling in a way that Paloma recognized as masking her disappointment. She pulled Paloma in for a hug. "Drive safely."

Before letting go, Paloma kissed her cheek, and before anything more could happen, she quickly got into her car and drove away.

At noon the next day, Paloma sat in her office and logged into a video call scheduled by Jace's niece. A moment later, she was face-to-face with a woman in her late twenties with thick, straight black hair, red-rimmed statement glasses, and a professional yet wary smile: a person she knew but no longer recognized.

"Hey, Olivia," Paloma said. "The last time I saw you, you were eating Teddy Grahams and talking nonstop about *Toy Story.*"

"Well, I still do both of those things," she said. "I go by Livvy these days, by the way."

"Got it." She stopped herself before making an offhand joke about going by a couple of different names herself over the years.

"Thank you for making time to meet with me," Livvy continued. "We're planning to send the first press release on Tuesday announcing the full lineup, with you as the headliner. Did you look it over?"

Paloma had read the release many times because seeing her given name in print again was jarring, and seeing how she was being promoted left her uneasy. "Yes, and while I appreciate all the hype you're trying to build around me coming back to the Artemis, you're laying it on kind of thick."

"How so?"

"You call me 'the local garage band legend and international sensation,' for a start."

"Aren't you?"

"It depends. Am I a sensation because of my music or because of the mystery surrounding my disappearance?"

"Does it matter if it puts butts in seats at the Artemis?" Livvy said, unsmiling.

It was no surprise that Paloma was not Livvy's favorite person. Paloma recalled how smitten Jace was by little Olivia and her sister (what was her name . . . Kristin? Kirsten? *Kristi*—that was it) when Joyce's adoption finally went through. She not only showered them with presents, she also went out of her way to spend time with them at parks, pools, and when she couldn't get away from work, in the dressing room backstage at the Artemis with crayons and earmuffs to block the noise and sleeping bags for when they'd had enough of the late-night shenanigans. Paloma had really enjoyed going on a few outings with Jace and the girls, who she remembered as being tiny for their ages and shy around strangers; when they smiled in her presence, she felt like the first human who discovered fire. Seeing Jace's delight in their company, Paloma had assumed she'd reconsidered the possibility of starting their own family, but when she'd attempt to bring it up, Jace would redirect and dodge.

As much as Paloma hadn't been forthcoming when she was with Jace, she could see in retrospect that Jace hadn't been much better. She'd told Paloma how much she liked being the "cool aunt," yet she'd never admitted flat out that she didn't want to be a parent. Instead, she'd dangled the parenting possibility in front of Paloma like a reward for getting through the next tour or recording session. "Once we get through this, we'll make time to talk about it," she'd say, but that time never came. Maybe she'd been as scared as Paloma had been to admit a truth that was likely to drive them apart.

Little Olivia had idolized her aunt Jace, so she probably only remembered Paloma as the bad lady who made Aunt Jace very sad. Now that she was an adult, Livvy may not have changed her mind; she seemed ready to avenge any hurt Jace had suffered. For the sake of making amends with the two of them, Paloma knew she needed to stay humble.

"I'll do whatever it takes to make this show a success," Paloma said.

Livvy focused her gaze offscreen, perhaps looking at her notes. "So after the release goes out, I expect we'll get immediate media interest, but I want to pitch a few key publications to get them to interview you and Sabine."

"Together?"

Livvy's eyebrows knitted. "Oh, no. Sabine hates you. We may have to create floor plans to keep the two of you from interacting during the show."

Paloma sighed sharply, realizing Jace had downplayed the issue.

"It took a few weeks before Sabine would even entertain the idea that you'd be on her stage again," Livvy said with a tone that indicated she wasn't exaggerating.

"Do you hate my guts, too?"

"Whether I do or don't isn't important," Livvy answered evenly. "My one job is to ensure we raise enough revenue to make Aunt Jace's fundraising goal. Since that means working with you to promote the shit out of your comeback, I will treat you like the best of besties."

"Likewise," Paloma said. "I am equally committed to making this work."

"Happy to hear that." Livvy looked down at her offscreen notes again, then shared what appeared to be a genuine smile. "I need to get background info from you to prep the pitch, so I have a few questions, the first one being, what exactly have you been doing the last twenty years?"

Paloma was ready to share a version of what she'd told Jace a few weeks before: anxiety, too much fame too fast, dropping out to save her mental health. But looking at Livvy, she just couldn't do it. She couldn't lie to yet one more person, and she had to stop lying to herself, too. When she left New York for Stone Beach, it wasn't to salve her nerves or shelter her child from the limelight, as she'd told herself every day since New York. No, she'd run because she'd been too scared to take charge of her own life, mistakes and missteps and dreams and all. That had to end. Now.

"Before we talk through this, is your aunt around? I need to tell her something."

"Sure, let me find her."

When Livvy disappeared from the screen to fetch Jace, Paloma typed a text:

> Kaden, I know how much pain and frustration I've caused you, and I understand you may not want to speak to me soon, or ever. Just know that I'm so proud to be your mother, and I hope one day you'll understand why I did what I did then and why I'm choosing to move forward now. I love you more than I can say.

As she hit send, Jace appeared on screen. "Hey," she said, smiling. "What's up?"

Jace was a fantastic negotiator because she was so skilled at hiding her emotions. Paloma had seen her in action dozens of times and admired how she could sail through any high-pressure meeting, even with the most difficult promoters or label execs, without losing her cool. She'd say something witty to break the tension; she'd flatter without going over the top; she'd deflect and distract to keep the attention focused on the matter at hand instead of herself. Even after they'd been dating for several months, Paloma hadn't always been sure if Jace was telling her how she really felt about her, only because she'd seen how easily Jace could seal off her feelings.

That emotional scaffolding was firmly in place as Paloma began their conversation by recapping their last year together, outlining how their relationship had been faltering for months, with the European tour becoming a breaking point. Jace nodded as Paloma ticked off the major problems they'd already covered at her kitchen table back in June. But as Paloma described how lonely she'd become within their relationship, how she'd longed for someone to listen to her without trying to change her mind—and how Nolan offered her that right when her relationship with Jace had frayed so badly she didn't know how to repair it—Jace's reserve began to crack. The words themselves—*I never planned this . . . it was a total surprise . . . I didn't want to hurt you . . . at least I could finally be a mom*—seemed to physically take her apart. It was horrible to watch; Paloma knew how much of Jace's self-worth was invested in her self-control.

"I should have broken up with you before all this happened," Paloma said, tears clouding her view of the computer screen. "I deluded myself into thinking everything could magically work itself out because I loved you so much, but that was impossible. We wanted different things, different lives. That doesn't excuse what I did or fix what I did to you, and I am so, so sorry."

The world seemed to stop turning while Paloma waited for Jace to respond. She expected her to walk away or say something sardonic and cutting, but Jace was silent and immobile, looking offscreen as the seconds ticked by. Paloma was about to hang up when Jace squared herself in front of the screen, her face impenetrable once more.

"I have three questions. One, is there anything—*anything else*—you haven't told me?"

Paloma shook her head. "No. That's all. That's everything."

"Two, are you still involved with Nolan?"

"No. He got cast in that movie and moved to California while I was still pregnant. We're co-parents and friends, but that's it."

"And three, are you completely committed to making this benefit a success?"

"Yes, I'll do whatever you need me to do. You have my word."

"Good," Jace said, her voice heavy. "Livvy and the rest of the team will get back to you shortly. See you in September." Then the screen went dark.

21

NOT LONG AGO

AUGUST 4, 2023

"Hey, P! You home?"

Bud had already come in the front door before Paloma could answer with a muffled grunt. She watched him from her spot lying on the couch as he set plastic containers on the kitchen counter. At eighty-four, his brush cut was white and his gait was measured. He made a to-do about stacking them straight in size order, always the mechanical technician even all these years after he retired from the line at GM.

"It's about time I got these back to you," he said. "Let me tell you, any time you want to make that egg casserole again, I'm happy to take your leftovers."

Ever since she'd moved to Stone Beach, Paloma had made sure to spend as much time with Bud on his own as she did with Bobbie because, as quiet and accommodating as he was, he often got overshadowed by his extroverted wife. She felt she owed it to him because from the moment Paloma had arrived in their home as a terrified teenager, he'd done right by her at every turn. He'd found her a waitressing job when she was in high school by talking to a friend from the plant whose father-in-law was hiring. For Kaden's third birthday, he'd made a wagon out of gorgeous cherry wood with a tiny personalized license plate. He'd drop jars of homemade strawberry jam and butter pickles off every summer. He took Kaden and Paloma on numerous long walks through sand dunes and along the water, collecting the beach glass and sand-polished stones they'd find and making them into lamps and jewelry. And as blunt as Bobbie was about how to handle a situation, Bud cared more about how everyone was feeling to the point where he seemed to pick up on Paloma's moods like a change in the weather.

Which had to be why he'd chosen this particular moment to bring back a bunch of used take-out containers that Paloma had left with them weeks before. He wanted to check on her, and for that, Paloma was grateful.

"Hey, how you doing, girl?" he said, sitting at the end of the sofa next to her feet. "Last night at the Cherry Mill, you seemed out of sorts during your set."

She sat up, smoothing back her hair and hoping she looked like she'd been taking a refreshing mid-morning nap instead of refusing to get off the couch to deal with her current situation. "Well, it's been about three weeks since Jace fell off the map and almost two months since I heard from Kaden. I've barreled through most days and have been okay, but then there are days when I feel like a living, breathing country song."

"Aw, that's awful," he said, putting an arm around her shoulders. "But you're not alone, you know. You have plenty of friends."

Paloma squeezed his hand. "Oh, I'm not sure about that. Now that the show is being publicized, I had to let people around here know I'm not who I said I was."

"How'd they take it?"

"Not well." She blew out a sigh and turned to face him. "Folks at the grocery store keep asking for my autograph, which is flattering but really weird. Tony and Kevin believe I didn't tell them because I think I'm too good to play with them, which honestly is not true. What hurts most are the parents of Kaden's friends who I've known since he was in preschool who say they need time to process this and don't want to talk to me right now. The number of people I've hurt just keeps growing, and I feel like it's never going to stop."

She hated crying in front of Bud because he was so tender-hearted, he often started crying, too. But she was so glad to be comforted when he pulled her into a big bear hug, hushing her tears.

"Honey, I know this is really tough, but I promise it's going to get better," he said with a squeeze before letting her go. "Owning up to your past takes guts, and the people who are your real friends will respect that. Just give them time."

"Do you respect me, Bud?" she asked, wiping her eyes.

He smiled fondly. "I respect you. I love you. I gotta admit, I don't always understand you, but I'm always here for you. So is Bobbie. No matter what. Got it?"

"Got it," she said, overwhelmed by the decency and love of this dear, extraordinary man.

"Good," he said with a nod before getting to his feet. "Well, I don't want to keep you from your nap."

She stood as well. "Naptime is over. I have to get ready for a meeting with Jace's niece about the show. She'll be here within the hour."

"So you'll have time for a shower then?" he asked as he walked toward the door.

Paloma sniffed her armpit. "I'm not that bad, Bud."

He turned and smiled. "You could be better. Love you, P."

Earlier in the week when Livvy had scheduled a time to visit Stone Beach to prep Paloma for media interviews, she'd mentioned she'd be bringing someone to talk about equipment and staging. Paloma hoped against hope that someone would be Jace.

After their last conversation, after so many days of her texts and phone calls being ignored, Paloma reluctantly tried to stuff her feelings for Jace back into the psychic box she'd been hauling around every day since New York, assuming she could lock them down like she'd done for years. Instead, they were popping out all over the place. She'd been looking out the window toward the lake, then could have sworn Jace was standing behind her. She'd gone to the grocery store at the center of town and stopped cold when she recognized the bouquet Jace had brought her the first time they'd re-met. She'd even woken up that very morning flushed and gasping after dreams of the two of them naked and intertwined on a too-small bed as if they were back at Jace's place in Hamtramck.

When her doorbell rang, Paloma's heart sank when she saw that Jace hadn't come. She was surprised, however, to find a gangly and very, very stoked young person with a piercing through the bridge of their nose and an awestruck expression taking up her front doorway.

"Holy shit, you are *Paloma Doralle*!"

"Hi," Paloma said tentatively. "Are you from the Artemis?"

"Yes, Rennie is from the Artemis and is also one of your biggest admirers," Livvy said wearily as she maneuvered around them with a grim expression and a laptop bag. "In fact, they've been talking about you nonstop for the entire ride up here."

"Sorry, I should have introduced myself," Rennie said, "but shit, you're *Paloma Doralle,* and I forgot my own name for a second!"

It had been a long time since she'd talked with a fan who was this sincere, and Paloma was charmed. "Nice to meet you, Rennie. Please come in."

Paloma settled them on the deck then brought out a charcuterie board, crudités, and a basket of crackers. "What would you like to drink? Red? White? Beer? Pop?"

"White, please," Livvy said.

"Water for me, please. I'm the DD," Rennie said.

When she came back with their drinks, Rennie was beaming. "Your place is unbelievable, Paloma. That deck. That kitchen. That lake! Everything is so—"

"HGTV?" Livvy said.

"Airy," Rennie said, loading chèvre onto a seedy wafer and topping it with a blueberry. "Is this how everyone lives in Stone Beach?"

"Actually, not many people live here year-round," Paloma said. "A lot of the cottages aren't winterized; they're just tourist rentals or summer vacation homes for people from downstate. And the folks who stick it out are pretty eclectic."

"That must have worked out well for you," Livvy said, not making eye contact as she put a slice of prosciutto onto her plate. "It's an ideal place to disappear and raise a kid out of the limelight."

"It's a nice place," Paloma said, her tone purposely friendly. She sensed that Livvy was no fonder of her than when they'd chatted three weeks before, probably because Jace had to have brought her up to speed about Kaden and everything else.

"So, Livvy told me you've become a music critic," Rennie said, seemingly oblivious to Livvy's tone. "Went over to the Dark Side, huh?"

That made Paloma laugh. "I hadn't really thought of it that way."

"It's ironic, because the press didn't really get you when you were performing," Rennie said, stabbing a cube of Swiss with a toothpick. "Most of the reviews I found online didn't give your musicianship or your songcraft enough credit. They didn't analyze your riffs, your hooks, your stage presence. They mostly harped on the fact that you were a woman in a man's game and that you were bisexual—and it was obvious they didn't understand what that even meant. If they'd been writing about me like that, I would have lost my mind."

"It worried Jace more than me," Paloma said. "She was all about building my reputation. I just wanted to play music."

"Is that why you've done a lot of articles about female artists and queer musicians?" Livvy asked, slipping an orange notebook out of her bag.

"Yes," Paloma said. "At first, I didn't want editors to pigeonhole me or assume I couldn't review a Metallica concert because I was a girl. But then I figured it was good to have someone like me writing about those bands because I'd see them as musicians first and foremost and evaluate them on their own terms. Some bands center their music around their female or queer identity, and others happen to have queer musicians and sing about whatever is important to them—and some do both. Anyway, they have to be good at what they do."

"I admire you for that," Rennie said, picking up a spear of blanched asparagus and crunching thoughtfully. "That's the kind of review I hope to get someday."

"You play?"

"Yup," Rennie said with a self-deprecating nod. "Write my own songs, too."

"Do you like their stuff?" Paloma asked Livvy.

To Paloma's surprise, Livvy responded with a bashful smile instead of words, which earned an impish grin from Rennie. Now it made more sense why they'd decided to come all this way to meet with her instead of scheduling a Zoom call: They wanted an excuse to spend time together in a lakeside town.

The three of them chatted and munched, Rennie peppering Paloma with questions about everything from music theory to preferred guitar pick brands and Livvy taking copious notes. Food and wine, plus the breeze off the water, seemed to have smoothed out Livvy's mood, and she got less pointy and more easily amused as the afternoon went on. Once Rennie had enough info to prep the technical crew, Livvy took over the conversation.

"Have you ever had media training before?" she asked.

"I mean, I've been doing concert and music reviews for a long time, but I don't do interview pieces, and I never got any 'training' before getting interviewed myself," Paloma replied.

"Well, that's why I'm here," Livvy said. "I'm happy to say that Platter.com confirmed they want to do an exclusive, in-depth article about your career and influence as well as the Artemis benefit. Their writer wants to book an afternoon next week to meet you in Detroit, grab lunch, and chat. It's my job to make sure you're ready to answer whatever questions he might throw at you, and I also want you to be able to redirect the conversation if it starts going off track."

"Will you be there?" Paloma asked, hoping the answer was yes.

"I'll be there to introduce you, but Platter insists that their interviews be one-on-one without any publicists or PR people at the table to make the conversation 'authentic.' They'll tape all the audio, so be prepared to sign the waivers they're sending over."

Paloma nodded, reminding herself that she promised Jace she'd do whatever was needed. "Will do."

Livvy took a printed page from her laptop bag and handed it to Paloma. "Here are the talking points about the benefit I'd like you to work into the conversation. Like, how the Artemis was the launch-pad for your career and so many other bands; the venue is more than just a landmark: it's a symbol for the city of Detroit and its place in musical history; a few nice things about Sabine, even though she still pretty much hates you."

"Don't worry. I'll be an adult about all this."

"Do you feel comfortable covering this stuff?"

"Of course," Paloma said, skimming the neatly bulleted list. "My history with the Artemis, my first concert there, *Cutie Pie*'s album release party, sitting in with other bands. None of that should be a problem."

"Great," Livvy said, taking out another piece of paper. "And here are the topics that might come up during the Platter interview. I don't think there are any surprises."

Paloma scanned the document. It read like an FBI dossier with her deepest, darkest secrets typed up and ready to be used against her. She put it face down on the table. "How many people other than Jace know this information?"

"Only me, because I need to know the facts to be ready to manage our messaging and coach you on how to answer tough questions," Livvy said. "No one else involved in the production knows any of this."

"I can confirm that," Rennie said. "Like, I have no idea what you two are even talking about."

"And we need to keep it that way," Livvy said with a telling glance toward the door.

"Right," Rennie said as they stood up. "Liv, I'll drop our stuff at the Airbnb then go to that bookstore with the rainbow flag we saw when we drove through the main part of town. Just call me when you want me to pick you up." They turned to Paloma. "Thank you so much for being a great host. Shit, thanks just for *being.* Call or text me if you think of any other tech stuff you want me to take care of, okay?"

"Thanks, Rennie. I appreciate it."

"My pleasure." They looked at Livvy and winked. "See you soon."

Paloma watched Livvy watch Rennie walk away and stifled a giggle. The girl's dark eyes were bright, her mouth turned up at the corners, her head tilted slightly to one side. She was clearly infatuated, and it was delightful to see.

"Rennie seems like a good soul," Paloma offered.

Livvy nodded shyly. "They are the coolest person I've ever met." She took out her laptop while Paloma re-reviewed the list of topics.

"Just because they ask these questions doesn't mean we have to answer them, right?" Paloma asked.

"Correct, but sometimes it's a better strategy to be straightforward and tell them what they want to know. Lack of information makes people curious. They'll frame you as difficult or, frankly, make shit up if you don't give them anything."

Paloma understood her point. "I'm open to talking about what was happening with me: the anxiety, the grueling schedule, taking a drastic step to change course that, looking back on it, I wish I could have handled differently. But as for Nolan and Kaden, I want to leave them out of the conversation. Nolan and I signed nondisclosure agreements when I got pregnant to protect our privacy and our son's until he turned twenty-one late last year, and now that Kaden is an adult, it's up to him when it comes to talking about his life and his parents. While I felt I had to tell Jace about his existence, I don't want to talk about him publicly unless he's comfortable with me doing so. Understand?"

"Yes." Livvy leaned back and crossed her arms. "I'm surprised no one discovered your name, or Nolan's, on his birth certificate."

"Michigan birth certificates aren't public record. If someone leaked that information, they'd be breaking the law."

"Huh. Learn something new every day." Livvy thought for a moment. "Here's my advice. If they happen to find out you had a baby years ago, tell them you're not revealing the name of your child's father, and your child will be the one to decide whether or not to tell their own story someday, then move back onto the benefit as quickly and smoothly as possible."

Paloma nodded. "I'm okay with that."

"Any other topics you want to try to keep off limits?" Livvy asked as she typed.

"Anything about other LGBTQ musicians in Detroit. I can speak about my own experiences, but other people were in the closet for a host of reasons. I'm not about to out them now."

"That's fair. What else?"

"Anything about Jace's and my romantic relationship," Paloma said quietly. "The business partnership, sure, but the rest isn't anyone's business."

"I hate to tell you, but that may come up," Livvy said. "You two being together was an open secret, certainly around here. If they interview anyone local, they might mention it."

"I want to talk about my music instead of my personal life," Paloma asserted.

"Copy that. But what about when they ask you what happened that night, after you performed on *Letterman*?"

"I'll stop the interview," she blurted defensively.

"I wouldn't advise that," Livvy said. "You stop the interview, they'll just rehash all the old rumors."

"I am not putting Jace through this publicly. Or Nolan. Or Kaden."

"Paloma, you have to accept that's the question everyone wants answered. You have to be ready to address it. You don't really have a choice."

Paloma didn't respond, yet Livvy's eyes were unflinching. "I want to protect Aunt Jace as much as you do. I'm just as invested as you are. We have to figure out how to navigate this, all right?"

Paloma's stomach felt like it was full of tar. Extricating herself from her web of deception had left her feeling lonely and bereft. But maybe she could find some solace in doing the right thing.

"All right."

Livvy nodded. "Good. So I'll ask you once more: Paloma, what happened that night?"

22

WAY BACK WHEN

APRIL 5, 2001

Forty-five minutes into her flight from Detroit Metro to JFK, Paloma sat in the airplane lavatory, staring at the two pink lines on the pregnancy test, willing her fingers to stop shaking.

It wasn't really a surprise. She figured her period was at least three weeks late. Her boobs felt like they'd grown two cup sizes, and she needed to pee every couple of hours. That morning, she'd whipped over to Walgreens to get a kit and zipped the slim white box into the inner pocket of her purse. She'd planned to test herself when she got to her hotel room, but fidgeting in her first-class seat, her brain felt like a bag of ants. She couldn't wait that long.

Still, it was a shock, and she was so stunned she could barely move. She was sure Jace would figure out by looking at her that something had changed. Then again, since she'd been avoiding Paloma's gaze pretty much since the end of the European tour, she probably wouldn't notice.

Last summer, Paloma had used every drop of adrenaline to perform all the dates, not wanting to disappoint the fans, or Jace, but by the end of each show she felt like a mannequin, hollow and brittle. She didn't leave the hotel on their days off, dread pinning her to the mattress. Jace had been worried enough to call a doctor in Paris; his diagnosis was nervous exhaustion that ought to be cured by a few days of rest. Paloma insisted that Jace go out and tour the City of Light without her. Even as she assured Paloma all she wanted was for her to feel better, she could tell by the sharpness in her voice that Jace was disappointed and frustrated with her, having never experienced a moment of nervousness or exhaustion in her life. In Amsterdam, they'd gotten into a fight when Paloma delayed the show by an hour after shutting herself in her dressing room to try to pull herself together. Jace had brought the argument to a screeching halt when she yelled at her through the door, so everyone could hear, "Drop the diva bullshit and get on the fucking stage!" Later apologies didn't really patch things up, and they'd barely spoken on the long flight home.

Back in Detroit, the distance between them continued to grow. Paloma holed up in her garage studio, attempting to develop the material for her next album but coming up empty. After months of this, Jace had to renegotiate the record's release date, pushing it off until the spring, and she scrapped the tour she'd planned for Paloma to launch the album. Even with the new deadline, Jace made it clear that Paloma had to release a single by Valentine's Day or she'd forfeit her advance.

Bored without any concerts to organize, Jace would go to the Artemis most nights to watch a show or lend Sabine a hand, returning in the wee hours. On those nights alone, Paloma would lie on the couch in her studio, headphones on, listening to anyone's music but her own, wondering what she ought to be doing with her life.

Or she'd call Nolan, who was eager to help her find out.

Since her birthday, they'd been meeting for coffee every couple of weeks to chat and talk shop. Their friendship was easy and unburdened by past history. They'd discovered they had a lot in common beyond their shared experiences in and around Detroit, and Paloma was grateful to be able to commiserate about their less-than-loving childhoods, the pressures of being creative on a deadline, and the terrifying space between what others expected of them and what they really wanted. The chats often turned flirty, and Nolan had even insisted on giving her a brand-new Nokia cellular phone for Christmas in case she wanted to talk to him on his dime. Paloma was determined not to take the romantic bait. She needed a friend more than an affair, and she thought the magic of the holidays just might help her patch things up with Jace. And she was right, for a while.

Joyce had invited both Jace and Paloma to stay at her place to be part of her daughters' first family Christmas, and they agreed to set their problems aside for the week to make it special for Kristi and Olivia. Paloma had brought her acoustic guitar to teach them carols, and Jace bought them a shit-ton of musical toys and helped them stage a concert in Joyce's basement. Being around the girls' excitement and wonder lightened their mood to the point they'd agreed to put the past rancor behind them. By the time they'd gotten back home and attended the annual New Year's Eve party at the Artemis, they appeared to be a happy couple, even to themselves.

The fresh start of a New Year had inspired Paloma to get back to songwriting from a more honest perspective: She had no one to satisfy but herself. She wasn't a raw, raging kid anymore who had to be catchy, angry, and loud to earn the moniker of being an "indie musician." After two albums with a major label, she couldn't care less if she was called a "female musician" or a "lesbian musician," either, because both were essential. Ever since singing with the orchestra at the Royal Albert Hall, the musical ideas in her head were lush and more dramatic. And if she could finally achieve her dream to compose poetry instead of scribble out lyrics, maybe she'd capture a tiny fraction of the astonishing love and admiration she still had for Jace, glowing bright in her mind's eye, framed by the glittering lights of Joyce's Christmas tree.

By the first week of January, she'd recorded "Heart Fire" with Mary and Colin, plus a cellist and a pianist, at the Tempermill in Ferndale. After playing through it for the first time, she looked toward the engineer's booth and caught Jace's gaze. Paloma was sure she was the only one who could tell that Jace was close to tears. When the musicians took a break and Paloma pulled her aside to ask if she thought the song was bad, Jace said no. "It's beautiful. I just hope we can live up to it."

Jace wasn't wrong. The glow of the holidays dimmed, and the unease resumed. Paloma was in no mood to get back on the hamster wheel of recording and promoting and performing ad nauseam, but Jace would not talk about delaying the release of the album until the fall ("Not now"), or finding a gay-friendly couples' therapist to resuscitate their sex life ("Not now!"), or giving a concrete answer about becoming a parent after stringing Paloma along for years ("Oh my God, NOT NOW!"). They decamped into their separate routines once again, with Jace spending her evenings at the Artemis and Paloma buying a pullout couch for her garage studio so she could avoid going back inside once Jace had come home.

She had not bought the couch so that Nolan would have a place to sit when he dropped by one February evening while Jace was out managing a quadruple bill at the Artemis. She had not meant to burst into tears when she saw him and turn into a complete basket case, babbling about how she couldn't live with Jace any longer and hyperventilating over the thought of moving out on her own. She hadn't asked Nolan to hold her, whispering in her ear to breathe in synch with him to calm down, assuring her that everything was going to be okay, that he was here for her. She hadn't predicted he would cup her face in his large hands and tell her she wasn't abandoning Jace if she left: She was reclaiming herself. She hadn't planned to kiss him, or take off his shirt and throw it on the floor next to her sweater and jeans, or pull him on top of her across the narrow sofa cushions, or cry out with relief and release.

The shame swept in immediately afterward. Things had been bad between them, sure, but Jace didn't deserve this. Paloma promised herself she'd find a way to reconnect with her, to make things right and bury this awful night forever. She'd sent Nolan home without a kiss goodbye, tidied up the studio, and went back into the house to take a long, hot shower. When Jace got home, she was sitting at their dining room table. With a rehearsed smile and a steady voice, Paloma told her she'd done some thinking and agreed with Jace that she should do a string of local performances to road test her new song and prep for the album release. When Jace asked if she wanted to come to bed, though, Paloma went cold with terror. She dodged the offer, telling Jace she'd had a nap after dinner and wasn't tired. Jace went to their room, and Paloma sat and stared out the kitchen window, sick with guilt, until the sky turned light.

Over the next few weeks, Paloma threw herself into performing, agreeing to whatever Jace recommended. And after Nolan left her a voicemail on the phone he'd given her, saying he was going to be in California for a few weeks and that he wished her well, she blocked his number then turned off the phone and hid it in the back of her closet.

"Shit, what am I going to say to Nolan?" Paloma whispered to herself in the metal confines of the airplane bathroom.

She returned to her seat, a couple of rows ahead of Jace, Mary, and Colin. When Jace had booked the flights, she'd seated everyone in their own row. Tensions within the group had been high ever since they'd come back from Amsterdam. Mary had renewed her threat to leave if she didn't get a larger royalty from the upcoming third album (presciently called *Breakage*), even though she wouldn't contribute a single lick or lyric. Colin's dependability was next to nil, and to ensure he'd make his flights and get to rehearsal and the performance on time, Jace had paid his brother to accompany him for the entire trip. And even though Paloma and Jace's professional relationship had gotten smoother, their personal life together continued to be thorny, so they kept their distance at home and on the road.

Before she sat down, she saw Jace farther down the aisle, reading a *Rolling Stone* magazine in blissful ignorance of what Paloma had done. Sorrow stabbing her in the gut, Paloma clicked her seat belt and closed her eyes for the rest of the flight.

They landed, and Jace sent the musicians on to check into the hotel so she could supervise getting their luggage and equipment to the correct locations, making them all swear to be at the Ed Sullivan Theater no later than two o'clock for sound check. Unlike their earlier tours in New York, when they'd stay in a series of low-end motels in cheap, often dangerous neighborhoods, tonight they'd be at the Marriott Marquis in the heart of the city. The Letterman folks had two Town Cars waiting for them. Lugging her purse and her Stratocaster, Paloma took the first one and rode off alone, knowing Mary would be much happier to ride in the other car and bitch and moan to Colin and his brother about Paloma and Jace all the way from Queens to Midtown.

Paloma got to her room and deadbolted the door before she lay on the bed with arms spread wide. Before the panic could start gripping her brain and her lungs, she closed her eyes and talked herself down.

Your wish is coming true, she told herself.

You are going to have a baby, and you'll love them more than any kid has ever been loved.

This baby is going to love you no matter what. They'll be there when the applause stops.

It's going to be amazing, and you can do this.

Everything is going to be okay.

Following a deep inhale and exhale, she sat up on the edge of the bed, unzipped the interior pocket in her purse, and calmly pulled out Nolan's cellular phone, which she had packed alongside the pregnancy test.

"Hey," he said sleepily when he finally picked up. "It's been a while."

"Yeah," she said hurriedly.

"I saw you're going to be on *Letterman* tonight. Congratu—"

"I'm pregnant."

There were a few seconds of agonizing silence before she heard a quiet "Oh, wow."

"I'm going to keep it."

She heard a rustle, like he was sitting up in bed. "Oh . . . okay."

"I mean, I don't know when I'll have this chance again."

"Paloma . . ."

"You know how I've wanted to be a mom since forever and now, well— "

"Let me absorb this . . ."

"I'm not expecting us to be a couple. And I'm not expecting you to be a parent, unless you want to be. Do you want to be?"

"Paloma, can you slow down? Please?" He sounded exasperated but not angry. "It's early in the morning here, and I was asleep literally a minute ago, and this is a life-altering conversation we're having, so I need you to slow down."

"I don't have much time," she said, standing and starting to pace. "I've got to be at sound check with Jace in two hours, then I have to play on the most monumental show on television as if nothing has happened. After that, I don't know what I'm going to do."

"It's not much different than what you told me you wanted to do back in February. Tell Jace that it's over. Find a place of your own and separate your finances. And make decisions based on what you want, not what other people want."

"I *said* all that. That doesn't mean I can *do* all that."

"You know you're going to have to."

She stopped pacing and looked out the window over Times Square. Colorful signs flashed for Broadway shows and restaurants and all kinds of high-energy family fun. "How are you feeling about this? Gut level?"

It was clear he was fishing for words. "This is wild. This is a lot to take in. Look, I've thought about wanting to be a father more than once, but I sure didn't think it was going to happen this way. I'm guessing you didn't, either."

"No," she said with a halfhearted laugh.

"You and I are going to have to figure out a lot of shit pretty quickly. You have my promise that I am not going to abandon this kid, though. I will pay my fair share, and I'll want to be a part of their life."

She heard him hesitate. "But . . . ?" she prompted.

"I'm not going back to Detroit. I've decided to relocate to LA."

She sat on the edge of the coffee table. "You are?"

"I just got cast in a movie," he explained. "Since *O Brother, Where Art Thou?* came out, all these roots music projects are in development, and they need musicians who can play that stuff on camera and advise the production. I start shooting in the fall, and after that, who knows? But I need to stay in California to get all this off the ground."

She hadn't expected him to rush to her side, and given what she'd seen of LA from performing there, she had utterly no desire to move to southern California simply to make it easier for him to be a part-time dad. If he'd asked her to marry him, she would have laughed him off. Still, she was disappointed that he didn't ask her anyway; she would have appreciated the offer to step in and save her from doing this on her own.

There was a knock at the door and a muffled, "Luggage, Miss Doralle."

"I have to go," Paloma said.

"Call me later. We'll figure this out."

She knew he meant well, but it was not his job to decide. It was hers. "No, I'll figure this out."

They said their quick goodbyes, and Paloma let the bellhop in to deliver her suitcase and garment bag. She called room service and ordered a huge breakfast because she was starving; eating for two was going to be an adjustment after years of grabbing food here and there. As she waited for it to arrive, she stared at her luggage, crammed full of cosmetics, hair products, and outfits and shoes for before, during, and after the appearance. So much stuff that meant so little to her; bags and bags of things she'd never miss. She could leave it all behind without a second thought.

That got her thinking.

She thought through everyone she knew back in Detroit, trying to identify anyone she could call on for help who wouldn't tell Jace.

Without exception, they were all "their" friends: hers and Jace's together. She couldn't expect them to keep a secret. She squashed the idea of calling her parents as quickly as it appeared, and she'd only call Dustin if there was literally no one else to turn to.

Her breathing began to race, and she felt clammy, like she had fallen to the bottom of a deep, cold well. She hadn't felt this isolated and alone since her parents threw her out and she moved in with . . .

Of course.

Room service arrived, and she wolfed down her Western omelet as she developed a plan. She counted the cash she had on hand then used Nolan's phone to call Amtrak. After chatting with a helpful representative about the cost and schedule for trains from NYC to Philly, she called Northwest Airlines to confirm she could purchase a one-way ticket at the terminal to fly from Philadelphia International to Detroit Metro. She memorized the fastest route to walk from the theater at 53rd Street and Broadway to Grand Central Station, ripping out the Manhattan street map from a tourist magazine that was on the coffee table.

Her breakfast fortifying her resolve, she pulled up a number from her own phone's contacts and, switching to Nolan's again, dialed a number with a 231 area code. The voicemail kicked in with a recorded message of a woman who sounded like she was reading from a script, as if she wasn't sure she was using her newfangled answering machine correctly: "Hello, you've reached the Morries. Please leave your name, your number, and a good time to call you back, and we'll talk to you soon. Goodbye."

In the middle of the *boooop!* a woman answered. "Hello?"

"Bobbie, it's Paloma."

"Paloma! It's been ages! How are you?"

"I'm good. Say, I—"

"I was just talking to Bud about you being on that late night show tonight! That's so exciting! We're gonna brew a pot of coffee after dinner so we can stay awake and watch."

"Thank you, I really appreciate that," Paloma said, willing herself to dial back her anxiousness and stay focused on the task at hand. "I'm really sorry. I don't have much time to catch up right now because I need to ask you something. Remember how you said to call you anytime I needed a place to stay?"

"I do," Bobbie said. "That still goes, even with us living up in Stone Beach now. You sound frantic. Are you okay?"

"Yes. No. Yes. But I need to ask you for a huge, huge favor."

"Okay. Don't go anywhere." Paloma could tell she'd put her hand over the receiver, yet she could still hear Bobbie clear as a bell as she yelled, "Bud? Get on the phone. Paloma needs help."

The two stayed silent for several minutes while Paloma gave them a rundown of what had happened over the last few hours. She outlined her plan, gaining more confidence as she explained it as if it were a well-considered, foolproof idea instead of running away from the mess she'd made. She had barely finished when Bud spoke up at last.

"Bobbie, you have enough gas in your car to get us to the airport?"

In the midst of sound check, Paloma looked out into the empty seats of the Ed Sullivan Theater, feeling like she had trespassed into a shrine. She was performing on the stage where Elvis and the Beatles had made fans lose their minds. This had been the ultimate idea of "making it" when she started years ago, a promise Jace had made to her when they didn't know how everything else in their lives was going to turn out. Now, it would be their swan song.

Once the show's producer gave her a thumbs-up, Jace pulled them to the corner of the stage. "All right, let me reiterate what they told you about the run of show and what I told you about the rest of our trip. There's food waiting for you in your dressing area—and Mary, before you say something, yes, I asked about your rider, and no, they were not able to accommodate it." Ignoring Mary's huff of disgust, she continued. "Hair and makeup will come for touch-ups at four, so be dressed and ready. The show starts taping at five o'clock. They'll take you to places on stage left during the second guest interview, so keep your eyes on the monitors and plan your pee breaks accordingly. Throughout the evening, do not approach Mr. Letterman. If he wants to greet you, he will come to you. After the show wraps, I'll stay here until the gear is taken care of, and Town Cars will be waiting on 54th to take you back to the hotel. If you'd like to join me to watch the show at eleven-thirty, drop by my room, but in case we don't cross paths before then, I'll see you in the lobby at nine A.M. tomorrow to catch the shuttle to the airport. Got it?"

Mary and Colin mumbled in the affirmative; Paloma nodded, doing her best to appear in control.

"Good." Jace stepped in closer, like a coach in the midst of her players. "This is a big fucking deal, and you've worked incredibly hard to get here. You're going to get thousands of new fans because of this one performance, and you've never been more ready." She looked at each of them, ending with Paloma, her sternness softening. "I'm so proud of you."

She gave Colin and Mary brief hugs, stating, "Have a good show," before pulling Paloma in tight. "I'll be in the back just like always, watching you set the room on fire," she whispered hot and fast. "I love you."

"I love you, too," Paloma whispered back, so overwhelmed it was as if she'd stepped outside of her own body and someone else had said it for her.

Just then, a PA stepped in to guide the musicians through the warren of corridors back to the green room, so Paloma didn't have to watch Jace walk down the aisle and out of the theater, her head held high.

23

NOT LONG AGO

AUGUST 4, 2023

Now that she'd heard every detail, Paloma couldn't parse Livvy's reaction. Her PR officiousness was gone; she had no retort or advice at the ready. Instead, she was quiet, her lips tight, her eyes thoughtful. Paloma was about to ask if she had any other questions when Livvy finally spoke up.

"How well do you know my mom?"

"We met several times. Really nice lady. A lot like Jace, but more easygoing. She came to a couple of my shows, and of course, we all spent your first Christmas together at your house."

"Did she ever tell you why she adopted us?"

"No. We mostly made small talk, and we never had a personal conversation. It was clear she adored you, though. I'm sure she still does."

"She's someone who can't keep still when Kristi and I are home because she wants to do everything for us," she said, chuckling. "It's become a running family joke. Kristi will put a glass on the counter on purpose and start a stopwatch to see how long it'll take before Mom wanders by and puts it in the dishwasher. Her record is six seconds."

Paloma smiled. "That's great."

"She's great," Livvy said. "When she adopted us, Kristi was seven, and I'd just turned four. The day before the adoption ceremony, Mom talked us through what to expect: We'd get all dressed up, then we'd meet a nice man in a black robe called a judge in a special building called a courthouse, and he'd ask her lots of questions before he signed an important piece of paper and banged a wooden hammer on his desk, and then she'd be our mom forever. I burst into tears and said I didn't want to go. Mom was caught off guard, so she tried to make me feel better by telling me about all the good things that were going to happen: We'd each get to choose a stuffed animal from his toy box to take home, and we'd go out for pancakes for lunch. Didn't work; I was terrified. So she rocked me and said, 'I love you and Kristi so much. I want to be your mom more than anything else. Nothing matters more than you two, and I will never leave you. Ever.' Then I said, 'I know that, Mommy, but don't let that man bang a hammer! That would be scary!' "

Paloma was glad to see Livvy's sly smile, giving her permission to smile as well. "Oh, you poor girl."

"Mom says that's why I'm hopeless with a toolbox," she said wryly. She tilted her head and looked at Paloma as if she were trying to read her mind. "Is that what you felt, back in New York, knowing you were pregnant? Nothing mattered more than that kid?"

Paloma nodded. "Not my stardom, not my career, and I hate to admit it, not even Jace."

Livvy sat back. "I still don't support what you did, but at least I can understand why you did it."

"Thank you," she said, relieved and grateful. "So what do you recommend I tell the reporter if any of this comes up?"

She thought for a moment. "Tell him you chose to step away from performing for personal reasons, and just like you did in 2001, you're keeping the details private. And if your son decides to share his story, hopefully it can be on his own terms."

Just then, Paloma's phone pinged with a text message:

Mom, can I call you?

Her brain went on high alert. "Livvy, I need to take a call. Can you sit here until I'm done?"

"Actually, I was about to text Rennie to pick me up. I've got all I need for now, and I'll touch base with you the day before the interview."

"Okay. I'll see you then if I'm not done before you go."

Paloma left Livvy on the deck and went into her office, closing the door. She texted him *Yes,* and he FaceTimed her immediately. Her heart ballooned as soon as she saw him, his scruffy beard completely grown in, wearing the Beatles in Berlin T-shirt she'd bought him last Christmas.

"Hi, honey. I'm glad you called."

"Hey," Kaden said. He was sitting in his bedroom at Nolan's, with the Hollywood Bowl lithograph over the headboard. "I have to tell you something."

Her stomach tightened. "Sure. Go ahead."

"A few weeks ago, Dad set me up to shadow these engineers at a recording studio in Burbank so I can learn the equipment, get some hands-on experience, all that. These guys have worked with everybody, and they shoot the shit all day about all the recording sessions they've done. They know Dad and assumed I grew up in LA, but when I told them I'm from Michigan, that must have rung a bell, because Sol started talking about working on an album twenty years ago for 'that Detroit chick with the song on TV right now—you know, Paloma Doralle,' and before I could stop myself, I said, 'That's my mom.'"

This wasn't the direction she'd expected this conversation to go. "Oh."

"Sol was impressed, and he remembered a lot about you," Kaden said, sounding surprised. "He said you were really disciplined in the studio and knocked out each song like your life depended on it. He said he always knew you were going to break big. I don't think he'd lie, by the way; it sounded like he really respects you."

The fact that an engineer admired her work ethic was remarkable. The fact that her son would pass along a compliment after not talking to her for weeks was incredible. "Thanks for letting me know. That's really nice."

"Mom, I don't get it."

"What do you mean?"

"You weren't just popular," he said. "You had talent. You were admired in the industry. You had a hot career going when most musicians can barely get a gig. How you could walk away, give everything up, just to have a kid? It doesn't make sense."

She looked at her son, with his outsize talent and limitless possibility, just discovering love and adulthood. "I didn't give anything up. Raising you was what I wanted to do. I made the right choice, and I wouldn't have it any other way." She caught herself. "I mean, other than this fucking mess I created and dragged you into."

"Yeah, other than that," Kaden said with an eye roll.

"Can you forgive me?"

He nodded slowly. "Yeah, Mom. Of course."

Her body felt lighter, freer. She had nothing to hide anymore. She could finally be herself.

She smiled at him. "So, if you're talking about me as your mom, may I talk about you as my son? Not that I'm going to spill our family business to a reporter, but you're on your way to having a stellar career, and I'd like to brag about you if I have the chance."

He winced. "I guess so, as long as I don't come off as some sort of nepo baby."

"And it would mean the world to me if you and I could perform together at some point."

"Um, sure. We could do that."

Paloma smiled. "What are you doing September ninth?"

Once she and Kaden wrapped up, Paloma walked out of her office and onto the deck. Livvy had departed, so she was alone with the waves and the breeze and the sun, all joining forces to create a ribbon of undulating light across the water to the shore. She leaned on the railing and looked out to the horizon, so distant and vast it seemed to bend with the Earth. All that open water; so many journeys ahead.

She heard a sharp knock at her front door. Thinking Livvy might have left something behind, she glanced through the house on her way through for anything out of place.

Paloma opened the door to find Jace staring at the floorboards of her porch, her hands in the pockets of her denim jacket. She raised her gaze and asked, "May I come in?"

Paloma nodded dumbly, too stunned to respond. It wasn't until Jace was standing in her entryway that she was able to speak. "I didn't know you were up here."

"I knew Livvy was coming to meet with you, and I hitched a ride, hoping we could talk," she said. "I won't stay long. I just wanted to say something."

Paloma braced herself for the official, inevitable parting of ways. "Sure."

Jace looked pained and weary, as if she hadn't slept well the night before, or the night before that. "I haven't been honest with you."

Paloma was confused. "What do you mean?"

Jace ran her fingers through her hair and exhaled. "When you came to my house, I told you I was searching for a way to live on purpose, as if I didn't know how. But I already knew."

"You did?" Paloma asked carefully.

She nodded. "After New York, I built a wall around my life. I told myself I had to focus on my business, and I already had my family and plenty of friends. I thought that would be enough, but it wasn't. And when I leaped at the chance to save the Artemis and be the hero, I thought that going back to managing musicians was what I needed to feel complete, but that wasn't it, either. Then I saw you again, and I realized we forged a molecular bond the moment we said hello to each other at that club in Ann Arbor that's never broken." Her shoulders rounded, and her eyes were rimmed with tears. "What I need, what I want, is you."

Paloma's heart caught in her throat. "You deserve so much better than how I've treated you."

"That's in the past. We know how to do things right this time."

"By being open and honest with each other," Paloma said, stepping toward her.

"Listening," Jace said, putting her arm around Paloma's waist.

"And not running away so we can work things through," she said, catching a stray tear with the back of her hand as Jace pulled her closer. "Because I love you, too."

Their first kiss in a long, long time was sweet. Jace's lips were soft, her touch tender. She cradled Paloma's head with her hand, and as their kiss deepened, Paloma was glowing with desire and grace and overwhelming joy.

They broke the kiss, and Jace still held her tight. Paloma adjusted Jace's glasses and stroked her soft, silvering curls. "So, open and honest is how we are now?"

Jace released her. "Yes."

"Then I have to tell you: I'm not leaving Stone Beach."

"I understand."

"My life is here."

"We'll figure something out."

"My son is here—well, not anymore, he moved to LA—shit, I'm an empty nester now—and oh, he's the drummer I just locked in to play on the ninth, by the way, but—why are you looking at me like that?"

"I just love hearing your voice," Jace said, her eyes blissful. "I love how the more worked up you get, the more your hands move around like you're conducting a symphony. I love that even after years away from the Artemis, you stride across that stage like you own it. I love that you survived your awful parents with your heart and your voice intact and that you gave your son the commitment and protection you never got as a kid." Jace was very close now, her fingers threading through Paloma's hair and tracing her cheek. "I love that you cook like a pro, and you still sing along to the car stereo, and you have never looked as beautiful as you do now, with the light and the lake behind you."

Paloma slowly licked her lips. "You sure you can't stay a little longer?"

Jace replied with another bone-melting kiss.

24

NOT LONG AGO

SEPTEMBER 9, 2023

Paloma hadn't stayed in a high-end hotel in decades, and she had to admit, doing so now was pretty sweet. The comforter was comfy. The toiletries were luxe. And thankfully, the king-size bed had plenty of room for both her and Jace, because they weren't slim youngsters who could fit on a futon anymore. Not that they would ever choose to sleep on a futon at this stage in their lives. They were grown-ass women, after all.

She woke up before the sun rose and looked over to the right side of the bed. Jace was zonked out on her stomach, her face crushing the puffy white pillow, her lips parted not so much seductively as functionally, since she'd acquired seasonal allergies over the last couple of years and had trouble breathing lying down. Her hair was mussed, and one foot was sticking out of the covers. Without being conscious enough to worry about the image she was projecting to the world, she was completely relaxed and vulnerable. Paloma smiled fondly before snuggling up and putting her arm around Jace's bare waist.

Their evening of makeup sex a few weeks ago, overdue since 2001, had been fervent but fitful. As much as they'd expected it would be like riding the proverbial bicycle, the road to romance was bumpier than it had been in their late twenties. What used to make Paloma moan in seconds now took a while to rev up, and since the batteries in her Pocket Rocket needed replacing, it took longer still. Jace had become extra sensitive in certain places, which was delightful to discover but resulted in helpless giggles instead of orgasms. Plus, each of them had learned some new moves over the years—understandable since neither of them had joined a nunnery since they broke up—but Paloma had to stop herself from obsessing over who'd taught Jace some of the more adventurous stuff. (Was it that woman from speed dating with the questionnaire that Jace had told her about?)

Yet between Paloma's spontaneity and Jace's determination, they'd had a great, *great* time and spent the rest of the weekend together. Rennie had even thrown Paloma a grin and a thumbs-up when they drove up with Livvy to gather Jace for the ride home, which was more endearing than embarrassing.

They'd managed to see each other a few times since. Paloma snuck down to Clawson the following weekend, and Jace found time to drive up to Stone Beach before going into overdrive for the benefit. And now they were able to take advantage of Paloma's comped hotel room ahead of the show. Paloma didn't want to think about how they were going to manage this ridiculous commute over the long term, but she trusted that they'd talk and work it out.

At dawn, Jace's phone pinged loudly. She startled awake and jostled Paloma as she grabbed her phone off the bedside table. She put on her glasses and sat up, scrolling through her messages and cursing. Paloma sat next to her and cuddled close, whispering, "Good morning."

"Good morning," Jace replied, distracted.

"Anything wrong?"

"There was a brownout at the venue last night. Louis said he has to reset all the light cues, and the box office manager is on her way in case that screwed up our reservation system," she said, typing a reply.

"In other news, the mayor wants to stop by for photos with Sabine right before doors open, and Jerome texted me at two in the morning to see if one of my crew could help him get photo releases from everybody waiting in line to get in the show. And so the chaos begins." She put her phone back on the table, then kissed Paloma's forehead. "I'm sorry, but I've got to go."

"Do you want breakfast or coffee?" Paloma asked, watching Jace pull together some clothes from her overnight bag. "I think the café is open downstairs. I can get you something."

"No, I'll grab something on the way out," Jace said as she started the shower. "Just go back to sleep, babe."

"You sure?"

"Yes, it's fine. Thanks, though." She closed the bathroom door.

Paloma dozed while the water whooshed and came to once Jace was dressed and tying the laces of her boots. In her black T-shirt and black jeans, she was breathtaking.

"Anything I can help with at the theater?" Paloma asked, appreciating her view of Jace's very fine ass.

"No, we'll handle it," she said, standing and putting her phone and room key in her pockets. "Besides, you're 'talent.' You don't have to show up until sound check."

Paloma reached over to the floor and picked up the hotel robe she'd cast off the night before. She walked into the bathroom and brushed her teeth. "Do you want me to bring your tux later?" she asked before swishing water in her mouth.

"I'm taking it now," Jace replied curtly. "I'm fine."

Paloma walked over to loop her arms around Jace's waist. "Are you really?"

Jace rested her hands lightly on Paloma's shoulders. "Yes."

"We agreed: no more saying what we think the other person wants to hear."

Jace crumpled a little. "I am under an insane amount of stress right now. My crew has done everything possible to ensure the show is flawless, but right this moment I'm processing the very real fact that something could also go horribly wrong and derail the whole night, and there may not be anything I can do to fix it. But it's my job to handle all this so you and Sabine and the bands and our audience will never know there was ever anything amiss." She looked at Paloma. "And I haven't had my coffee yet, so I'm testy."

"I have complete faith in you, with or without caffeine," Paloma said, giving her a light kiss on the lips, followed by a more insistent one. Jace pushed the lapel of Paloma's robe back and nibbled her neck, which still had the power to turn her insides into warm honey. But just when Paloma was about to drag her back to bed, Jace pulled away.

"I've got to go," she said, sounding supremely frustrated. "I'll see you at the Artemis. We'll have a car waiting for you outside the lobby at four-fifteen, okay?"

"Okay," Paloma said, a little breathless.

Jace slung her computer bag over her shoulder and was reaching for her garment bag when they heard a *ping!* With a sharp sigh, she took her phone out of her back pocket.

"New chaos?" Paloma asked.

"At least it's the kind I like," she responded. "I just got a message from the Artemis Reconstruction Fund. There's been a last-minute donation of twenty-five thousand dollars."

"Wow! Who from?"

As Jace read on, her eyes got wide. "It's from Madeleine Grady-Poole."

"Who's that?"

"The Adoption Academy fundraising exec," Jace said, mystified. "The one who fired me."

Paloma came over to read over her shoulder. "Any note?"

"Let me see," Jace said, rolling down to the bottom of the auto-generated message. "All it says is, 'Honoring Jace Randolph and the talented team at Function Fest,' then it has her phone number."

"Is she coming tonight?"

Jace popped over to the sales report. "I don't think so; she didn't reserve tickets. Shit, I always figured she was loaded. Now I have proof."

"You gonna call her?"

"Yeah, I have a few questions for her," Jace said, still seeming pleasantly shocked. "Hope she can wait until this circus has left town, though." She slipped her phone back in her pocket and, garment bag in hand, kissed Paloma's cheek. "Love you. See you!"

"You too!" The door closed.

Too wound up to go back to sleep, Paloma showered and puttered around the hotel room, running through a five-point plan she and her therapist had developed to cope with the stress of the evening:

- Eat and stay hydrated.
- Focus on your friends in the audience, who'll make the crowd more personal and less intimidating.
- Just because there's an after-party doesn't mean you have to go if you don't want to.
- Don't invent problems. Control what you can and let the rest go.
- And stop to smell the flowers.

With the last tip in mind, she buried her nose in the bouquet that Sabine had sent, chock-full of the freesia that smelled like her gothic perfume. She chuckled, remembering what her card had said: *Jace loves you, and I love who Jace loves. Friends again? Hope so! XO*

Riding the elevator down to the lobby café, she texted Kaden to see if he wanted anything; his silence told her he and Cindi were still asleep. Taking her food back up to the room, she arrived in time to receive a series of texts from Bobbie, one of the few people Paloma knew who was up at this hour:

Hello Paloma from Bobbie and Bud! We are so prud of you!

*proud

Brake a leg tonight!

*break—I hate texting so much!!!

Much love and see you back in Stone Beach!

Once she finished breakfast, she realized she had nothing else to do except go with the flow of the day. She was having lunch with members of the Rousers, the Queenlords, Zoodiac, Britt Ney, and other bands performing at the benefit followed by a photo shoot, but otherwise she was unscheduled. She decided to keep herself occupied by cleaning out her email before getting back to work on a song she was writing for an alternative-ska band out of Minneapolis. At the top of her inbox was an email from the Artemis Reconstruction Fund account with the subject line: *Someone made a donation in your honor!*

"Aw," she said, surprised as ever that anyone would send in their hard-earned money and name her as the reason. Most of the donations so far had been from fans of *Olympia, California* or former Detroiters who lived out of state but virtually bought a "ticket" as a contribution to the cause. But when she saw the message from this pair of donors, her heart stopped.

We saw on TV that you are the star of the show tonight. We'll be there in spirit. You make God happy by being yourself. Keep shining!

Mama and Daddy

They'd given fifty dollars, which was how much they used to tithe to their church each week, even before rent or groceries: "God's money," they'd call it.

She reread the message to see if there was an email address or phone number, but there was none. She hit reply to see if she could reach someone to track down more details, but she got an automated message that the account wasn't monitored. Her pulse thumping, she realized the fundraising team had their hands full and wouldn't be able to get back to her with more info anytime soon, and she wasn't about to pull the "Do you know who I am?" card to get them to do a last-minute favor. And it wouldn't be fair to call Jace, who already had enough going on today. Instead, she hit speed dial.

"Good morning, *Paloma Doralle*!"

"Bobbie, hey there," Paloma said, steadying her voice.

"I am so glad to be able to call you by your actual name again," Bobbie said. "I never could get the hang of calling you 'P. D. Smith.' It never fit you. Too dull."

"Listen, I have—"

"Aren't you supposed to be sleeping until the afternoon like the rest of the rock stars?"

She forced a laugh. "No, I'm up early. Hey, I have a question for you. Did my parents ever contact you after the emancipation hearing?"

"No," Bobbie said. "I haven't heard from them since they gave us guardianship. Why do you ask?"

"Because they made a contribution to the benefit."

"Oh, my."

"I haven't heard from them since I was fifteen, and they do this." She took a screenshot of the message and texted it. "What does this mean?"

Bobbie was quiet for a moment. "I don't know."

"Are they trying to fuck with me, now that I'm back in the news? Get in my head?"

"I don't know."

"Do they think fifty dollars is going to make up for all the shit they put me through?"

"I don't know, hon."

"Why would they do this?" Paloma asked, feeling sick to her stomach.

"I don't know, and neither will you unless you contact them."

"That's a hard pass," she said, anger burning the back of her throat.

"Then you can frame this however you want to. You can believe they're effing with you since they were so abusive in your past. You can ignore them and pretend this didn't happen."

"Too late for that," Paloma said with a bitter laugh.

"Or you can see this as a sincere attempt to make things right, even if it's too little, too late. No matter what you believe, or do, it's your choice."

Paloma took in a deep breath, and her eyes settled on her beloved Stratocaster, always at the ready in its well-worn case. That guitar had helped her spin her hurt and longing into a career and a calling. As much as her parents had clung to their church and their God to quell their fears and make up for their faults, she doubted they'd ever experienced the bliss Paloma had whenever she played and sang. She scanned the room, looking at Sabine's flowers, the T-shirt she'd picked up for Kaden to wear to the show, and Jace's neatly packed overnight bag. She was surrounded by forgiveness, none of it deserved, all of it freely given, and had broken out of the cage of her own mistakes. What was the point of carrying her parents' burden any further?

"I forgive them," she said quietly. "I forgive them and wish them well."

"Good for you," Bobbie said soothingly. "You made your own way in spite of them, and by now you've earned the right to your own happiness. I mean, look at everything that brings you joy right now. Your music. Your son. Fantastic neighbors. Jace."

Paloma smiled mid-sniffle. "That's absolutely true."

"Jace *is* making you happy, right?"

"So far, so good. And I'm trying to do the same for her."

"Glad to hear it. Keep it up, hon."

"Okay, that's our cue," Kaden said as the announcer called out Paloma's name and the audience reacted with a roar. He adjusted the silver cowboy hat on the chain his father had given to him, squeezed his mother's hand, then followed Mary onto the Artemis stage.

From the wings, Paloma watched Kaden get into position at the drum kit, wearing his black "Save the Artemis" T-shirt with the arms cut off. Mary walked into place as the cheering swelled, with her raven hair brushing her shoulders and the ropes of heavy silver chain around her neck. Paloma checked her own outfit—a studded leather vest over a cherry-red velvet tee, her black jeans tucked into oxblood Doc Martens—and made her entrance.

The crowd was on its feet, screaming and applauding, creating a wave of sound that crested and crashed to the stage over and over. Paloma acknowledged the audience before taking her Strat from a stage tech and strumming a few notes to ensure it was turned on, even though she couldn't hear anything through the monitors over the cheering. She came to the microphone standing down center and called out, "Hello, Detroit! I missed you!"

The volume exploded again, and Paloma scanned the floor. She'd asked that the house lights be up when she came on so she could see who was in the audience. Off to the sides were many of the musicians who had gone on earlier in the evening, reveling in the sound of the city they'd created together. Throughout the crowd were people she recognized from different points in her career—venue owners, bartenders, the director of her first music video, even some dedicated fans she'd gotten to know after years of their coming early to be in the front row and staying late for autographs—all beaming. The rest were old and young, hip and ordinary, tattooed and strait-laced, everyone alight with joy.

And squinting at the spot next to Louis in the back, she could see the glint of Jace's glasses in the lights. Paloma knew they were home.

She checked in with Mary, who was ready to go, and Kaden, who tipped his sticks to her in a salute. Back at the mic, she screamed with delight, "Okay, kids, let's play!"

The opening chords of "Why Don't You?" rang out across the hall, and from that moment until the final chorus, Paloma was at one with the audience. Many of them knew the lyrics better than she did after her long hiatus, and they chanted over her vocal like they were pledging allegiance to her and her music. The same happened when she played "Wreckage" from *Cutie Pie,* and she was having so much fun, she almost didn't want to stop. Seeing the red LED clock at the back of the house, however, she knew she had only so much time to wrap up the set with the song everyone had been waiting for.

As the applause relented, she changed out her Stratocaster for an acoustic then rested her hand on the mic and leaned in. "Thank you for that warm welcome, and thank you for being here to help the Artemis keep its doors open, not just for musicians like me, but for fans like you." She shaded her eyes and looked over the audience. "How many of you are here for the first time?" A sizable number responded. "Fantastic! And how many of you saw me play here when I was just coming up?" Grinning as the noise rose another couple of notches, she said, "All right, all right. I'll bet that you new folks and you long-term fans may have a favorite song of mine in common."

Unbidden, the crowd began chanting, *"HEART FIRE! HEART FIRE! HEART FIRE!"*

"I thought so," Paloma said, nodding. "Before we get into it, let me introduce these fine people on stage with me. On bass, please give it up for the marvelous, the mighty Mary Piotrowski!"

Mary stepped forward and bowed her head as the applause rose.

"And, on drums, a genius way beyond his gene pool, please welcome my son, Kaden Greene!"

Kaden stood, grinning with pride as he soaked up the love and support of the sold-out crowd at his first gig at the Artemis.

Paloma turned back to the mic. "It's been a long, long time since I've played my biggest hit in front of a live audience, so I want to make this extra special by having a few more friends join in." As she spoke, many of the musicians in the audience came on stage, grabbing their instruments and drumsticks. "Please welcome the Arsenal of Detroit Rock and Roll, everyone!" The crowd went bananas.

Once everyone was settled in their places, Paloma readied her guitar and told the rapt crowd, “You are going to be witnessing history, folks, with the cameras rolling, too, so put your phones away so you don’t miss a thing. Here we go: one, two, three, four.”

Paloma began the first verse solo, with the mic and her acoustic guitar being all that stood between her and the audience:

I thought love was a judgment.
Since I was unworthy then no one would love me at all.
In the cold, my heart kept on beating,
Banging loud in my chest as I climbed up and over the wall.

She came to the first chorus, and Mary and Kaden began to play, restrained and solemn:

I thought that love would never be mine, I would never deserve it.
Desire was a sin, and joy was a hell of a joke.
Then you pulled me out of the dark. All at once, my life had some meaning.
We’re on fire. We’re desire, kissed with smoke.

The rest of the musicians on stage joined in, fueling the intensity of the second verse:

I learned love was destruction:
All my hopes ripped to shreds and my dreams left to die on the floor.
I had no one and nothing.
I would stagger along, praying someone would just end the war.

The singers on stage joined the vocal, *ahh*ing in three-part harmony as Paloma crooned the second chorus:

I thought that love would never be mine, I could never survive it.
It would start off with roses and end with a kick to the throat.

Then you brought me into the light. All at once, my life had new meaning.
We're on fire. We're desire, kissed with smoke.

She turned to the group to lead an instrumental verse, moving to the middle of the stage, glorying in the wall of sound she and her friends were creating together. When she arrived at the front once more, the circle connecting musicians to audience, from the proscenium arch to the exit doors, was almost complete. All Paloma needed was to see Jace standing in the back: the clasp that held the chain together. And there she was, standing just inside the ring of light at the edge of the crowd, holding up her hands in the shape of a heart.

The musicians brought the volume down as Paloma began the final verse:

You said, "Love can be freedom."
We could be—you with me, us together—a part of the world.
You, with your laugh and devotion,
Are the warmth that I need, 'cause you see, you're my heart fire girl.

The final chorus started, and as the audience sang along with her, the song vibrated every atom in the room:

I thought that love would never be mine, I could never believe it.
I longed for a voice to call out, but then none ever spoke.
Then you took me into your arms. All at once, my life had real meaning.
We're on fire. We're desire, kissed with smoke.

The musicians repeated the first three lines of the chorus before Paloma brought the song to a close, just her and her acoustic:

We're on fire. We're desire, kissed with smoke.

Back in the day, whether playing a college cafeteria or a three-night run at the Paradise in Boston, there had always been a cadre of folks who would hear the opening notes of a Paloma Doralle song and immediately outscream the rest of the audience. After the shows, Paloma and Jace would spin stories about why those people overreacted the way they did. Maybe that was their favorite song of Paloma's, or maybe their favorite song ever. Maybe they felt cool for recognizing the tune when others were hearing it for the first time. For all Jace and Paloma knew, that could have been the exact moment when the mushrooms kicked in. Whatever the reason, Paloma could never quite believe that her music could mean so much to complete strangers.

This time, Paloma understood. The tune she'd strung together after pacing in her garage studio for two frigid days in 2001 harmonized with the experiences of everyone in the room and thousands of others around the world. The lyrics she'd written to memorialize and repair her relationship with Jace defined *their* perseverance, *their* longing, *their* hope. "Heart Fire" wasn't really her song anymore. It was everyone's.

The applause went on for what seemed like forever. As the other musicians moved to the rear of the stage, Paloma extended her hands to her bandmates to join her for a bow. When she looked at Mary, she saw she was crying. When she looked at Kaden, he brought her in for a gangly hug.

She only wished she could bring Jace up with her, to show her off to the world, but she knew that would be the last thing she'd want. Paloma had her job to do that night; Jace had hers.

At last, Paloma came back to the center microphone. "Folks, thank you so much for coming out tonight to save the Artemis Club. I don't have enough time to tell you how this place changed my life. I'm sure it changed a lot of yours, too. And that's all thanks to one woman: our host, our champion, the Greek goddess herself: Sabine Galanis!"

Over hoots and whistles, Sabine emerged from the right side of the audience, her silver top hat catching the light as she moved through the crowd, beaming and waving like a beauty queen in her black bead-encrusted evening gown and satin opera gloves. She turned to Paloma and blew her a kiss, then retreated into the dark.

With the finale coming up, even more musicians joined the folks already on stage, including Tony and Kevin from the Cherry Mill, who had been thrilled to be included. As they assembled, Paloma told the room, "Well, folks, the big clock on the wall says that we're going to have to wrap things up." Over boos and whistles, she continued. "The regulars who come here often know that when you hear a certain song play over the PA, the concert is about to start. Tonight, I figured it was the perfect way to end a perfect evening in the Motor City." She looked around to make sure everyone was ready to go, and with a "One, two, three, four!" the horns struck up the intro to "Detroit Dancing Days" by Melodee and the Makers.

The all-star ensemble rollicked through the Motown classic, but with it running less than three minutes and the audience still going strong, Paloma kept the groove going by throwing out names of towns all over Michigan then tossing in the names of bands when she ran out of cities. This evolved into a call-and-response with the audience:

Dancing days at . . . *The Artemis!*

Dancing days at . . . *THE ARTEMIS!*

After a few more rounds, Paloma spun and lifted her Strat over her head, signaling the group to find their place in the final chord and play out with horns blaring and drums rolling until she brought her guitar back down, slicing the air and bringing the benefit to a close.

JACE AND PALOMA

BONUS TRACK

BONUS TRACK

NOT THAT LONG AGO

JUNE 8, 2024

Jace pulled up in the city parking lot a half block from the Artemis Club and waited until the Buzzies' "Super Tan" faded out completely before turning off the ignition and unplugging her phone. After mourning the loss of her iPod for more than a year, she'd accepted that while the click-wheel era of portable music was over for good, she could take advantage of the dazzling breadth of obscure, weird, and phenomenal music via streaming anytime, anywhere. Even better, she could continue to turn her unquestionably good taste into playlists to foist on her friends. It was time to evolve instead of complain. She wasn't going to dwell on the past.

Jace walked through the main doors and stood at the back of the empty performance space. The bartenders were pouring bags of ice into tubs and filling garnish trays with maraschino cherries and lime wedges while the technicians tested the light cues. Everyone was focused but having fun, joking around as they prepped for a sold-out crowd that would undoubtedly give them plenty of stories to tell their friends the next day. Anyone who worked at the club night after night, from the security guards to the cleanup crew, knew they had jobs other people envied. They were like astronomers, witnessing stars before anyone else caught a glimpse. And the music—fresh, raw, and honest—bonded the freaks and nerds and good-timers and troubled souls together in ways they never could with their blood relatives. They'd found their people at the Artemis, and if they ever moved on, they were always welcome to return.

Thanks to the success of the benefit, Sabine had paid off her debts in full, including the fee for Jace's production team, and still had enough left over for some additional upgrades. Compared to when Jace first walked into the joint, the Artemis was practically a palace. Framed posters from nearly a hundred years of public performances were hung gallery-style in the lobby. The original light fixtures had been restored and rewired for energy-efficient light bulbs. The main floor was easy to keep clean; the bathrooms had automatic air fresheners and high-powered hand dryers. The HVAC aggressively controlled the temperature so that even when the floor was packed and the patrons were dancing their asses off, it was rare that they'd break a sweat. Baskets of individually wrapped pairs of foam earplugs had been installed at the main doors, and water coolers lined the back of the performance space to keep everyone hydrated for free. Risers ran along the sides of the main floor lined with rows of seats for those who wouldn't or couldn't stand for the duration. And the rickety merch table had been replaced with a long, polished counter, offering band swag at one end and Artemis gear at the other along with the music of local artists on vinyl. Again.

The bar menu—and it was remarkable that there *was* a menu after decades of yelling drink orders at whoever was pulling the taps—illuminated the flat screens on the wall and featured options that would have been the stuff of fantasy when the Artemis opened: local craft beers and hard seltzers; specialty cocktails and mocktails inspired by the acts performing that evening; and along with the traditional bags of popcorn, meat- and vegetable-forward tacos that were available every night, not just Twednesdays. These days, Eau de Artemis Club smelled delicious.

Sabine was experimenting with the programming, too. In addition to the typical weekend slates of three bands playing long after midnight, she'd had success in hosting "School Night Specials" on Thursdays that were guaranteed to wrap by nine P.M. and featured local bands whose members were juggling kids and day jobs and appreciated getting home at a decent hour as much as their fans. "More music and more musicians for more people" had become her business model.

Thankfully, Sabine wasn't trying to handle it all by herself anymore. In addition to the office assistant and house manager she'd brought on to run the day-to-day, she'd also hired a promoter who had an ear for music, an eye for talent, a brain that could anticipate every aspect of producing a show, and a love of chaos. Starting next week, Jace would be back on the Artemis payroll.

And it was da bomb.

Function Fest was still in operation, but Jace had been downshifting over the past several months, trimming her client list to focus on a handful of events for organizations that truly gave her joy. One of these was Adoption Academy, which had survived an embezzlement scandal involving the former CEO and his buddy the board member. Thanks to recently appointed CEO Madeleine Grady-Poole, the organization had returned to its original mission, and thanks to Madeleine's sincere apology and generous donation to the benefit, Jace agreed to put them back on her roster. Based on Jace's advice, Madeleine ditched the black-tie bullshit to put the "fun" back into "fundraiser." The planning committee for the upcoming Holding Hands event included some of the kids supported by the charity, and it was shaping up to be epic: a picnic with a rock-and-roll theme offering instrument demos, karaoke, dance-offs, face painting and spray-on hair color, and a G-rated sing-along led by a grizzled punk guitarist calling himself Grandpa Slamdance.

As delightful as planning this sort of event was, Jace knew it didn't scratch the same itch as the live music business, especially when she was surrounded by people she loved.

"Hey there!" Sabine had materialized at her elbow, decked out in a charming black-and-white checkerboard frock, her silver hair in two braids studded with black velvet bows.

"Hey, boss!" Jace said, greeting her with a hug.

"Boss? Oh, right. That's me!" Sabine giggled as she adjusted the delicate chains around her neck so that her spiked heart pendant was front and center. "Are you hungry? I have pizza. Want to join me?"

Sabine keyed in the code to the door lock for the office and Jace followed her in, walking past what would be her desk starting Monday. Sabine had attempted to clear out some of the ephemera to give her more elbow room but hadn't made much of a dent. Jace really didn't mind. Her laptop wouldn't take up much desk space, and every scrap of paper preserved a priceless memory.

She helped herself to a corner slice of veggie and sat across from Sabine, who had settled behind the metal monstrosity of a desk that she refused to upgrade. "Did you get a chance to see Jerome's rough cut yet?"

"Yes," Sabine said, flustered. "I love what he did to capture all the performances, but I'd be happier if I was never on screen. God, I look so old."

Jace took in the lines radiating around Sabine's dark eyes and gave her a sly smile. "If that's what old looks like, everyone should be so lucky. You're flawless, my friend."

"Thank you. You're too kind."

"Besides, that documentary is documenting you and your club. You're supposed to be front and center." Her phone buzzed with an incoming text, which she read and responded to. "Livvy said she just parked and is walking over."

"How's the research going?"

"She doesn't like me to ask about it, but I think it's going well," she said, finishing her last bite. "She spent the last few days in Stone Beach following Paloma around, recording her stories. Livvy's biggest complaint is that Paloma has so much material and so little time to talk about it, now that she's back in the recording studio. At least the album will come out with the memoir so she can market them together."

Sabine chewed thoughtfully. "Are you really okay with her ghost-writing Paloma's biography? She's going to learn a lot about your personal history from Paloma's point of view, and as we know, that was not always a pretty sight."

"Livvy asked me about that before she signed the contract," Jace said. "I told her to be fair and compassionate. Paloma and I did a lot of things we aren't proud of now, but we were often fucking amazing, and we can't share one side without the other."

"Hello, ladies," Livvy said as she entered, holding up her laptop case. "Sabine, could you please store this in your safe? I'm not lying when I say there's fifty years of Paloma's life on that hard drive."

"Sure." Once Sabine had locked up the computer, she picked up a manila envelope. "Livvy, I've been meaning to show you these. Jerome scanned them to use in the documentary, and there may be some Paloma will want to include in her book."

Inside were a couple dozen black-and-white eight-by-tens, some antiques in cardboard frames, others more recent with borders riddled with staple holes. "Oh wow, I remember these, Sab," Jace said, sitting next to her niece. "You had them up in those glass cases on the hallway walls. It was like a living history lesson."

Livvy flipped through the older photos, careful not to damage them: a photo of the Artemis exterior taken by the Detroit Chamber of Commerce in the 1920s; a close-up of the Goddess of the Moon and the Hunt soon after the club opened, regal and unblemished; the club's founder Stavros Galanis, silent-movie-star handsome with his wavy dark hair and keen mustache, standing in front of the venue entrance, nearly bursting with pride.

"Your great-uncle Stavros would be so proud of all you've done here, Sab," Jace said.

"I'd like to think so."

Livvy held up a slick photograph of Sammy Sinister, head down and right arm raised and ready to swoop in for another explosive guitar lick. "I didn't know he played here."

Sabine nodded. "The first time was in 1969. Stavros's son Nick said it was the worst decision of his life to book them. Then again, Nick was not a fan of 'reefer music,' so I'm not surprised."

"This is a Lana Berlin photo, right?" Livvy asked, finding a signature on the back.

"Yes."

"Do you know her personally?"

"Absolutely lovely woman," Sabine said. "I sell prints of her work at shows sometimes, and when I run out, I call her and she drops off another stack. If you want to use any of her work in your book, I'll put you two in touch."

"Wow," Livvy said, examining the promotional shot the legendary photographer had taken of the Screds on Belle Isle. She went through the shots from the '90s, shaking her head in wonder. "God, everyone played here. Did you have a sense of how influential some of these acts would become when you booked them back then?"

"A lot of them didn't even know if they'd have another gig, much less a career," Jace said. "Most of them were just happy that they'd booked a venue that had some local cachet."

Livvy chose another photo and examined it closely before handing it to her aunt. Late twentieth-century Paloma was framed center stage, the lights pouring over her from all angles, sequins on her T-shirt sparkling like stars. The shot caught her mid-lyric, her right hand a blur over her guitar, joy and power radiating from every pore. "This one is great," Livvy said. "Do you know who the photographer was so I can look into rights?"

"Actually, that's one I took, and you're welcome to use it," Sabine said. "There should be a few more in that bunch of color photos, too."

Livvy scanned the pile. "Ooh, candid shots! Look at these, Aunt Jace. When were they taken?"

Jace picked up a handful. "The *Cutie Pie* release party in '99," she replied fondly. "Look at us . . . oh, look at us."

There was Paloma, Jace, and the Seal-Eye reps posed in front of a poster-sized version of the album artwork. Eager fans handing Paloma CDs to sign. Colin wailing away on his drum kit, and Mary facing down the audience with a menacing glare. All of them young and fearless and ready to take over the world.

It occurred to Jace that someone was missing out on the nostalgia party. "Where is Mo?"

"She's been hovering at the bar," Sabine said with gentle irritation. "She isn't convinced that the new bartender knows how to mix tonight's signature cocktail. And to think, when I hired her, all Mo could do was pop the cap off of a beer bottle."

As if they had conjured her, Mo appeared in the office doorway, wearing a black baseball cap with the Artemis logo and a dark blue work jacket. "Sab, I'll jump in when the bar orders get backed up."

"No, they'll have everything under control, I promise. Come have some dinner."

"Yes, missus," Mo said, getting a couple of squares of pepperoni onto a paper plate before sliding a folding chair next to Sabine and giving her a smooch on the lips.

"Did you see these photos?" Jace asked, holding up one of Mo in the midst of a big-hearted laugh, with Sabine beaming at her.

"Oh, you look gorgeous, Sab," Mo said with an adoring glance.

"Looking at this, it's a wonder it took more than twenty years for you two to finally get together," Jace said to Sabine.

"Sometimes love has to wait for people to be ready to admit it," she said. "We were never on the same page until, after all that time, we finally were."

"Tectonic plates move faster," Mo muttered as a bit of sauce dripped onto her wedding band. "I like your shirt, Jace."

Accepting the compliment, she sat a bit taller, adjusting her black denim jacket so that everyone could see the bright red T-shirt with the lemon yellow Wonder Woman logo across the chest. "Thanks. It was a gift."

They chatted and ate until the large digital clock over the doorway said 8:55. Jace stood, tossing her trash in the bin. "I need to get in there to hear the opener. Anyone else want to join?"

"I'll join you in a bit," Livvy said. "I had a couple of questions for Sabine and wanted to jot down some notes before I forget."

"Go on in," Mo said. "We'll find you later."

Jace went to the back of the room, introducing herself to the two techs who were running lights and sound before standing in her usual spot. The first of the three bands playing that night was a four-piece group from Ypsilanti calling themselves Obvi. Made up of Eastern Michigan University students, they'd only been together a few months and were more loud than good at this point, but they had a daffy rapport that caught Jace's attention. And even though the audience was sparse this early in the evening, many of them were folks who probably had never been to the club before, which was fantastic. New blood meant new business.

Three numbers into their set, Jace felt an arm link with hers and a soft kiss on her cheek. "Hey, babe. Sorry I'm late."

Jace turned, taking Paloma in her arms for an extended hug before walking her out of the noisy room and into Sabine's now empty office. Paloma dropped her duffel bag in a corner and spotted the pizza boxes.

"Ah, I so love tradition," she said with a laugh, snagging a stone-cold veggie slice. "I didn't stop for dinner on the drive out here; I haven't had anything since lunch."

Jace and Paloma had gotten into a rhythm of commuting every other weekend to stay at their respective houses. It was still a weird, exciting combination of hanging out with an old friend and chatting up a fascinating stranger. They'd spent so much time apart, so many years living their lives solo, they'd agreed to take this next phase very slowly. No rush to move to the same part of the state; no need to spend every weekend together. There were plenty of ground rules, too. Jace wasn't managing any part of Paloma's business, and Paloma was not guaranteed to book a slot at the Artemis, although frankly that was a guideline more than a rule since she reliably drew a large crowd. Neither one was to offer advice uninvited. And their most important rule was to always be honest with each other about their feelings or opinions. At this age and place in their lives, they were finally able to talk to each other without holding anything back, knowing that the other person cared and was ready to listen, even if she didn't always agree.

Paloma was wearing what she called rock mama drag: a long-sleeved black tee under a scruffy Soundamania tour shirt, olive-green cargo capris, and a newish pair of checkerboard Vans. She'd told Jace she admired Sabine for going gray with style but hadn't taken that step herself. Her new stylist in Detroit had convinced her to crop her hair into a cheeky ash-blond bob that echoed her '90s look. She looked at Jace as she finished her snack and smiled proudly. "Looking good, Wonder Woman!"

That made Jace feel like hot property. "Livvy told us how much she's enjoying talking to you. Are you sick of her yet?"

"Of course not. She keeps telling me how cool I am. I'll talk to her until she begs for mercy."

"That'll work for me. I'm glad to have her around."

"So is Rennie," Paloma said.

Jace rolled her eyes. "Hoo boy."

"Why are you so grumpy? The two of them are adorable together."

"I dunno. Dating a musician is tricky."

Paloma chuckled. "Shit, if she doesn't know that from growing up with her aunt Jace, she'll never learn that lesson. Besides, you're the one booking Rennie's band here. If you'd just say no, they'd spend more time getting rich from their coding gig to better afford keeping Livvy in comfort."

Thankfully, Rennie's ability as a guitarist was beginning to meet the demands of their unflappable enthusiasm. Purple Betty had just brought in a new keyboard player, too, so their sound was locking into place: early '60s pop squirted through a broken speaker. Sabine had been right: Rennie had just needed time and space to bloom, and now they were building a following in the city and elsewhere in the Midwest.

Jace gazed at Paloma's relaxed sense of joy. She wasn't about to take credit for her happiness—Paloma owned that completely—but Jace was glad to see it more and more. "I'm so glad you're back in my life," she said, her face aglow.

"Thank God," Paloma said, her smile warm and broad.

They chatted while Paloma wiped out the rest of the pizza, then Livvy stuck her head in the doorway, looking peeved. "Aunt Jace, are you coming? They're almost done with sound check."

"Of course."

Paloma headed toward the door then turned and pulled Jace toward her. Her kiss was raw and deep, her fingers teasing Jace's scalp until she shivered. Jace hummed as Paloma's lips dotted across her jaw and the bowl of her neck. As pragmatic as she wanted to be about their future together, Jace couldn't imagine life being any better than right now: in the arms of the woman who thrilled and delighted her damn near every moment.

Paloma pulled back and smiled. "That's to thank you for making me breakfast tomorrow. I'll have more to add when we get to your place."

"You'd better."

By now, the main floor was full. Sabine waved them over to sit next to her and Mo in the riser seats. Jace inserted her earplugs and took a chair as Paloma sat on the aisle. From their vantage point, she was pleased to see how varied the audience was in every way. Everyone was welcome at the Artemis, now more than ever.

As the minutes ticked by with no one on stage, someone started a chant that soon took over the room:

When I say purple, you say Betty
Purple! BETTY!
Purple! BETTY!

At last, the Voice of God came over the PA: "Please give it up for Purple Betty!"

Jace and Paloma leaped to their feet and cheered as Rennie came to center stage. They were grinning and waving to the whoops and hollers from the crowd as the bassist, keyboard player, and drummer filled in behind them. Having evolved their look over the past year, Rennie was now sporting a long, bumpy pixie cut dyed blue-black and wore a fierce amount of eyeliner. Clad in an embellished violet-colored military jacket, tight black jeans, and motorcycle boots, they were devastatingly sexy.

"Hey, y'all!" they shouted, settling the guitar across their hips. "I have to say: You are the tastiest humans in all creation. It'll be hard to concentrate with all of y'all standing in front of us, but we'll find a way." They turned to their bandmates and counted off: "One, two, three—GO!"

The aural assault began, and Jace couldn't help but grin. This was Detroit garage music for the future, and it was having the same effect on her as it had when she first walked in the door of the Artemis. Adrenaline flooded her veins, and electricity raced through every cell. Her feet couldn't keep still, and she couldn't stop smiling. Paloma looped her arm around her waist and leaned into her as the music flowed through them, their bodies pulsing like a beating heart.

The music had changed, but the love had not.

AUTHOR'S NOTES

I moved to the Detroit suburbs in 2006 after the White Stripes had become a household name, which also brought some attention (not enough) to their incredible musical compatriots. While I've been privileged to see some of these bands more recently, it's undoubtedly a much different vibe now than when they were performing in long-gone venues like the Gold Dollar or places that are still open (as of this writing) like the Majestic and St. Andrew's before they'd benefited from major renovations, the publicity reach of social media, and the overall redevelopment of the city. Doing research for this book, I was honored and grateful to get firsthand accounts from several generous, kind people who made and promoted Detroit punk, indie, and garage music at the turn of the twenty-first century, including the following:

Ward Tomich is my cousin by marriage and one of the funniest people on the planet. Ward had been hired as a bartender at the Cross Street Station bar in Ypsilanti, Michigan, following a rigorous job interview: "Can you open a beer bottle?" He went on to become their music booker as it evolved into a venue that hosted an impressive array of bands that played in Detroit as well. Not only does he have a lifetime of shenanigans and musical memories for a book of his own (which I will happily share with everyone I know), but he also met the love of his life at Cross Street Station.

Valerie Tomich was an Eastern Michigan University student and a hardcore fan of many of the musicians who came through Cross Street and probably got her share of free drinks thanks to that cute bartender she married (see above). In addition to her current career as the high school teacher we all wish we'd had, Val is also an extraordinary visual artist. Check her out on Instagram @valtomichart.

Neil Yee owned the Gold Dollar from 1996 to 2001. He had purchased the building situated in a dicey part of Cass Avenue right before the city would have repossessed it for back property taxes, with the intention of it being a music and experimental performance space. The White Stripes made their debut there, and many musicians are on record as saying it was one of their favorite places to perform. I truly appreciated Neil's viewpoint as I created Sabine's fictional Cass Corridor venue, and I was grateful for his candor about Detroit's status in the national music scene. He sold the Gold Dollar well before the 2013 fire that reduced it to ashes, and its reputation continues to burn bright.

Kevin Herron, aka esQuire: The Boy Who Invented Rap, provided background on his experiences as a musical artist performing in Detroit and around the world. He was also a resident of Woodbridge, which remains a popular neighborhood for Detroit musicians to this day. Be sure to watch his music video for the single "Brandy and Xanax" to experience his unique DIY rap stylings and the go-go dancers who were part of his one-of-a-kind act.

Dave Feeny is a talented producer, engineer, and musician who happens to play hockey with my friend and neighbor, Vince Simonetti (thanks, Vince, for introducing us!). Dave's performing career began in the 1980s with Detroit-area bands like the Orange Roughies and Hysteric Narcotics and continued in the late 1990s and early 2000s with alt country bands Blanche and American Mars. He also played pedal steel guitar in Jack White's backing band for Loretta Lynn's 2004 Grammy-winning *Van Lear Rose* and appeared on *Late Show with David Letterman* in support of that album. Additionally, Dave owns and operates the Tempermill studio in Ferndale, where the Dirtbombs, the White Stripes, and many other amazing bands have recorded.

Stephanie O'Connor is my friend and co-worker as well as a dedicated Detroit indie music fan. I appreciated that she was willing to share her experiences from the audience's point of view.

Carrie Flinger and David Nantais are not only good friends and lovely people but they also own a gorgeous American Foursquare home in Woodbridge that they graciously invited me to tour.

I am also indebted to so many others who have supported me every step of the way. Thank you to my literary agent, Frances Black of Literary Counsel, who is an insightful, delightful partner in this business. My gratitude goes out to my editor, Katy Nishimoto, at The Dial Press, who invests so much talent, energy, and kindness into making my work the best it can be. Also, thank you to the dynamos at Dial, including Whitney Frick, JP Woodham, Debbie Aroff, Hope Hathcock, Madison Dettlinger, Avideh Bashirrad, and Raaga Rajagopala. And I'm so grateful to Dial's book team—Cindy Berman, Rebecca Berlant, Jennifer Backe, Rebecca Maines, Karen Ninnis, and Karina Jha—for their copyediting and production prowess.

Thank you to Tom Cole and Donna Cheng for the spectacular cover design.

Sheri Holman's storytelling genius is apparent to anyone who reads her books and watches her television shows. Thank you so much for helping me fulfill the promise of my premise. My love and appreciation go out to Gail Nelson, who is an exceptional friend, writer, and editor as well as an incredibly effective beta reader. Likewise, thanks and kudos to Tracy Garner, aka Jess Sinclair, whose writing and work ethic inspire me daily.

This book would not be here if not for my writers' group of more than fifteen years. Susan Chaplin, Lynne Golodner, Karen Hildebrandt, Pam Houghton, Kim Kozlowski, Carrie Nantais, and Anne Osmer: You are a constellation of stars.

James Robb, Gabrielle Sellei, and Michael Nosanchuk: I value your intellectual property acumen.

Love and hugs to my children, James, Hunter, and Davis, and thanks for your help as Gen Z and Millennial cultural advisors. And, Dani, you are the song my heart sings.

Thank you so much for reading, and take it from me: Life is short, so buy the ticket. Bring your friends and make some new ones at the venue. Spring for the T-shirt. Show up in time to see all the opening acts. Stay for the encore. And love who and what you love.

MOTOR CITY LOVE SONG

LISA PEERS

DIAL DELIGHTS

Love Stories for the Open-Hearted

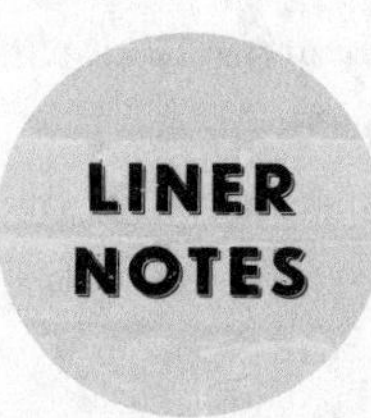

DIVING DEEPER INTO DETROIT'S INDIE MUSIC

All of the Detroit musicians and material mentioned in *Motor City Love Song* are fictional. While I wish I could share the imaginary catalogues of Paloma Doralle, Purple Betty, Tiny Teacups, and even Bitemother, the actual musicians who inspired me have incredible discographies and vast troves of video recordings online, and many of them continue to perform. So, if you want to learn more, where can you start?

To give you an aural snapshot of the music of the specific years of the story, I recommend you tap into your local used record store, public library, or Discogs to find the 2001 compilation album *Sympathetic Sounds of Detroit*. Produced by Jack White (and recorded in his house), it showcases some of the best bands of the era.

If you want to see what some of these bands were like live and hear about their experiences firsthand, hunt down the 2009 documentary *It Came from Detroit*, which is available for download and on DVD. It features amazing conversations with and performances by many of the folks who made the scene what it was.

There are several great books out there that provide history and commentary about the period. Two that I recommend are *Fell in*

Love with a Band: The Story of the White Stripes by Chris Handyside, and Joe Malloy's *Acid Detroit.*

And if you want to construct your own Detroit-themed garage and indie playlist, here are some great songs to get you started:

1. "View From Here," The Gories
2. "Like a Man," The Paybacks
3. "Go to Hell," Rocket 455
4. "Right Around the Corner," The Detroit Cobras
5. "Fox in a Box," Gore Gore Girls
6. "Go-Getter," Ko and the Knockouts
7. "You Go Bangin' On," The Go
8. "All the Stars," Demolition Doll Rods
9. "It Came from Japan," The Von Bondies
10. "Gay Bar," Electric Six
11. "Do You Trust Me?," Blanche
12. "Brandy and Xanax," esQuire
13. "That Ain't Right Little Girl," The Sights
14. "Michigan Blues," The Hentchmen
15. "Hot Women (Cold Beer)," Goober & the Peas
16. "Let's Shake Hands," The White Stripes
17. ".32 Blues," Soledad Brothers
18. "Motor City Baby," The Dirtbombs

GOING UP NORTH

Even as her story begins in and around Detroit, Paloma spends a significant part of her later life in the northern part of Michigan's lower peninsula, the area known to Michiganders as "Up North." Stone Beach is a fictional lakefront town that incorporates aspects of several real, wonderfully beautiful places I am privileged to visit several times a year, thanks to the hospitality and friendship of our generous neighbors Lois DeBacker and Chuck and Alice Moss. Swimming and beachcombing, shopping for souvenirs and snacks, eating extremely well, watching the sun set over the water, and wishing we could stay a little longer: Trips Up North have been a treasured tradition for my family ever since we moved to Michigan, thanks to them.

I hope you will be able experience the beauty of Up North for yourself, and when you do, here are just a few of my favorite places to visit:

- *Empire Beach Village Park:* This is a fantastic public beach for folks of all ages, with a boat launch, playground, picnic pavilion, and plenty of parking. Stroll along the shore and keep your eye out for pieces of beach glass and smooth rocks polished by the sand and surf. It's a block from Empire's delightful main street and within sight of Sleeping Bear Dunes National Lakeshore, a gem of a national park just a few miles down the road.

- *Grocer's Daughter Chocolate:* In addition to a wide assortment of chocolates, this LGBTQ+-friendly shop is also great place to get coffee, ice cream bars, and gelato. You can also rent the Dark and Milk Chocolate apartments above the shop when you visit Empire. Can't wait to try their truffles and honey caramels? They ship throughout the US!

- *Cherry Republic:* Michigan's leading cherry retailer is based in Glen Arbor with locations in Traverse City and Charlevoix as well as other locations downstate. Their wide range of products is inventive and delicious, and they offer ample samples in their stores. And they also ship throughout the US and Canada, so you can enjoy a taste of Michigan wherever you live.

- *Boonedocks:* The fictional Cherry Mill in Stone Beach owes a lot to this relaxed, sunny bar and grill in Glen Arbor.

During the summer season, they sell candy and ice cream at their Sleeping Bear Sweets shop and host live music on the deck on Fridays and Saturdays.

- *The Old Mission Peninsula Wine Trail:* Spend a lazy afternoon enjoying a range of wonderful local wines and photogenic views. A couple of my favorite stops on the trail are Black Star Farms and Mari Vineyards.

- *Farm Club:* This is my favorite hang in Traverse City. About 90 percent of the food served at this farm-to-fork restaurant is grown on their property, and the menu changes with the seasons. During the summer, you can wait for your table on the lawn while sipping their wine, beer, and ciders. They also sell their produce and products year-round.

- *Rove Winery at the Gallagher Estate:* Located in Traverse City on the highest point of the Leelanau Peninsula, this is a stunning spot to enjoy a happy hour with live music while taking in the view of the vineyard and the rolling hills.

- *The Cook's House:* This "petite, chef-owned destination for sustainable fare," as their chefs describe it, is a James Beard Award finalist known for its ingenious menu and talented staff. Their five-course tasting menu of local ingredients exceptionally prepared, with each course paired with one of the world's best wines, is one of the best meals I've ever had.

- *Penny Lane:* At this resale shop on Front Street in Traverse City, sellers rent booths for their collections of clothes, shoes, jewelry, and whatnot on a weekly basis, so there's an ever-changing mix of great fits for terrific prices. I always seem to find something there that fits perfectly.

- *Bookstores galore!:* With all of the things to do during a vacation Up North, for me nothing beats sitting on the deck and reading a pile of books. Thankfully, nearly every town has an independent bookstore that offers everything from best sellers to local authors, and even upbeat LGBTQ+ romances! I'm particularly indebted to Horizon Books and Brilliant Books in Traverse City and the Cottage Book Shop in Glen Arbor for their support of readers and writers like me.

Wherever you end up, in Detroit or Up North, tag me in your photos on Instagram @lisapeersauthor! I want to hear all about what you discover!

© DAVIS KUREPA-PEERS

LISA PEERS is a writer with a passion for smart, funny love stories with well-deserved happy endings. She has acted professionally in San Francisco, produced TV and radio programs in Detroit, and is currently a creative director for an international marketing agency. A Harvard graduate with an MFA in acting from the American Conservatory Theater in San Francisco, Lisa lives with her partner, Dani, in metro Detroit, not far from their three grown children, along with their beloved cats and way too much yarn.

Instagram: @lisapeersauthor

ABOUT THE TYPE

This book was set in Minion, a 1990 Adobe Originals typeface by Robert Slimbach. Minion is inspired by classical, old-style typefaces of the late Renaissance, a period of elegant and beautiful type designs. Created primarily for text setting, Minion combines the aesthetic and functional qualities that make text type highly readable with the versatility of digital technology.

Discover more books by

LISA PEERS

Available wherever books are sold